CLEANUP ON AISLE SIX

Daniel Stallings

Pace Press
Fresno, California

Published by Pace Press
An imprint of Linden Publishing
2006 South Mary Street, Fresno, California 93721
(559) 233-6633 / (800) 345-4447
QuillDriverBooks.com

Pace Press and Colophon are trademarks of
Linden Publishing, Inc.

ISBN 978-1-61035-343-4

135798642
Printed in the United States of America
on acid-free paper.

This is a work of fiction. The names, places, characters, and incidents
in this book are used fictitiously, and any resemblance to actual people,
places, or events is coincidental. Whenever real celebrities, places, or
businesses have been mentioned or appear in this novel, they have been
used fictitiously.

Library of Congress Cataloging-in-Publication Data

Names: Stallings, Daniel, author.
Title: Cleanup on aisle six / Daniel Stallings.
Description: Fresno, California : Pace Press, [2019] | Series: Li Johnson
    murder mysteries; vol 2
Identifiers: LCCN 2019032413 | ISBN 9781610353434 (paperback ;
acid-free
    paper) | ISBN 9781610353564 (epub) | ISBN 9781610353564 (kindle
edition)

Subjects: LCSH: Murder--Investigation--Fiction.
Classification: LCC PS3619.T3497 C54 2019 | DDC 813/.6--dc23
LC record available at https://lccn.loc.gov/2019032413

Contents

CHAPTER 1

Oscar the Grouch

Hearts were hard to find in the grocery store.

But thanks to his connections to an offal supplier, he got what he needed.

The Butcher tore the paper off the beef heart, his fingers twitching. He watched it bleed onto the cutting board, fresh from the chop shop. His eyes sparkled, and he caressed his lips with his tongue. The first steps of revenge tasted sweet. He seized a well-loved chef's knife out of a kitchen drawer. And he drove the blade into the meat.

I'm killing you, Oscar. I'm finally killing you.

All the anger boiling inside him for months raced in waves of blood across his arms, through his fingers, down the knife, and into the heart. Therapy. This was the therapy he needed. He hacked at the heart flesh, tearing it, trashing it, whittling it down to a more human scale. He once put Oscar on a pedestal, followed him as a disciple. He bought every book the man wrote. Then Oscar unleashed the monster inside him.

You snake! You ruined me! You attacked my family! You destroyed my friends!

The Butcher ripped the knife out of the meat, his face smudged with tears. He smeared them away with the back of his blood-stained hand. His swollen eyes surveyed his handiwork. Not bad. Here was the main course on Hannibal Lecter's dinner table. A heart torn out of a human chest.

Just like mine. And he slammed the blade into his prey, leaving the knife jutting cockeyed out of the flesh. A knife in the heart. Far too fitting.

The Butcher's eyes, still blurred with tears, lifted from the wreckage on the cutting board to a line of books on his countertop. The titles mocked him. Oscar's books. He should have barbecued them, smirking as he watched the flames eat up all those lies. His hand pawed blindly at them, groping for the fattest volume. He let the book fall open and ripped out a page.

A small smile curled his lips. That felt GOOD.

He ripped out a few more. Then more. And more.

After he destroyed two chapters, he grabbed one of the torn pages, snatched a fat marker—a fitting shade of red—from the magnetic caddy on his fridge, and scrawled out a message. A little card to put with his present.

FIRST WARNING.

Now it was all ready to be wrapped and dumped on Oscar's doorstep.

"Resigning? What the hell do you mean you're resigning?"

Frank Dixon slammed the offensive letter onto his desk and launched to his feet. Angry arcs of color burned on his tan cheeks still pockmarked with old acne scars. His face became a perfect model of the Martian landscape. His thick lips twisted into a snarl.

"What are you trying to pull, Oscar?"

The man addressed as Oscar stroked the brass head of his ebony cane with a jaundiced thumb. He settled further into the leather visitor's chair across from the desk, where his boss held his stance like a king under siege in his fortress. A cold, reptilian sneer slithered out from underneath a black broom of a mustache.

"I believe I've come to the end of my time here at *The Shorewood Gazette.*" Oscar's words oozed across his tongue like syrup. The sneer widened. "It's not like you really wanted me here, Frank."

"My personal feelings aren't the issue here! You're putting the paper in a hell of a bind!"

"The newspaper has never cared for my work. The public loves it, but you could never appreciate what I brought to the table, if you pardon the pun."

Frank's scowl ripped through his face. "I'd be happier if you just toned it down in your reviews. Why do want to destroy people all the time?"

"Why should these establishments be permitted to serve substandard fare to their customers?" Oscar's tone was one of righteous indignation, the feeling a man who proclaims himself to be the Sword of God might feel. "The citizens of Shorewood have every right to—"

"You closed a café because they mistranslated a French quote! How in heaven's name is THAT news that the public needs to care about?"

"That imbecilic quote reflected the shoddy execution of their cuisine. They were no more French than I am."

Frank's scowl warped into a tortured, scathing grin. "Oh yes . . . a fact you mentioned several times on that disgusting blog of yours." His eyes searched for surprise in that poisonous yellow glare of his resident restaurant critic. He got none. "I bet you didn't think I knew about it, huh? Imagine my surprise to find out *The Gazette* got the DIET version of Oscar Lindstrom's patented blend of prejudice and condescension. What did you call your blog again? *Tough Bite to Swallow*? Well, it certainly was. I nearly choked on it."

Oscar's yellowing eyes narrowed. "I don't believe I have to mention the First Amendment in this case, do I?"

"Oh sure. Protected by all the buzzwords. Critique. Opinion. Freedom of the press. You're a shining example of how much murder we can get away with using our words."

Oscar drummed sallow fingers on the arm of the chair, keeping his sick eyes locked on his boss's red, bulging face. His sneer shriveled into a frown. "Despite your handicaps, Frank, you do have a way with words yourself. Look at the irony of what you just said."

"What are you talking about?"

"Words . . . and how we use them." A spark flared in Oscar's eyes. "You asked me to tone down my words. I think 'toning things down' has become the manifesto of *The Shorewood Gazette* under your editorship. Scaling back on bad words. Words that may . . . reflect poorly on certain . . . people."

Blood drained from Frank's cheeks, turning the landscape of Mars into the surface of the moon. His fingers corseted around a football-shaped brass paperweight his wife gave him for his birthday last year.

"You're talking in riddles, Oscar."

"I pay attention to things. The details matter. I despise it when details don't match up. Why, for instance, did you fire Esposito a month ago after she published one of her most successful articles?"

"Who I hire and fire is my business, Oscar. I have no reason to discuss them with you."

The lizard's grin snaked out from its hiding spot under his mustache. "I think I know why. And it would certainly be an ugly situation for you. Even uglier than your first divorce, eh, Frank?"

"YOU'RE one to talk about divorce, Oscar. What are YOU on now? Wife number three and mistress number seventeen?"

Oscar continued to grin. "That's hardly something to hold over someone. It certainly won't damage my career. Unlike the little secret you are treasuring, eh?"

The urge to pummel the paperweight into Oscar's bald spot flooded Frank's body. His hand twitched. He felt heat swarm up his neck and turn all his acne scars into microscopic volcanoes.

I'll slaughter him for this, said a dark demon in his heart.

Oscar had the last word. "I suggest you let me resign from this 'honored' publication and continue with my own way of executing the truth. You'll be much happier when I'm gone. I can already tell." He smirked. "Maybe then you can hire an inoffensive wimp of a restaurant critic who is perfectly happy supporting your 'tone it down' campaign." He stood, keeping his back as straight as the path of righteousness and thumping his ebony cane on the hard-wood floor. He endeavored to look sainted and dignified, a pillar of truth. "I have a mission. I'd love to stay and watch you writhe, but I have an errand to run before I go home to my perfect wife. I expect your decision by Monday. Have a good weekend."

Twirling his cane as he strolled out of the office, Oscar left his boss on the threshold of murder. Frank threw the paperweight at a potted fern, shattering it and spraying dirt all over the wall.

His stomach roared at him.

"Oh shut up shut up shut up," he growled back. "I heard you the first time. And the second time. And the twelfth time."

Liam Johnson stretched out the cramp in his fingers. He squeezed the freezer handle too hard. His silver-blue eyes scanned the prices on the frozen food, hunting for bargains. Shopping hungry and on a severe budget was a mistake, but his fridge was one meal away from being empty. And it had been like that for a week. How could he focus on saving money when he just wanted to empty the entire freezer section of Esther's Family Grocery and have a feast? His stomach whined again.

The miracle check he got this past July was a distant memory now. Everything was expensive. After losing his cruise ship job, the move from Long Beach to Shorewood hadn't been cheap. He checked off the costs in his head: back rent, moving costs, security deposit, food, utilities, more rent, transit pass, tuition, a couple of weeks of unemployment as he scouted for a new job. Money left his hands as quickly as he got it. How in the world did people manage to save any?

And he still didn't have a job. He pounded pavement all over the city, eating a hole into his dirty, threadbare sneakers. Li anticipated walking barefoot from interview to interview. This was turning into the longest September of his life.

"Well, buddy," he said to his moaning stomach, "looks like it'll be cereal all week. Might have to give up milk too, if the price is too high."

"Excuse me?"

Li jumped back, slamming the freezer door and tripping on his own feet. He fell hard on his back on the linoleum floor, making little stars dance across his eyes. Now every part of his body moaned.

A head hovered over Li's face, eyes etched with concern. "Dude, I'm sorry. I didn't mean to scare you. Here." A hand grabbed Li by the arm and hoisted him to his feet. Li begged the supermarket to stop spinning. "I hope you didn't hit your head. Floors aren't forgiving. My name's Reuben, by the way. What's yours?"

Li shook away the galaxy clouding his vision. Reuben started to take shape. Young man pushing his late twenties. He had a chocolate-colored apron and a regulation white button-down shirt stretched tight over a sizeable belly. The uniform for Esther's Family Grocery. He worked here.

"Dude, if you're not going to answer me, I'm calling the paramedics."

"Liam ... My name is Liam. Call me Li."

A wide grin spanned Reuben's tan Latino face. His dark chocolate eyes glimmered. He chuckled, making his stomach wobble. "Nice of you to return to the land of the living, Li. You sure you didn't hit your head?"

Li ran a palm over his short black hair. He had a bump all right. He winced when his fingers grazed it. "I'm okay. Just ... startled me, that's all."

"Do you need any help?"

Yeah, give me a job, Li thought. "No, I'm okay. Just browsing."

Reuben tilted his head and narrowed his eyes. His gaze traveled from the stress lines crinkling Li's forehead to the torn laces on Li's shoes. Li felt like he was naked in the middle of the freezer aisle. He pulled his flimsy windbreaker tighter around his body, if only to disguise how thin he was. His toes curled up his perforated sneakers.

Reuben clapped a hand on Li's shoulder, making Li flinch. "I'm probably going to make an ass out of myself, but are you in trouble? You look like you haven't eaten anything for months." His eyes dropped to Li's shoes, where a socked toe peeked out to say hello. "And you've got holes in your shoes. You're not ... homeless, are you?"

A laugh crumbled out of Li's mouth. His smile faltered. "Nah. That's the only thing I do have." Then, after hearing how bluntly he phrased it, he tried to crawl into his shoulders like a turtle into his shell. "Forget I said that. I'm fine. Really."

"You're not."

Li's eyes drifted to the packed shopping cart next to Reuben. "You're probably busy stocking the freezers. I'll get out of your way." He moved to escape.

Reuben snatched the back of his windbreaker. "Hold on. You've piqued my curiosity. What happened? Is there any way I can help you?"

"I can handle it." He pulled his jacket free.

Reuben grabbed Li's wrist. "Hey, stop trying to escape. I just want to help."

"You're busy."

"I can make time."

Come on, just leave me alone. Li could feel the ghosts of his rotten life rise from the pit of his empty stomach. "This isn't any of your concern."

"You know you don't have to suffer alone. I know a few people who might be able to get you back on your feet. I just wanted to make sure you were okay."

"Why? Why should you care?" Li's eyes flashed like the swords of crusaders. A hot plume of color rushed up his neck. He yanked his arms out of Reuben's grip. "I'm just a random customer trying to shop for food! Why should my problems be any concern of yours?"

Reuben folded his arms across his chest, his eyes smoldering like mugs of black coffee. He matched Li glare for glare. "I have seen a lot of people at the end of their ropes traipse in here. You are, by far, the youngest. How old are you? Eighteen? Nineteen?"

Li's eyes started to waver. "Twenty."

"Well, with those premature wrinkles you're getting, you look almost thirty. Some serious crap went down in your life. You shouldn't struggle like this. You should be hanging out with friends, going to school, laughing, having fun. Instead, you look on the verge of collapsing." Reuben's glare eased. "I got worried. You remind me of my kid brother. I didn't want to find your name splashed out in a suicide article. So what's up? Do you have family? Do you have a job?"

Li lost the glaring contest. His head drooped, and his eyes traced the cracks in the linoleum. Anything to stop the tears. His brain teased him with memories of his father, three years dead, and his mom and sister, who hadn't seen him in months. Then he remembered his empty fridge and drained bank account. His stomach wouldn't stop sobbing. His eyelashes started getting wet.

"Uh-oh," Reuben said. "I think I see waterworks. That bad?"

It would take way too long to explain, Li thought. "It's nothing ... Just ... It's ... Things have been hard lately."

"I'll ask again. Do you have family who can help you?"

Li mushed away the tears with the heel of his hand. "I ... I don't want to talk about them right now."

"Yikes. Well, do you have a job?"

"Still looking." He glanced at the holes in his sneakers. "For a while now."

Reuben's round face brightened with a huge smile. "Then just call me your guardian angel! Apply here!"

I must be hallucinating. "What?"

"One of our guys quit suddenly. Our manager hasn't put the want ad in the paper yet. The job's still open. Let me talk to Leo and get you an interview."

Li had to be dreaming. He pinched the skin in the crook of his elbow. It yelped in pain. "Wait ... Hold on. You don't know anything about me. Or my work ethic. I ... I could be scamming you with some made-up sob story."

Reuben tipped his head to one side, his mouth twitching with a suppressed chuckle. "You're seriously going to fight a job opportunity? In your position?"

"I'm busy trying to convince myself that this is a dream. Besides, how can you have any confidence in me?"

"You're clean. You haven't let your appearance fall apart. You're well-groomed and clean-shaven. Clearly, you're fighting for a job. You're not a slacker." He nodded toward Li's shoes. "You've worn your shoes down to nothing walking from interview to interview."

"That still—"

"Oh shut up, Li." Reuben winked. "Let's get you that interview. I'm sure Leo will jump at the chance to get a new hire so quickly."

Reuben nudged Li to follow him. Li walked in a haze, still unsure if any of this was real. Then the flimsiest of smiles played with his lips. Maybe he could get this job. Maybe his luck was turning around. Maybe—

He collided with Reuben, who had stopped abruptly at the end of the freezer aisle. Reuben's tan face surged with blood, staining his cheeks a dark cinnamon. His eyes darkened way past black coffee. More like two steaming tar pits. His mouth was one curl away from being a snarl. He stared at a man who just entered the grocery store.

Li followed the glare. The man had a face like a sick monkey. Thick, greasy remnants of black hair fringed a bald dome. Huge, round eyes the color of old wallpaper glue flanked a smashed nose with large nostrils. A black broom of a mustache bristled under his nose, hiding a small, cruel mouth. A sallow hand patched with black fur clutched the brass knob of an ebony cane. He returned Reuben's glare, but, if anything, it was more poisonous.

Li lifted an eyebrow. "Reuben? Are you okay?"

Reuben was lost in his trance. "Nothing. It's nothing."

Oscar could have skipped down the sidewalk of Shorewood Avenue. Instead, he ambled along, twirling his cane in his hand. He was even tempted to whistle. His lizard grin spread over flabby cheeks. Today was beautiful and perfect. The September sun, though hot, glimmered like a topaz jewel. Birds serenaded him. He made Frank want to slaughter him. All his plans were crystallizing. This was the point in a musical where the character would segue into song. Oscar couldn't be happier.

He stopped, his cane reverting to neutral. Or could he? There were a few niggling details left to iron out. Easily accomplished after dinner. And after he posted the latest review to his infamous blog.

The grin puckered into a frown. Unless that stupid son of his tried to edit his masterpiece. Then he'd be up half the night trying to pummel some discipline into that juvenile delinquent. It had been a long time since Oscar drew a bath for that boy.

The frown smoothed back into a smile. Jason was easy to handle. Everything was easy, it seemed. There were no hiccups.

He controlled the city more effectively than any government. And soon, he hoped to control the world.

At the next light—Prichard Avenue—Oscar turned left. This street began the small neighborhood where people with more comfortable incomes kept their homes. Not much farther now. The short walk from the grocery store invigorated his spirits. The scowls were just for show anyway. Lately, he felt as ebullient as a teenage boy reliving his first kiss. Maybe even his first orgasm.

He stopped in front of his home, his eyes making quick work of the daily inspection. The freshly shaved lawn swelled around Mrs. Lindstrom's perfectly circular flower beds, neatly packed into pools of fluffy white mums, flowers that wouldn't compete with the house. The paint scheme—dove gray and snow-white—gleamed like a new dime from the US Mint. The lines of the two-story house were rigid and straight, unadorned, unfanciful, from the roofline to the porch. Oscar gave his castle a sharp nod and skipped up the front steps.

The smell of braised beef short ribs, drunk with natural jus, swarmed to him as he crossed the threshold. Dinner. The perfect scent for a man's home, in his opinion. None of that cloying, flowery crap. Kathryn knew how to please him.

And there she was, waiting for him at the base of the staircase. Blue gingham apron tied smartly around her slender waist. Eyes of such a warm, deep blue that they could pass for violet. Skin like peaches and milk. Kathryn Lindstrom smiled at her husband. It was a smile so full of love. Her face glowed with it. She had tied her luscious chocolate curls into a sensible braid that trickled down her back.

"Dinner," Oscar declared. Why waste time with prolonged greetings?

"It's all ready, sweetie."

Her voice was warm and musical. Like the low hum of cello. Oscar smirked at how many men would wage wars just to hear her say that to them.

"Good. Perfect. Where's Jason?"

"Upstairs. He's posting your latest review to the blog."

Oscar's good humor shriveled into a dead husk. Dammit. The big dope had to ruin what was turning into a splendid evening. Couldn't he wait until after dinner to do it? The moron would probably foul everything up.

"JASON!" Oscar's voice carried upstairs with all the subtlety of a bomb. "DINNER! NOW!"

Kathryn showed zero reaction, her smile and loving glow never fading.

A scuffle of footsteps. Maybe a whispered oath. Oscar would skin Jason later for that little slip. He turned to his wife. "Kathryn dear, I believe it would be a good time to start prepping for the first course."

"Absolutely, honey." She settled a kiss on her husband's flabby cheek. "I'll have it ready in no time." And she swept through the huge archway to her right and into the adjacent formal dining room.

The scuffle of footsteps clambered down the stairs. Oscar winced at the noise. It was like an elephant doing ballet. Jason Lindstrom, a frown pinching his mousy-gray eyebrows together and his hair-thin glasses bouncing on the bridge of his nose, scrambled up to his father. He looked lost under the baggy long-sleeved sweater he wore. Oscar didn't conceal his disgust. Jason was twenty-five years old and completely hopeless! He was tardy. He was slow. He was inefficient. He was disrespectful. An altogether disappointing specimen.

"What have I told you about posting reviews?" Oscar growled.

Jason's voice, thin and high compared to his stepmother's, pushed through a tremor. "I-I was only setting it up, Dad."

"That's not what Kathryn said."

"Sh-she got it wrong, then."

"She doesn't get anything wrong, son. You get things wrong."

Jason's anemic complexion burned scarlet. His protuberant Adam's apple bobbed like a buoy in a storm. "I-I'm not wrong, Dad. I didn't do anything. I—"

"Stop talking. You know I hate excuses. Here's what you'll do." Oscar thrust a warning finger into his son's face. "Never touch my reviews again. If you do, I won't be responsible for your situation outside of these walls."

He started toward the dining room when his son's voice broke into a sharp retort, cracking from strain, a petulant whine. "You're . . . You're not the b-boss of me!"

Oscar turned and took stock of Jason's appearance. Anemic skin tone. Frail figure. Dry, colorless hair. That damn weakness in his eyes that was a curse from his mother's family. Everything screamed puny, shrunken, and brittle. Jason would crumble in the real world like chalk crushed in a fist.

"You're a slug, Jason." Oscar's voice was low and soft, the searching growl of a hungry wolf. "You can't take care of yourself."

"I can do better than you think I can!"

"Don't argue with me, Jason. You're worthless. Get in the dining room and eat dinner, or I'll make you get in the tub. Do you want that? Do you want another bath?"

Jason stumbled backward, his eyes huge and his lip shaking. "You . . . You wouldn't."

"I would. Now shut up and get in the dining room."

Oscar turned to leave, but his ears caught a few profane mumblings from his son. He whirled around and whacked the head of his cane onto Jason's shoulder. Jason shrieked.

"What have I told you about using that filthy language, you stupid boy?" Oscar growled. "Maybe I should have you drink your special bath water instead. That'll shut your disgusting mouth."

There was a split second of mortal terror in Jason's face. He stormed into the dining room, tears brimming against his eyelashes.

Kathryn's musical voice, the perfect anticlimax, floated through the archway to her husband's ears.

"By the way, dear, you got a package today."

CHAPTER 2

Victims

"Thanks for agreeing to work weekends, Liam. Everyone wants those days off. We're always horribly understaffed. You're a lifesaver."

Li, freshly turned out in his black pants, white button-down shirt, and chocolate brown apron, smiled. Actually, he hadn't stopped smiling since he heard the words "You're hired." His cheeks started to ache. "No problem, Mr. Lewitski."

Li's new boss flinched at the name. He swiveled on his heel and flashed a billion-watt smile at Li. "Call me Leo. Leo Lewis. Mr. Lewitski was my father."

"Oh ... um ... sorry, Leo."

"Don't worry about it. You'd want to change your name too if your parents named you Leonard Lewitski." He tugged on the sharp, black manager's vest he wore and flaunted the brassy name tag bearing the slim and sexy rewrite of his birth name. Then he straightened his manager's tie—black-and-gold pinstripe to distinguish him from standard employee black—and hustled along, Li shadowing him. "I think the best way to learn the job is to do it. Throw you to the lions. But I'll have someone train you on the basics and give you a good head start. Meet your training buddy, Reuben Rodriguez."

Reuben, who had been negotiating a barge of cereal boxes with a pallet jack, stopped and turned. He grinned. "I knew you'd get the job."

Li blushed.

Leo walked to the cereal shipment and patted it. "Reuben was just getting ready to build our weekly special display. I think that's a good way to break into your duties. You can help him out, Liam. Just follow his instructions. And if you have any questions, feel free to ask him or come and find me. Welcome to Esther's Family Grocery."

Before Li could say his thanks, Leo marched away, leading with his chest.

Reuben set the shipment down. "Now that you're working here, I can poke and pry into your sob story at will! It's nice to see you looking really happy though. You're smiling almost as much as Leo."

Li relaxed his grin and massaged his numb cheeks. "I'm just relieved to have a job. I feel ten pounds lighter."

"And you look ten years younger." Reuben pulled the jack out of the pallet and started wheeling it toward the back of the store. "I've got to get another shipment of Frosted Fizzle Bombs. Use your box cutter and unwrap this one. Then we can start building."

On Reuben's return, they set to work. Leo had specific guidelines for his displays. A pyramid. Always a pyramid. But one of exact dimensions and with the product name always aimed toward the customers. Li envisioned being a tomb builder in ancient Egypt.

"Why a pyramid?" he asked.

Reuben spread his hands and shrugged. "You got me. You've seen how it is around here. All the displays are pyramids. Even the produce. It's like working in Giza. Leo's got some half-formed reason of his own—some healthy eating pyramid thing—but I think he was Pharaoh Khufu in a past life."

Reuben helped Li set the exact dimensions for the display, and together they built the foundation. He also wheeled out detail after detail of Li's backstory. His father's leukemia. The family business failing. His father's death. Near bankruptcy. Being driven into the workforce as a teenager to pay the mortgage. Moving away from home to ease the financial burden. His mom and little sister breaking their backs to keep a roof over their heads. Being too poor to go to college. His self-assigned homework to complete his shoestring education. Bad luck with jobs. And the murderous set of circumstances that cost him his last job on the Howard Cruise Line.

"Damn," Reuben said, his eyes wide, "I knew you had crap happen in your life, but that's enough for an epic trilogy. How come you haven't collapsed under all that?"

"I just keep reminding myself of the lessons my dad taught me." Li fussed with the precise angle of a box. "Never give up. He didn't raise a quitter. Even when I felt like falling apart, I had to push through it. Life wasn't going to be easy for me."

"What brought you to Shorewood?"

"I had a little help. Mainly I just wanted to get the hell out of Long Beach. I grew up in this area. Jefferson, California. It's only a few miles away."

"Yeah, I've heard of—"

Li's stomach interrupted. By roaring. Li tried to shrink into his apron.

Reuben's belly wobbled when he laughed. "I thought that's what I heard yesterday! You okay? Do you have enough to eat at home?"

"Well ... I ... um ..."

Reuben raised a hand. "Mumble no more. I got the picture. I'm inviting you to dinner tonight at my place with me and my boyfriend, Noah. We'd love the company. And we need to get some food into you."

"Oh no! I couldn't. I mean ... you've already been so nice and—"

"Don't mention it! Seriously, come. Noah loves to cook for people. Heck, he's a hospitality major. We'd be happy to have you."

A grin stretched the full expanse of Li's face. "Gee ... I-I really don't know how to thank you. I'm kind of overwhelmed."

"Hey, I just like helping people. And I'm glad you're here. You're by far the fastest-learning and most organized trainee I've had. Not a single casualty. Let's get the stepladder and—"

Reuben's eyes seemed to double in size, frozen on something over Li's left shoulder. He forgot all about his trainee. He muttered under his breath, "No. He can't be here. Not again."

Li craned his neck over his shoulder, and his eyes locked on the customer from yesterday—the man with the monkey's face. What was he doing here on Saturday when he already did his shopping on Friday? Monkey Face saw them, and a grin that reminded Li of hungry lizards slid out from under his mustache. He walked toward them, swinging his cane.

"Oh God," Reuben whispered. "Go away. Leave me alone."

Li's eyes shifted to him. "Reuben, what is it?"

Reuben couldn't answer. He trembled all over. His eyes were darkening into tar pits again. He strangled the corner of his apron in fat, shaking fists.

Monkey Face was upon them. "Are you boys responsible for this . . . structure?" His voice was slimy, dark. It felt like oil pouring into Li's ears. He tapped the unfinished pyramid with the foot of his cane.

Li, his glance drifting between Reuben and the customer, cleared his throat. "Um . . . yes, sir. Do you need some help?"

"Oh, I don't think I'm the one who needs help." His eyes oozed with venom.

"If you want to buy the cereal, we—"

"What makes you think that *I* would ever think of purchasing those processed cardboard pellets?" Spittle punctuated every hard consonant.

Judging from the man's jaundiced complexion—the price of overindulging in rich food and expensive wine—Li had to agree that this customer wouldn't be caught dead buying Frosted Fizzle Bombs. Or even enter this store in the first place. Monkey Face's poisonous eyes scanned the supermarket and seemed to find all the ugly details: the bubbling and cracking linoleum floor, the winking fluorescent lights, and the vague stink wafting from the men's restroom several feet away. "You both work in a dump," he said.

Reuben spat out a reply. Almost like he was trying to release the tension coiling around his body. "Esther's Family Grocery has been a fixture for families in the Shorewood community since 1968."

Monkey Face smirked. "And judging from these cracks spidering across the floor, it hasn't seen an update since then."

Reuben continued to twist his apron in his fingers. Like he was fashioning a garrote. His round, pleasant face twitched and squirmed, battling to keep back a flood of emotion. His eyes steamed. "Get out of here."

Li moved between them, the electric tension in the air squeezing against his throat. "I-is there anything I can help you—"

Monkey Face's cane whacked the bottom of Li's chin and snapped his mouth shut. He drilled his sadistic glare into Reuben's writhing face. "You're not very polite to your customers. Then again, your family doesn't know much about service."

Li could hear Reuben starting to hyperventilate. Reuben snarled at the man. The explosion was coming.

Monkey Face pushed the foot of his cane into Reuben's belly, drawing attention to his weight. His yellow eyes traced the Mexican heritage in Reuben's features. "Unusual setup for you, isn't it? A little far from the border. Shouldn't you and your family be selling food from the back of a—?"

That did it. In a heartbeat, Reuben's face swelled with blood, his eyes black and smoldering. His body flinched, a panther ready to strike. His hands, trembling and independent, launched forward.

Li gripped Reuben's shoulder with steel wrists and pulled him back. Reuben squirmed against his restraints. Li glared at Monkey Face, his eyes like titanium. "I'm not going to tolerate you making those kinds of insults. All you're doing is baiting him. If that's what you want to do, leave. I refuse to help a racist."

His voice carried bright and cold through the store, as firm and unshaken as a battle cry.

Monkey Face chuckled and twirled his cane. "You bore me." And to prove it, the man unlocked his jaws with a huge yawn. "I was going to suggest that you dismantle this monstrosity and construct something more . . . circular." His cane whirled over Li's heart as if reminding the boy what a circle looked like. "And try to keep the diameter on the small side. We don't need you to show off your building skills, however limited they are. Just replace that repulsive pyramid. Don't you agree that would be the best solution?"

He didn't linger for a reply. Turning on the heel of his wing tips, Monkey Face swept away from the pyramid and down an aisle, spinning his cane in his hand like a drum major. Li watched him go. It was a splinter in the eye, the idea that he didn't even need the cane. He just used it to intimidate, maybe even engender a sick form of pity he didn't deserve.

Li's thoughts were so uncharitable that they left the taste of vinegar on his tongue.

Reuben wilted, plastering still shaking hands to his face. Li thought he heard a smothered sob. "I have never come so close to assaulting someone in my whole life. I'm scared how far that went. Oh God. Why did he have to come here?"

"Reuben, who is he?"

"O-Oscar the Grouch."

The nickname almost made Li laugh. It didn't seem to fit the monster that came into the store. He swallowed the impulse. "Who's Oscar?"

"I don't want to talk about it."

"But he implied that he knew your family. What does he mean to—?"

Reuben dropped his hands, tears flooding the planes of his face. "I said I don't want to talk about it!"

No cane twirling today. Oscar thundered down Shorewood Avenue, entertaining the notion of tripping any kids who passed him. That smug little snot in the grocery store would learn a lesson from speaking to him like that. Oscar would bury him, plant him in an early grave. Furry knuckles cracked and popped as he squeezed the head of his cane.

He paused. His scowl eased into a smirk. Oh yes. That mouthy punk with the crybaby eyes would earn a special education courtesy of Oscar Lindstrom. He knew how to make people writhe in their own skin.

He started to twirl his cane. And this time, he whistled.

A jet-black sedan with tinted windows, conspicuous by its attempts to look otherwise, crawled up to the curb next to Oscar.

The driver's side window rolled down, and Oscar was not at all surprised at the person behind the wheel. The woman had the resources and the privilege to have a paid driver, but she insisted on retaining her independence. It was one of the things Oscar did not like about her.

The woman removed her sunglasses, revealing eyes tinted to match the windows of her car. Her hair, swept into a French twist, drew inspiration from a thunderhead, deep purple-black slashed with lightning bolts of gunmetal gray. An amused smile touched the wide mouth that held definitive court over the lower half of her face.

"You're a ways from home, Oscar," she said, her voice rich and throaty, a baritone Bea Arthur could appreciate. "Taking an afternoon stroll?"

"Ah, Constance Henderson. Are you having me followed?"

"If I did, I certainly wouldn't waste my energies announcing my presence to you, would I?" Her lips, colored a deep rose, parted in a grin that showcased the best teeth orthodontia could provide.

"I should hope not. That would be a waste of the taxpayers' hard-earned income if their mayor's wife spent it on counterproductive espionage."

Constance tilted her head and graced him with a slight titter. "Still using big words hoping someone will think you're smart?"

"Oh no, my dear Constance. Only trying to impress you. It worked once."

"Thankfully, it didn't take." Constance turned her head to look down Shorewood Avenue and the streets that branched off it like legs on a centipede. "Heading home to that little chippie that calls herself your wife? Or heading off to see the little chippie who knows that's all she means to you?"

Oscar gave her his famous sneer. "I didn't think you had it in you to be jealous."

Constance let a laugh—cultured, refined, the laugh a politician's wife is supposed to give—tumble from her lips. "Jealous? Of you? Of them? Oh sweetie, I learned a long time ago not to be jealous of people like you. As for them"—she lifted her shoulders in an offhand shrug—"I just feel extraordinary pity."

Oscar showed no anger or resentment. In fact, he seemed pleased by her judgments. "As I pity your husband, my dear. I don't think Mayor Henderson quite understood the storm he got himself into."

The extreme tips of her smile tweaked downward. "Yes, well, we're all entitled to a few mistakes." She slid her sunglasses onto her face, camouflaging her dark, glittering eyes. "I suspect you are up to your old sins again, Oscar. I feel compelled to remind you what my Mama's Bible used to say about that. 'Be sure thy sins will find thee out.'"

Oscar allowed a small snicker. "And I feel compelled to remind you that 'old sins cast long shadows.' Your past will come back to haunt you. Especially since I'm in it."

The window scrolled up too quickly for Oscar to catch her reaction. But he knew down in his soul that he had her crushed under his thumb. He watched as her sedan merged into traffic and sped off for the safety of City Hall.

Another win for Oscar Lindstrom. Another victim caught in his coils.

The office phone, irritable, inconsolable, shrilled at Frank Dixon, clawing at the dense fog of gloom and misery he closed around himself. He mumbled a rainbow of swear words, the first hooks of a headache tunneling into his skull. Massaging his left temple, he straightened in his leather desk chair, contemplated letting voice mail take the call, and then clenched the receiver in his fist.

"Dixon speaking." He wondered if his greeting sounded as dead to his caller as it did to him.

"What are you doing in your office on a Saturday, Frank?" The man's voice, rich with bonhomie, started to chuckle. Frank wished he could see the humor just as easily.

"Thinking, Tom."

Tom's voice sobered. "I guess you do have a lot to think about. Heard Oscar practically skipped out of your office, doing that thing where he twirls his cane. We all know that means bad news. What did he do?"

"He resigned from the paper."

"Then shouldn't you be the one skipping and twirling?"

It hurt to smile, but Frank couldn't help it. "If the man wasn't such a snake, I might."

"Uh-oh. I don't like the sound of that. What is he holding over you?"

Words, Frank thought.

"It's nothing."

"Which is exactly what you said when Cindy divorced you. Come on, Frank. We're fishing and hiking buddies. Maybe I can help."

Frank felt a spear of migraine nail him between the eyes. He pinched his eyelids shut and massaged the acne-pocked bridge of his nose. "I just think it was a mistake to let him go."

"How do you figure that?"

Frank hesitated. "Well . . . he is a main draw to the paper. I can't ignore the sales spike on Wednesdays when his review comes out."

Tom cleared his throat, working a little injury into his words. "Ahem . . . I'll remind you that my sports column has a pretty damn strong following, Frank."

Frank was floored by the laugh he heard tumbling out of his mouth. "Ease up, Delancey. You're still batting a thousand for us." He sank back into a frown. "Oscar has too much influence. He's turned *The Shorewood Gazette* into a pamphlet for witch hunts. I keep remembering that new holocaust he stirred up after the Bauer incident." Bauer . . . the name brought a sour glaze to his tongue.

"And you think he's going to turn his weapons against you?"

Frank decompressed with a sigh, relieved to hear someone else voice his dark, twisting terrors. "Uh-huh. Can't you talk to him, Tom? You're his friend."

Tom Delancey chuckled. "Whoa, back up there, Frank. I don't think anyone can claim to be Oscar Lindstrom's friend. More like neighbors by accident, colleagues by choice, acquaintances by necessity. You'd be better off getting a girl to talk to him. Is Juliana still around?"

Frank winced. "Had to let her go."

"Damn. She'd be a winner. I never underestimate the drive of a ginger to get a job done." Another chuckle.

All this good-natured ribbing made Frank want to throw his paperweight again. He glanced at it. The brass football was dented and smudged with dirt. He wished it was blood.

"I'm sick of being cooped up here, Tom. I think I'll head up to Harper Lodge for the weekend. Take Maryann with me. Why don't you come along and bring whoever the latest lodge bunny is this time?"

"Her name's Staci, and I don't think they appreciate being called lodge bunnies."

Despite the distance, Frank could still picture Tom's charming, cavalier smile stretching from cheek to cheek. Oh, to be a bachelor again. "Anyway, I'm sorry I can't help you, Frank. Taking Staci out to a ballgame at Jordan Field tomorrow. Sort of a last hurrah for the baseball season. We won't be back until late. I promise to have my article about the game ready on Monday." Tom's tone sobered again. "Hey, listen. Whatever it is Oscar has on you, it always seems worse than it really is. Don't let him get to you. That's the part he loves the most. He wants to see you squirm. Take care, buddy."

The line went dead, just like Frank's hopes for his career.

Was it his career he worried about? At the moment, he would gladly surrender the editorship for the chance to dump his problems on some other sap. Or was he afraid of Oscar's influence, the way he could manipulate people into believing anything he wanted? He had a strong core of followers. They had faith in every lie he told them. A new, paralyzing realization caught at Frank's chest, stopping his heart. Oscar Lindstrom was nothing more than a modern Adolf Hitler.

Frank should have killed him when he had the chance.

Li hitched a raisin of a backpack higher on his shoulder, waiting for a response to his knock. He bobbed on his feet, trying to shake off the aches that came from walking all the way to Reuben and Noah's apartment. He had heard the duct tape he used to hold his sneakers intact crinkle with each step.

The door flew open, and Reuben was all smiles. "Hey! You made it!"

"Yeah. Sorry I'm late. I missed the bus, so I had to walk over here."

Reuben's glance dropped to Li's feet. "In duct-taped sneakers? Your feet must be killing you. Come on in! Don't need to loiter in the hallway." He hollered over his shoulder. "Hey, babe! Our guest is here!"

Reuben pulled Li inside the apartment. It was a cozy place, meant for two. The living room, kitchen, and dining area all opened onto each other. All the furniture had a lived-in, hand-me-down feel, an eclectic collection of loaned pieces to help furnish a young couple's nest. Li could sense all the family dinners, game nights, reunions, and story times around the tables, sofas, and chairs. His heart twinged. He started to calculate how long it would take to save up for a bus ticket to visit Mom and Anna in Jefferson.

Reuben strolled into the love nest kitchen and pecked his boyfriend's cheek. "Smells delicious, honey." He turned back to his guest. "Li, this is my boyfriend, Noah Larsson. Noah, this is the guy I told you about."

"I heard Reuben was picking up strays again." Noah wiped his hands on a dish towel and shook Li's. The sparkle of welcome in his emerald-green eyes complimented the shimmer of his blond hair. His smile, wide and generous, sat a little off-center on his face. "I'm glad you could make it, Li. Make yourself at home."

Reuben nudged Li in the ribs. "Yeah, don't stand around. Take a load off. Here, let me help you with that." He slid Li's backpack off his shoulder. "Why'd you bring a backpack anyway?"

Li, his head spinning from the ocean of hospitality, shuffled into a chair at the dining table. "Sorry about that. I'm taking an

English class at Shorewood Community College. I have an essay due in a few days, and I still have a lot of work to do before I go to the library to type it up."

Reuben sat next to Li, waving aside the explanation. "No big. We were students once. I remember bringing my laptop on a date with Noah, so I could finish a business model for class. Boy, I'm lucky that he gave me another chance after that." His eyes softened as he watched his boyfriend cook. "I'm the luckiest guy on the planet." Then they swiveled back to Li, bright and glistening. "I have an idea! Instead of going to the library, why don't you type up your essay here? I've got the computer and printer. It'll save you on printing costs."

Li's cheeks flushed pink. "Oh no. I couldn't impose on you like that."

"Don't be silly. It's not an imposition. We want to help you get your education."

Li felt a strange bubbling in his chest. Did he dare call it happiness? He had never met such nice, open, friendly people before. He had to think of some way to repay them for all their generosity.

Noah called out from the kitchen. "I hope you like fried chicken, Li."

Li's stomach, deprived of a big meal for so long, went insane. It's like they knew his one weakness. "Fried chicken is my favorite meal ever. Can't get enough of it."

Noah flashed one of his half-smiles. "Awesome. Must have been intuition."

Dinner was amazing. The chicken, juicy but not greasy, warmed his whole body. The skin—his absolute favorite part—was crisp and spicy. It was paired with creamy mashed potatoes, rich scratch gravy, buttery corn on the cob, homemade coleslaw . . . the list stretched on forever. Li ate far more than he should have.

Noah shared details about their lives, how they met, their respective families. Li filled Noah in on his life. Reuben entertained them both with stories about work that made Li nearly bust a gut from laughing.

Reuben took a big bite of his drumstick. "I'm not saying Leo's a bad guy, but where did this guy learn about work ethic? Must have charmed his way through high school and peaked at college. Good schmoozer, but don't ask him to stock anything. I once found him putting overstock milk on shelves in the breakfast aisle. He said it made it easier for customers to get their milk when they bought their cereal. With that megawatt grin of his, you could almost believe it."

Noah smirked at his boyfriend. "Don't go falling for a fancy smile, babe."

Reuben settled a long kiss on Noah's cheek. His voice softened. "I already did that."

"Did you tell Noah about that customer today, Reuben?" Li asked.

Walls were thrown up. Every muscle in Reuben's body tensed. Like a runner anticipating a starter's pistol. "We're not going to talk about that."

Tiny wrinkles furrowed the space between Noah's eyes. "Honey, what's wrong?"

"We're not talking about it." He mouthed a single word to his boyfriend. Oscar. Noah's eyebrows lifted in unison. He rested a hand on Reuben's and stroked it with his thumb. Reuben gently squeezed Noah's fingers.

Noah deflected the tension. "So, Li, how're your mom and sister?"

Li pushed the remains of his dinner around his plate. Now he felt like the one throwing up walls. "They're . . . fine. I think."

"You think?" There were whispers of concern in that emerald-green stare.

"Well . . . I haven't seen or spoken to them in months. I don't have a phone, and neither do they. It's too expensive." He sighed. "Everything is too expensive."

"Isn't there someone who could get in touch with them?"

"There's our neighbors, the Watsons. Family friends. Sometimes we use their phone."

Noah fished a cell phone out of his jeans pocket and held it out to Li. "Here. Call them."

Li's eyes, wide and disbelieving, bounced between Noah's face and the phone. "Oh, I couldn't—"

"Seriously, call them. I think it'll do you some good." He pressed his cell into Li's hand. "I know my mom loves to hear from me. You can use our bedroom for privacy. Go on. Don't worry about the cost. We'll take care of it."

Li shambled into the bedroom, the phone weighing tons in his hand. Why was he so scared to call his family? Did he have this premonition of disaster? Was his family in even worse trouble than before? With his fingers like lead, he dialed a number he knew by heart and waited as the rings stretched for centuries.

"H-hi, Mrs. Watson. It's me, Li Johnson. Oh . . . yeah, I'm okay. Um . . . I-I was wondering if I could talk to Mom and Anna. That is if they're not too . . . Oh, they are home. Great! I mean . . . if it's not too much trouble. Yeah, I'll hold." His throat started to ache. "Anna Banana? It's LiLi. Have you started terrorizing pedestrians with your driving yet? Well, I'm your big brother, so I can tease you if I want, baby sister. Yes, I know you hate it when I call you that." A smile pulled at his lips. "Your seventeenth birthday is coming up. Got any ideas what you want? Uh-huh. . .Uh-huh . . . Well, I'll see if I can make it up there. Yeah, I moved to Shorewood, so I might be able to visit you soon. I miss you too, sis. Hey, put Mom on. I love you too, Anna Banana." Li felt his cheeks grow moist. "Hi, Mom. Mom, why are you crying? Oh . . . I miss you too. I told Anna that I moved to Shorewood, and I might be able to make it up to Jefferson for her birthday. Yeah, I'm okay, Mom. Yes, I have a place to live. Yes . . . Yes, I'm still eating. Mom, I'm okay. Really. I made some really cool friends. You and Anna take care of yourselves. Watch that arthritis of yours. Well, someone has to look out for you, Mom." He sniffed heavily, brushing away a loose tear. "I love you, Mom. I miss you guys a lot. I-I'll come home for a visit. I promise. Talk to you again soon. Oh, and Mom . . ." His mind drifted to the ashes in the little urn on his mother's mantle. "Tell . . . Tell Dad I love him."

He clicked off the phone, which had grown blurry from the tears gleaming in his silver-blue eyes. He chuckled weakly and fisted away more tears. He didn't expect to get so emotional. He hobbled out of the bedroom, his hands unable to stem the crying. He handed the phone back to Noah. Despite the waterworks, Li smiled, and his cheeks were glossy and rosy. "Thanks, I ... I-I really needed that."

"You okay? How's your family?"

"They're fine. It's ... I just haven't heard their voices in a long time. It was nice. They sounded ... happy." He sniffed and wiped his eyes on his sleeve. "Aw geez ... I can't stop crying. I must look like a total crybaby to you."

Reuben's smile was warm and understanding. "You really miss them, don't you?"

Li remembered a treasured photo in his wallet. A happy family of four playing in the beach sand. "I miss all of them. Guys ... I really don't know how to thank you for all this. I'm feeling overwhelmed. This is seriously the nicest thing anyone has ever done for me since ... since my dad died. Thank you so much. I think if you gave me anything else, I'd completely fall apart."

Reuben chuckled. "Well, we were going to save it for after dessert, but what the hell? Merry Christmas Happy Birthday *Feliz Navidad!*"

He handed Li a box. Li's fingers shook as he pried it open. Inside was a clean, shiny, brand-spanking-new pair of sneakers.

"If they don't fit, we can always—"

Li heard nothing more after that. He cried his soul out.

CHAPTER 3

Tonight

Oscar uncrumpled the blood-streaked note for the seventh time. His eyes devoured the angry, trembling block letters screaming at him in all capitals. Obviously, a pitiful attempt to disguise one's handwriting. Couldn't these neophytes do a little research before executing these remedial acts of revenge?

He didn't even care that a page from his first book had been violated. And this special delivery was so bad that Kathryn didn't shriek when she unwrapped the package. Ever practical, she tossed the gift into the garbage.

But Oscar kept the note. It amused him.

He looked out of his spotless home office window, witnessing the invasion of clouds pulling over the roof of his house. The weatherman reported an overcast day and a moonless night. Oscar took this as a thumbs-up from Mother Nature.

His poisonous glare returned to the message in his hand. Surely this idiot wouldn't try something tonight? Then his bloated lips oozed into a smile, and the waxen texture of his cheeks seemed to glow as he outlined his plans. He gave a chuckle permission to wobble in his throat. A childish moment of doubt. Nobody did anything on Sundays. Day of rest. No hotheaded crybaby would interfere with the day's goals. Not when they were glued to the idiot box watching *Sunday Night Football.*

Oscar crumpled the note into a ball and pitched it over his shoulder into the trash can. Perfect shot. Like always. He smirked at the view, at the blanket of gray clouds trying its best to smother the sunlight.

"Tonight," he muttered.

Constance Henderson kept her jaw set, her chin aloft, and her eyes level with her duplicate in the salon's mirror. Selena, buxom and blonde, ran a comb through the trademark black-and-silver hair. Selena was the only stylist in the salon who didn't insist on removing the gray. Constance liked that.

"So where are we going today, Mrs. Mayor?"

Ah ... Mrs. Mayor. The title that defined her as the First Lady of Shorewood.

She favored the girl with a political smile. "What would you suggest for a covert mission?"

Selena giggled. "If it was me, I'd do a low chignon just about here." She cupped her fingers around the nape of Constance's neck. "And give you a stronger fringe. Something simple. Nothing flashy that would draw attention to itself."

A bun and bangs to hide my eyes, Constance thought. "It sounds perfect."

Selena's comb whipped through the stormy hair. "Shall I trim the ends for you?"

"Only if it's necessary."

Constance shut out the world again, sheltered in her thoughts. It didn't matter if the girl believed the covert mission story or not. All Constance cared about was information. Information fueled clout. And clout, the brass ring she spent her whole life reaching for, could smooth out any hiccup in an otherwise flawless situation.

Her thoughts soured. *Damn Marshall! Damn him! Damn him! Damn him!*

However, she could handle Marshall. Oscar was the man she had to control. Constance felt her blood beat in her jaw. She knew he was planning something. Something huge. She had never seen him so happy before, and a happy Oscar was a plague to the city of Shorewood.

"I'm going to take off about an inch, Mrs. Mayor. Just the ends, okay?"

"What? Oh ... oh yes. That's fine."

She remembered Friday. She watched him saunter home. Oscar had been on the cusp of singing and skipping. Her sources said he resigned from *The Shorewood Gazette* that afternoon. Her internal sirens blared. Oscar wouldn't leave a job where he had power unless he had a very persuasive reason. Cutting off all ties.

Separating himself from a powder keg. And there was his threat on Saturday. Veiled, yes, but it was there. A deadly threat wrapped in pleasantries. What did he plan to do with his information?

But his walk home didn't start at *The Gazette* offices. That was farther across town. And he had the smug smile of a man whose plans were crystallizing. The place where he started that walk made him deliriously happy. She could feel his fur-patched paws clamp down on her throat. Where had he been? What did he do there?

"I hate cloudy days," Selena moaned as she styled Constance's bangs. "They're too gloomy. The weatherman said it would be a cloudy night too. No stars or moon or anything. It'll be like living in a cave."

A cloudy night. Perfect night for espionage.

"It's just winter reminding us that it's coming, Selena. Did the report definitely say there would be no moon?"

She knew where Oscar had been headed. Home to his chippie.

But where the hell did he come from?

The report was accurate. The plush bank of clouds filling the skies all day stayed resolute. Shorewood was pitched into darkness by seven o'clock, the sky so clean and black that it seemed God had rubbed out the moon and the stars. Rain threatened to arrive uninvited.

The gray house sat as still as a tombstone on the calm, quiet street. A screen in a second-story window jostled in its seat. Something inside pushed and prodded along the casing. After a few cricks and creaks, the window screen popped out of its setting. The gloved hands were expert in their movements. The screen didn't slip from their hold and withdrew into the house without so much as a scrape. Sly as a cat burglar, a man crept through the open window, perched on his toes.

This was the tricky part. The tree limb was pliable, given to sway at the slightest breath of breeze. Keeping one hand glued to the sill, the man reached out for the branch. It moved, unprovoked, and grazed his gloved fingertips, slipping through them.

The man swore. He was a lively swearer when certain monsters weren't around.

Another unprovoked sway brought the limb into his palm, his hand closing upon it like a bear trap. He pulled on the branch, wishing he could drag the whole tree closer, fighting to ignore the beading of sweat on his forehead. Now came the scary part. He had to do it. He couldn't wait until Wednesday. There wouldn't be any more Wednesday jaunts after Friday's bombshell. This was an emergency. Calming his heartbeat with a soul-reaching breath, the man pushed off the wall with his feet and let go of the sill, his free hand swinging for the branch.

His hand made contact, and he strangled the limb with his fingers. Thank Jesus for his slender frame. He swung his legs up until they twisted around the branch. Even though he'd done that move thousands of times, it still boggled his mind. He shimmied across the branch toward the tree trunk, where the descent would be lifetimes easier.

His feet made a soft *flop* in the well-gardened grass lawn. Cats aren't the only ones who always land on their feet, he thought. Sparing a brief glance at the open window that would accept his return, the man raced off into the Shorewood night, his sneaker-steps muffled by the grass he took care to stay on.

Jason Lindstrom had escaped from his prison again.

"Sunday nights are slow, Li. Be prepared for long hours and no action. Nobody really buys groceries at this hour. It'll be a grave-yard in here."

Reuben taught Li how to use the handheld scanners, and they were busy logging price changes on boxes of oatmeal. Li stocked them onto the beige metal shelves. "I don't mind quiet nights. I kind of need one after last night."

"Speaking of that, Noah and I would love it if you came again sometime. We promise not to make you cry."

Li laughed. "Oh don't worry about it. After tasting your boyfriend's food, I'm tempted to move in with you guys."

Reuben's grin brightened his face. "Why do you think I love him so much?"

"Are you going to marry Noah?"

An unexpected blush filtered into Reuben's cheeks, giving them a healthy russet glow. His smile shrank into that of a shy child's. "I really, really, *really* want to. There's just so many questions though. Are we ready? Are we too young? Besides, I wanted to wait until Noah got his master's degree." He closed the narrative with a sharp nod. "Then I'll marry him. It's a done deal."

"I'm looking forward to the big engagement." Li scanned more boxes, his fingers dancing over the keypad like he had been working here for years. "So ... um ... can I ask you something?"

"Of course you can."

Li fiddled with a few buttons on the scanner, buttons he didn't need to push. "Well ... uh ... what's with you and Oscar anyway?"

Reuben's face hardened into sandstone. "Nope. Not going to talk about that. No way."

"He really pissed you off though."

"I'm not listening to this."

"Reuben, I—"

Reuben slammed a box on the shelf, making other boxes fall over. "Fine. I hate him. I hate his guts. Satisfied? No more discussion."

Li lifted his hands in surrender. "Okay okay, I was just worried. You said you were close to assaulting him. You've been so nice to me, and it was scary to see you get that angry. What would happen if you ran into him again?"

"Oh, I better not. Twice in a weekend is already too much. I'd bash him in the head."

"Don't make jokes like that!" Li's memories zoomed back to the cruise ship where he last worked. A body. Artfully displayed. Roasting in the summer sun.

Reuben turned dark, bleak eyes to his trainee. "Who said I was joking?"

Thunder rolled over the roof of Esther's Family Grocery.

"Looks like our forecasters forgot to mention the rain." Leo Lewis, millionaire's smile pinned to his face, strolled down the breakfast aisle with the swagger of a man who has conquered the world. "It's going to be a wet night. How's it going over here, boys?"

Li tried to make eye contact with Reuben and failed. "Almost done, Leo."

"Hey, you remembered. Excellent. I have another job for both of you. Unfortunately, I have to split up the dream team."

"Fine by me," Reuben said. He mumbled to himself: "I think I need to be alone for a little bit anyway."

Li's stress lines, which had been smoothing out for the past two days, returned in sharp relief on his young face.

"Reuben, I think you can handle the rest of these price changes. After the oatmeal, we need to do some on the canned pasta. Aisle five."

"Sure thing, boss." Reuben's words dropped from his lips like lead sinkers, thudding on the tortured linoleum.

"Perfect. Liam, could you use the long dust mop and sweep these floors? Make them sparkle? The dust mop is over in produce."

Li fussed with his necktie, casting concerned looks at Reuben. "S-sure."

"Great. Wonderful. I'm lucky to have you both here." Leo strode off again, chest out, chin up.

"Reuben, I just want to say that—"

Reuben forestalled him with a hard look, holding out an open palm for the handheld scanner. The frown tucked into his face told Li everything he needed to know. Li blushed, handed over the scanner, and left for the produce section.

He found the dust mop leaning against the self-serve nut bins and started weaving the bristled head around the pyramids of oranges, apples, potatoes, and onions. Reuben was right. The supermarket was a graveyard tonight. Li could count off the number of customers on one hand. He saw a lady—definitely a lady by the way she held her shoulders and chin—in a black silk jumpsuit taking a rather overt interest in the prepared salad mixes.

Almost like she refused to let Li see her face. He shook the idea out of his head and began sweeping the perimeter, scanning the store for other customers.

There was a young couple exchanging furious glances with each other in the snack aisle. A man in a dripping, yellow slicker returned the glassy stare of a dead fish in the seafood counter. A stoner tried to open a can of SpaghettiOs with his fingers. A sad crowd. All of them too absorbed in their own bubbles of consciousness. Two months ago, Li would have given his eyeteeth to have this sort of freedom and peace at work. Now nobody wanted him.

But, he mused, recalling the deadly interference at his last job, this sure beats the alternative. *Let's keep everyone alive this time, okay?*

He wove through the aisles next, eyes still searching the customers, this time to check for vital signs. He felt this weird churning in the core of his stomach. Like motion sickness. He pictured Reuben's face from yesterday—cheeks saturated with blood, eyes dark with murder, snarl warping his smile. All of it aimed at a man nicknamed Oscar the Grouch. Who was he? What did he mean to Reuben?

Speaking of Reuben, he was in aisle five, apron smudged with bright red stains, waving a Wet Floor sign over a damp patch on the linoleum floor. He snarled at the stoner, who giggled at the splashes of red on his distressed jeans and steel-toe boots. Li scurried out of the aisle before Reuben targeted that snarl at him.

Li rounded the endcap and swept down the spice aisle. He shoved Reuben's problems out of his brain. They were none of his business. He didn't have to—

Thump. The dust mop bumped into something big and thick blocking the aisle. Li's heart stuttered. He pulled back the dust mop, lifting a sad, dirty curtain on a horrible sideshow. A man lay across the breadth of the spice aisle, his back facing Li. He must have been sick. Or he fainted. Li had to get help. Or try to revive him.

He would have … except for that spreading halo of blood around the man's head.

The dust mop clattered on the floor. Li stumbled backward, plastering both hands to his mouth and banging into the shelves behind him. Spice shakers cartwheeled to the ground, some of them shattering and coughing up clouds of pepper, cinnamon, and oregano. Li sneezed, and his eyes started to flood with tears. He didn't know if it was from shock, terror, or the spicy, vinegary scent of blood washing over him.

Don't go into shock, he told himself. *This isn't your first . . . your first body. Breathe. Do what Doc Innsbrook told you on the cruise ship. Breathe.*

Li coughed and wheezed, pulling himself out of the spice-rich fog. He tiptoed toward the unconscious man. His feet blundered over a five-pound bag of sugar lounging near the swelling ocean of blood. *Blood. Oh God, I hate blood.* Careful not to tread in the puddle, Li stretched out a trembling hand and rolled the man on his back. The man plopped onto the tile with a wet squelch.

He looked even uglier than Li remembered. The face sagged like a popped balloon. A fat, purple bruise sat squarely on the bald crown of his head. Blood oozed like strawberry jam through a crack in his skull. His eyes were accusatory, blaming Li for the mess on the floor he had been ordered to clean.

But Oscar the Grouch wouldn't levy another critique about Li's work ethic.

He was dead.

Li scuttled away from the accusing eyes, the body, *the blood.* Hyperventilation seized his lungs. Swallowing a thick draft of air, he staggered toward the front of the store. He slipped on a few wet spots on the floor, crashing to the ground. His wide, tear-streaked eyes met the dead man's glare. YOU DID THIS, they screamed. YOU DID THIS! YOU DID THIS! YOU DID THIS!

Now he knew how Medusa's victims felt.

Li crawled out of the spice aisle, swayed to his feet, and started to shout, unaware how weak and shrill his voice was.

"Someone! Anyone! Call the police!"

CHAPTER 4

Police

He was a dead ringer for Sidney Poitier.

Or better yet, for Sidney Poitier playing Mr. Tibbs in *In the Heat of the Night*.

Detective Antoine Hughes brushed the peppering of raindrops off his close-cut black hair, resisted shaking the water off his bullet-gray overcoat, and let his eyes settle on the activity in front of him. Esther's Family Grocery was a hole in the wall, especially with the new Whole Foods in town. He doubted if Esther's had ever been as busy as it was right now.

Adam, his shadow, sauntered up behind him. "Boy, this is probably the busiest this place has ever been. I've never been here before. I shop at Whole Foods."

Detective Hughes shifted his appraisal from the store to his partner for the case. Adam Schafer-Schmidt was young, which, to the senior officer, meant he was just over thirty. His rain-slicked dishwater-blond hair made him look even younger. The kid was up for promotion to detective, and the chief thought it was best to get Adam's feet wet early on a potentially big case.

Detective Hughes glanced at his sodden shoes and wished the idiom hadn't been so appropriate.

"The meds here, Adam?"

"Yes. They arrived a few minutes before we did."

"Who is it?"

"Dr. Reynolds."

Detective Hughes let the muscles around his heart relax. "Good. Rick's sound. Doesn't keep us waiting. Let's get this over with. It's a foul night to be out."

Detective Hughes and his partner strode past the checkout stands, where customers and staff clumped around with space-ship eyes and rubber necks. They didn't have to go far. The crime scene—if it was a crime—splashed out before them like an ugly piece of pop art. *Cleanup on Aisle Six*, it would be called. Flashy and trashy.

A young man wrapped in a black turtleneck sweater and boot-cut Levi's crouched next to the body, shaking his head. A frown pinched together his dark, high-arched eyebrows.

"Whatcha got for me, Rick?"

Dr. Eric Reynolds, Shorewood medical examiner, spared a glance at the detective. "Glad it's you, Tony. I wouldn't want a rookie to mess this one up."

"Spare the barbs, Rick. I've got a fresh one with me."

Dr. Reynolds peered around Detective Hughes, where Adam scribbled notes in a palm-sized notebook. "Adam's good. He keeps clean, has a nose for trouble, and has no agenda. Better than most."

"Got a name for this one?" He thrust his chin at the man on the floor.

"Oscar Lindstrom. I recognized him from his picture in *The Shorewood Gazette*. He writes the Tough Bites column."

"Oh . . . the food critic guy. Heard he's kind of nasty."

"Let's just say the ugliness wasn't confined to his looks."

"Harsh. Well, what happened?"

Dr. Reynolds swung his eyes back to the blood-rimmed body. "I think it speaks for itself."

It certainly did. The man lay on his back, arms flopped open. A bushy, black pelt of an overcoat swallowed his body. Insulted eyes glared at the stuttering fluorescent lights overhead. Blood leaked out of his head. Detective Hughes glanced at his partner. This kid held up extremely well. No sign of nausea or even horror. Just strict and professional. He approved.

He inspected the rest of the scene. A five-pound bag of sugar swam in the blood, an island in an ugly sea. One of those long-handled dusters lay farther down the aisle. Nearby, several spice shakers crumbled in a heap on the floor. Detective Hughes sniffed. Yep. The spices were in the air, mixing with the vinegary tang of blood. He had the flavor of blood and clove on his tongue. A unique experience.

"So how long has he been dead, Rick?"

"Not very long. An hour. Hour and a half tops."

"What killed him?"

"A big-ass crack in his skull." Dr. Reynolds used his rubber-sheathed hands to maneuver the head. A fat bruise bloomed on the scalp, followed by a bloody depression smashed into the skull. Not pretty.

"How do you suppose that happened?"

"Tough to say. When I get him over to the lab, I'll be able to examine him more thoroughly. But it's an interesting wound. Not a sharp edge, but ... I would say a rounded one. And something square or rectangular."

"Care to put that in more plain terms?"

"I'd say you're looking for something hard and square with rounded corners. That should be enough to get you started."

"Like that bag of sugar?"

Dr. Reynolds glared at the bag lounging in the man's blood. "Oh, I hate that sugar ..."

"Because it's bad for your health?"

"It may have been. You see ... superficially, it fits the criteria. Square with rounded corners. But I don't think it's strong enough. Look at the wound." He drew a gloved finger over the crack. "This was a single blow. And I mean a hard blow. Whatever hit him had done so with enough force to split open his skull. The bag of sugar wouldn't hold up. The paper would tear, and there'd be sugar everywhere."

"So something else hit him hard enough that it could be in a million pieces for all we know?"

"I'll check the wound for particulate matter, but I'd say the instrument that hit him held up afterwards. So we're talking thick, chunky, and hard."

"So why is the sugar even there?"

"I have no idea. And I hate that."

Adam cut in. "Maybe it fell from the top shelf. See?" He pointed with his pen.

Reynolds and Hughes followed the pen to the riser above a four-foot section of spices. Lined like teeth, bags of sugar matching the delinquent spanned the shelf, a gap marking where one had fallen. Detective Hughes saw that the shelf rose directly overhead where the body lay.

"So this bag fell from the riser and clocked the guy?" he asked.

"It's possible." Dr. Reynolds scowled at the sugar. "But it's still not hard enough to crack his skull like that."

"Enough for the bruise?"

Dr. Reynolds let his eyebrows merge over his nose, his forehead creased. "Yes . . . I think so. Provided that it fell and hit him. It won't work the other way."

"Other way?"

"Have you ever tried swinging a bag of sugar in your hand? It's really awkward."

"So you don't think this could be an accident?"

Dr. Reynolds challenged him with a higher-arched eyebrow. "Would you?"

"Murder?"

"Murder."

Detective Hughes unloaded a sigh and ran his palm over his hair. A few stray drops of water pelted the floor. "Okay, boys, we got a homicide. Let's round these folks up and start the legwork. Get that photographer, Adam. Anyone mind telling me what happened over there?" He pointed to the duster and broken spice shakers. "Who found the body?"

Dr. Reynolds hitched a thumb at a young man waiting near the endcap. "Kid who works here found him. I gathered he had a bit of a panic attack. We're lucky he didn't puke. I brought out a bucket just in case he couldn't hold it in, but I think he's holding up okay."

"Must not be his first body," Adam said.

Detective Hughes cursed Adam and his ability to echo his thoughts.

"Hey, kid," he called out. "Come over here."

If Adam and Dr. Reynolds were kids to Detective Hughes, this one was practically a baby. Hardly out of his teens. Smooth, pale skin contrasted with a hard set in his chin and jaw. Stress lines—old ones, too—wreathed his mouth and eyes. Short, sharply groomed black hair crowned his head. The boy had a remarkable pair of eyes, a mottled silver-blue that reminded Detective Hughes of mountain lakes on overcast days. They were wide, searching, intense with ... fear? Yes, he supposed there was fear in them, but it wasn't the terror of a nameless evil a kid never encountered before. These eyes had knowledge in them. They knew evil. It was fear with roots.

Interesting.

"What's your name?"

The boy's mouth trembled. "Liam, sir. Liam Johnson."

"You work here?"

"Yes, sir. Evening shift today. I'm a new hire, sir."

Polite kid. Respected authority. Point in his favor.

"How did you come to find the body?"

Liam told his tale, exact in his details. Detective Hughes summed it up: "So you were asked to sweep the floors. You turned the back corner from aisle five and accidentally ran into the body. You saw him, dropped the duster, and retreated into the shelves, knocking off the spices. Then you turned him onto his back, saw he was dead, and called for help."

"I also slipped on some water that was on the floor." The boy massaged his elbow. "Right after I saw that ... he was dead. I slipped, hit the floor, and then scrambled out to get help."

"Where did you slip?"

"Maybe a couple feet from the body. Towards the front of the store."

"Who phoned it in?"

"My boss, Leonard Lewitski. He goes by Leo Lewis around here. He thinks it sounds better." Liam blushed. "Sorry, didn't mean to talk like that. Anyway, he ran up when he heard me shout, saw the the body, and ran to the phone."

"Where did he come from?"

Liam frowned and narrowed his eyes. "From the direction of the bakery, I think. That's just to the right of the big doors when you enter the store."

"All right. Now back to the body. You said you turned the body over to see who it was. So that means the body is not in the same position when you originally found it. Is that correct?"

"Yes, sir."

"Okay. Where's that photographer?" A uniformed officer cradling a Nikon in his callused hands materialized at his side. "Good. Take a few pictures of the scene as is. Then we'll have Liam here put it back the way it was when he found it. Make sure we label these pictures properly, boys."

After a few explosions of light from the camera's flash, Liam turned Oscar's body onto its right side, a tight grimace crimping his mouth shut. The camera flashed away again.

Detective Hughes nodded slowly. "So he's standing here at the spice shelves, scanning for an ingredient, let's say. Maybe someone knocks into the shelves on the other side, tipping the sugar bag over. It hits him on the head, bruising him." Now the mental picture started to grow fuzzy. "Does it knock him out? Stun him? Is that when the killer walks by, sees his advantage, and bludgeons him with some impossible weapon? What do you think, Rick?"

Dr. Reynolds stuffed his now gloveless hands into his jeans pockets. "Too soon to tell, Tony."

Liam fidgeted and fussed with his black necktie. "Excuse me, Detective, but I don't think he was standing when it happened."

Detective Hughes drummed his fingers against his leg, biting back the urge to check his watch. "And why do you think that, son?"

Liam wrung his hands together for a second or two. He released a breath and walked up to the edge of the shelves. "I'm about the same height as Oscar, right? See how the top of my head is almost in line with the riser? It's not very high up. Makes it easier for customers to reach it."

"Get to the point, son."

"Erm ... yes, sorry. Anyway, *if* the bag of sugar fell while he was standing, it would only fall over about two or three inches before hitting him. Hardly enough to bruise him as badly as he appears to be." An odd ripple of light, like sunshine off a knight's helmet, worked across the boy's blue eyes. "Unless . . ."

"Unless?"

"Unless he was squatting." Here Liam squatted in front of the shelves, shrinking into the linoleum. "Now the distance between his head and the shelf increases exponentially. When the bag falls, it has time to build up momentum and hit him harder than it would have if he stood."

"Sound reasonable. Rick?"

Dr. Reynolds's dark eyebrows almost disappeared into his hairline. He laughed. "I'd say it's spot-on, Tony! Nice bit of headwork, kid. I was thinking along those lines myself. I believe that's a sound explanation for the bruise."

Detective Hughes wasn't inclined to look as impressed. "So Oscar was squatting when the bag hit him. What was he looking at?"

Liam swept a hand along one of the lower shelves. "Spices and seasonings. We've got everything from allspice to cinnamon to dried sage to pepper to cumin to thyme to—"

"Yes. Thanks for your help, kid. Stick around for a while. I'll have more questions later. And keep your little discoveries to yourself."

"But I—"

"Did you get his statement, Adam?"

"Every bit, Tony."

"Good. Then we don't need to have him linger near the crime scene." He shooed Liam out of the spice aisle, then wiped his forehead with the back of his hand. "Let's keep our findings to ourselves, boys. I don't want a bunch of little Sherlocks tramping all over my evidence. How's the search? Find anything good?"

Adam handed his superior a slip of paper zipped into an evidence bag. "I think you might want to see this, sir. We found it in . . . kind of a strange place."

Li fumbled over his feet when the detective shoved him out of the spice aisle. He jerked his apron to straighten it and overcorrected his tie. Of course, it wasn't his problem. The police could handle it. He didn't have any reason to care about Oscar's death. He could ignore the odd motion sickness and the tight threads of fear around his throat and just focus on—

A flutter of neon yellow disappeared down an aisle. Li caught the barest ripple of motion out of the corner of his eye. His thoughts took him to regions he wanted to avoid.

Reuben?

He shuffled into the neighboring aisle—pasta. Empty. Not a soul in sight. But Reuben worked here just before Li found Oscar. By himself. His only witness was too stoned to remember him. He was close enough to see something. Hear something.

Do something.

Li remembered those warm, friendly eyes smoldering like two lethal beds of tar. The fingers throttling the corner of an apron. A man on the verge of assault.

Li shivered and tucked his arms around his body.

"You complete moron!"

Voices. Heated, tense, muffled into whispers. Li's thoughts screeched to a halt. He peeked through the perforated backing of the canned pasta shelves. Two silhouettes loitered in the juice aisle. Two voices floated through the perforation. One was female, brusque, efficient, sharp. One was male, apologetic, frantic.

"What the hell are you doing here, Frank?"

"Honestly, Connie, I didn't know you were here!"

"I know that. Don't you think I realized that?"

"I wouldn't imply—"

"Stop talking, Frank. The plan was that you stayed away from my husband and me."

"I wasn't following you, Connie! I swear! I followed Oscar!"

Li sucked in his breath. Someone here hunted Oscar.

Connie shushed him. "I suggest you keep that little confession to yourself, Frank. You don't want to tip the police off, do you?"

"Connie, what are we going to do? Oscar's dead. I mean . . . are all of our problems over? Are we free?"

"Of course not. Oscar was murdered. Tony Hughes isn't the kind of man that shirks his duty. Keeping him from the truth will be an uphill war. And his partner, Schafer-Schmidt, is no weakling. Nickname at the station is Wolf. Known to be relentless, a hunter."

"How do you know all of this?"

Yes, Li thought. *How do you know?*

"I have my sources, reliable as any reporter's."

There was a faint lilt of irony in her voice. Li suspected that meant Frank was a reporter or worked on a newspaper. Did he work with Oscar?

"Here's what you're going to say, Frank. You were buying last-minute groceries for a staff party you're holding this week. It would help if you actually had the party. I'm sure Maryann can throw something together. Where did you spend most of your time here?"

"Seafood."

"Damn. That's a harder sell. No matter. Use your imagination. Whatever you do, do not mention Oscar in any way. Don't get overly maudlin about his death. That's a red flag for any cop. Just pretend you were ignorant that Oscar was here. Simple. Straightforward. And if you say anything about Marshall or me, I'll see you hanged as a horse thief. Understand?"

One of the silhouettes bobbed its head wildly. A nervous nod.

"Good. See that you do that. I'll do what I can to smooth things over with Tony. Won't be easy. He's not like Roy. Roy is butter in my hands."

Smoothing things over with the police. Li's stomach twisted into knots.

"We need to discuss what you're going to say about his death on Monday, Frank."

Frank's voice didn't sound so weak now. It was dull and harsh. "I can just print the basics. Oscar's resignation won't come into it at all."

Li lifted an eyebrow and leaned farther into the shelf. *Oscar resigned? From what? From* The Shorewood Gazette?

"Perfect. If anything, you could suggest that Oscar was killed by some maniac drug fiend or something. I think I saw a whacked-out punk shuffling around here tonight."

"I'll save the speculation for later. Just the basics will be enough to disarm—"

"Wait a minute. I thought I saw something in the next aisle."

Air evacuated from Li's lungs. He jerked backward, accidentally grazing a can of SpaghettiOs with his arm. It whistled against the metal shelf.

Connie swore. "I think someone's listening to us. *Get him.*"

Li fled from the shelves and collided with Reuben's belly. He bounced off and crashed to the floor, landing on his injured elbow.

"What do you think you're doing, Li?"

Massaging the new bump, Li craned his neck over his shoulder and caught a blur of yellow and black, like a giant wasp, flit down the back aisle of the store. His gaze swung to Reuben's face. Dark eyes like black ice bored into his. A frown tugged at Reuben's mouth, pushing out his bottom lip. His helpful hand was slow to react.

That look on Reuben's face, cold, hostile, solidified the vague, wispy fears in Li's heart. Reuben, his coworker. Reuben, his new friend. Reuben, his savior. Could it be? Did he—?

Li brushed invisible dust off his apron and avoided that cold, dark glare. "I ... um ... I was just ..." All his arguments crumbled before reaching his lips.

Reuben knotted his arms across his chest. "'Cuz it looks like you're snooping to me. Or do you always stuff your head into shelves?"

"I ... uh ... I thought I heard something."

"What?"

"Oh, it ... it's not important."

Reuben's eyes whittled into tight slits. "So you're eavesdropping on something boring?"

Li wiped the veneer of sweat on his palms onto his pants. "I ... uh ..."

"You know, Hughes hates snoops. I don't think it's smart to play detective while he's on the case." He waved a hand at the security cameras stationed around the perimeter. "Don't you think the cameras will catch your little Sherlock act?"

"Cameras," Li muttered. His eyes sprang wide open. "Reuben ... the security cameras! The police can watch the tapes and find out who killed Oscar!"

Reuben broke out in applause, his smile snide. "Oh, brilliant deduction, Holmes! I'm sure Hughes hasn't even thought of that yet!" His smile withered into a scowl. "Unless the cameras shorted out like they did during our last little drizzle. The electrical here is shoddy at best. And those cameras are dirt cheap. For all we know, the police will be treated to a late show of white noise."

Li pinched his mouth into a grim line. "Wait a second. How do you know Detective Hughes?"

Reuben's eyes seemed to frost over. "Nope. I'm the one asking questions now. Why are you really over here?"

"Reuben, I—"

"Were you spying on the cops? Trying to solve Oscar's murder for them?"

"No! I was just—"

"Or were you trying to find something on me?"

A cold weight plopped into Li's stomach. He dropped his eyes to his feet.

Reuben shook his head, reminiscent of a parent disciplining a child. "I can't believe you, Li. Don't you think I have eyes? I saw you sneak down this aisle. I know I worked here by myself. I know my alibi rests on some dude who won't even remember tonight. But do you really think I killed Oscar?" His eyes started to simmer. "Well? Spit it out. You think I'm a crazy killer, don't you?"

"I never said that!"

"But you're thinking it. It's written all over your face."

Li bobbed on his feet. "You ... You did say you hated him."

"Thanks for the vote of confidence, buddy."

Reuben spun on his heel and started to march out of the pasta aisle. Li seized him by the back of his shirt. "Reuben! Wait! I didn't say I want to believe it! I . . . It's just . . . I mean . . ."

Reuben ripped himself free. "Save it. You've said enough."

"Would you let me finish?"

"You can barely form a complete sentence! What, you think I *want* to hear you accuse me of murder? Because that's what you're going to do!"

Li restrained him with a hand on the shoulder. "I haven't accused you of anything! Can't I speak for myself for once?"

Reuben charged at Li and pinned him to the shelves with his belly. His eyes fumed, and his cheeks burned with blood. "Fine, buddy. Say it. Make it short."

"H-how do you know Oscar?"

Dark brown eyebrows scaled Reuben's forehead. "Seriously? That's your question? What about 'Did you kill Oscar?' or 'Why did you bash in his ugly face?'"

"I want to know how you knew him. He knew you and your family. You're hiding something."

"I'm allowed to keep some things private, Li."

Li's eyes blazed like steel in a forge. "You think so, buddy? Because I guarantee that the police will find out about it."

A shadow of fear flickered on Reuben's face. "I . . . um . . . Sometimes I'd read his column in *The Shorewood Gazette*. Tough Bites. Just a restaurant review. It's nothing."

"You're evading the question."

"Yeah, well, I don't like your questions." He pulled away from Li. "If the police find anything about Oscar in my past, it's their problem. Not yours. This is none of your business." He swung away from Li and stomped toward the end of the aisle. There was the flimsiest thread of tears brewing against his eyelids.

Li called out to him. "And what will Noah think if his boyfriend is held for questioning about killing a man he hated?"

It was the cheapest shot he could have made. Li's stomach wrenched at his words. *Oh crap. Did I really just say that?*

Reuben's shoes screeched on the linoleum. He swung around. Now his eyes screamed murder. His voice shook, and he had trouble keeping his fingers from curling into fists. "You know what, Li? I think you can take care of yourself from now on. Have a great life, jerk."

He stormed away with a full hurricane over his head.

Nice going, Johnson. Care to say something else stupid? Maybe something that can get you arrested? You seem to be on a roll tonight.

Li clutched his face in his hands, rubbing his temples. His temper and his mouth betrayed him. Again. So much for his luck turning around. He slouched out of the pasta aisle, dragging his feet on the cracked linoleum. And each little fissure in the floor reminded him of the crack in Oscar's skull.

Murder. Oh God, another murder at my job. Exactly what I needed. Li scuffed the floor with his new shoes and hobbled toward the waiting crowd. He didn't get far. Over his shoulder, he heard some official mumblings and the brisk patter of feet. He jerked his head toward the noise.

Detective Hughes, hands jammed into his overcoat pockets, strode out of aisle six and scanned the cluster of faces in front of him. "Who's in charge here?"

Leo faltered forward. He tried to slap on his million-dollar smile, but it came across as a fifty-cent failure. "I-I am, Detective. Leo Lewis, manager of Esther's Family Grocery."

Detective Hughes let his gaze rove over the young manager. "I'd like to talk to you first. Find out how this place works. Is there somewhere I can set up shop for a bit? Get these preliminary interviews out of the way?"

"Y-yes, sir. My office. It's up the stairs here." Leo pointed to a staircase rising from a little hallway behind the checkout stands. They led to a mezzanine level overlooking the supermarket behind a row of one-way windows. The manager's office and security rooms were hidden there.

Detective Hughes cleared his throat. His voice was deep and official, a man used to respect. "I know it's been a long night and you all want to get home. I personally don't want to stay here until two a.m. However, I want to be thorough. And the best way to do that is to have your complete—"

"Of course, we'll cooperate, Detective Hughes. I can't think of a single citizen who wouldn't."

Li gaped at the woman with the nerve to interrupt the detective. That voice, deep and robust, commanded attention. The lady in the black silk jumpsuit marched out of the crowd, hand outstretched as if expecting the detective to kiss it. Her hair, its colors a reflection of the storm outside, had been bundled into a fat knot at the nape of her neck. Strong, level bangs tickled her eyelashes.

Detective Hughes had an excellent poker face, but there was a microscopic lift to his eyebrows. "Ah, Mrs. Mayor. It's a surprise to see you here."

"One of these unfortunate coincidences. How are Maddy and the kids?"

"Um . . . just fine."

Li arched an eyebrow high into his forehead. *Who's Mrs. Mayor anyway?*

The lady beamed at the detective, her dentist-adored teeth sparkling. "I'm sure I can speak for the entire Shorewood community when I say we will do everything in our power to assist you in solving this heinous crime. I will happily volunteer to be interviewed first as an example for the people."

If Li wore glasses, he would have peered over the rims. *Example for what? That the police aren't scary? Or do you want to impress your version of tonight's events on the police?*

Detective Hughes's smile could compete with Leo's. "That's very kind of you, Mrs. Mayor, but I believe I wish to keep the investigation moving in a certain direction. I promise to get your statement at the earliest possible convenience."

Mrs. Mayor kept her smile civil, but her eyes, dark as the thunderclouds brewing above the store, narrowed. "I understand, Detective. Very proper of you. Give my best to your wife." Chin held high, she paraded back into the crowd.

Detective Hughes addressed the assembly again. "Let's not waste any more time. Mr. Lewis, I'll start with you. Let's go up to your office. As for everyone else, Officer Schafer-Schmidt"— he gestured to the man standing close enough to crowd out his shadow — "will fetch you one by one. Please stay available for questioning. Nobody leaves the store or town without my permission."

He clapped a hand on Leo's shoulder and guided him toward the stairs. Leo looked like a man walking to the gallows. Detective Hughes stalled at the base of the stairs, doubled back, and scanned the crowd. His eyes settled on Li.

He thrust his chin at the boy. "You come with us, Liam. I have a few questions for you."

CHAPTER 5

Third Degree

Li's knee jittered, and he rubbed his sweat-coated palms on his apron. His eyes darted to the sad gray clock on the sad gray wall. Twenty minutes since Detective Hughes shut him away in Leo's office, in a little gray cell with gray walls, gray desk, gray chairs, gray filing cabinets, and even a gray view, since the windows hadn't been thoroughly cleaned in several months. A blizzard of papers scattered across the dented metal desktop suggested that Leo might be over his head trying to manage a grocery store.

Li started to rock in the metal folding chair, listening to the creaks of the joints. How long was he supposed to wait in here? Until he hammered a hole in the floor with his nervous foot? Until he—?

Detective Hughes charged into the office. He fished a notebook and pencil out of his overcoat pocket, shoved aside a few documents on the desk, and slammed the notebook onto the bare spot. He dropped into an aging swivel chair and knotted his arms across his chest. He pulled his lips into a smile, but his eyes, a hard, polished buckeye brown, glared with all the potency of a basilisk. Li shrank in his chair.

"So," the detective said, keeping his tone smooth, "I hear you've been snooping."

Li chewed his bottom lip. "Sir?"

"We really don't have the time here to be playing dumb. I know you were eavesdropping on someone in the aisle next to the crime scene."

Li's eyes bulged. "How did you—?"

"You and your friend need to have less public arguments."

Color tinged Li's cheeks. His gaze slumped to his tightly knotted hands.

Detective Hughes leaned forward. "You should listen to your friend. I don't care for snoops. They like to think that because they are lifelong members of the Sherlock Holmes Fan Club, they can stick their noses into whatever crime they want. And it turns into a headache trying to sort all their information. This case is already a migraine."

Detective Hughes massaged his left temple and flopped back into the chair. Li saw infant stress lines crease around the detective's eyes. His mouth spoke before his brain could reconsider. "The cameras shorted out, didn't they?"

Detective Hughes shot the boy an unsavory look. "How do you know that?"

"M-my friend suggested it. Our wiring is really poor, and the cameras are junk. When the weather gets stormy, they tend to burn out."

"Not that they were very good to begin with, kid. Picture was damn blurry." The detective shoved out a sigh. "The cameras went on the fritz shortly after Oscar entered the store by himself around seven o'clock tonight. Almost a half hour before he died. I almost exploded. A simple case became a nightmare."

"Because of that woman, Mrs. Mayor? She seemed eager to push her way into this case."

A smile unraveled across Detective Hughes's face. "You better not let Constance Henderson hear you call her 'that woman.'"

"Who is she?"

An eyebrow arched. "Exactly how new are you in town?"

"I moved here a few weeks ago after I lost my old job."

"Then don't worry. You'll learn all about the mayor's wife in due time. Constance has more clout in her pinky than Marshall, her husband, has in his whole body. Still, they make a powerful pair." A shade of bitterness soured his words.

Li challenged him with an arched eyebrow of his own. "But you're not the kind of man who would shrink back from his duty, are you?"

The smile brightened. "If Constance Henderson clocked the guy, she'll look fetching in an orange jumpsuit. I can promise you that." The smile abandoned him. "Enough small talk. I have a few questions for you." He flipped open the notebook. "You told me you work the evening shift. When does that start and end?"

"Four p.m. to ten p.m."

"So everyone working in the store now"—he checked his watch—"at nine o'oclock came in at four this afternoon?"

"By now? Probably. But I wouldn't know for sure."

"You came in at four, didn't you?"

"Yes, sir."

Detective Hughes tapped the eraser on the pencil against his lips, studying Li's face as if it were a forged painting. "Tell me about the bags of sugar on the riser."

Li's eyes widened. "There aren't supposed to be any sugar bags on the riser."

"Oh? Why is that?"

"They're too heavy and bulky. They're supposed to go on the lower shelves."

"Ah, but you saw for yourself how they were placed directly over Oscar's head. Interesting, isn't it? Especially since your boss already admitted to putting the sugar there earlier in the evening. Around five o'clock, he said."

The muscles in Li's face relaxed. "Oh. Well, that makes sense."

"How?" The detective's voice sharpened and his eyes zeroed in on Li's. Li gnawed on his lower lip again. "Come on, kid. I won't tell your boss you blabbed. What do you know?"

"Leo . . . Leo's just lazy, sir. I think he's been pretty lazy all his life. He has us work all the important jobs while he schmoozes people. He rarely stocks. And if he did . . . well . . . he slacks off on it. Did he say if the sugar was overstock?"

"He did."

"That explains it. My friend told me he's done stuff like that before. He's too lazy to deal with the overstock the way we're supposed to, so he tries to stuff it somewhere. If he put those bags of sugar up there, I wouldn't be surprised."

"Your friend seems to possess a wealth of information."

Li swallowed and squeezed the corner of his apron, soaking it in sweat.

Detective Hughes scrawled a few notes. "Did you see Oscar Lindstrom at any time today?"

"Not today."

"Earlier?"

"I saw him in the store on Friday when I was applying for the job here. But that was only for a few seconds. He came into the store yesterday though. Around three thirty p.m. He ... um ... He criticized the big weekly special pyramid I worked on."

"Criticized, eh?"

Li kept his eyes level with the detective's. He learned at his last job that he was received better when he didn't cower. "I think he was a critic to his soul."

There was no need to mention Reuben's look of murder, right?

"I see. And what did he do after that?"

"He went down an aisle, I think." Li's brow furrowed. "Come to think of it, it was the spice aisle. At least, I'm pretty sure it was."

Detective Hughes dragged the eraser across his top lip as if wanting to rub out his frown. "Are you sure about that? Did you see him later?"

"I never saw him again until I found his body, Detective. And I can't be sure that it was the spice aisle. I thought it was, but that's as accurate as I can be."

The detective twirled the pencil in his fingers. The gesture was graceful, almost balletic. It betrayed a certain smoothness underneath the case-hardened scowl.

"Here's something interesting: If Oscar Lindstrom came to the store yesterday as you claim, why did he come back today? If he did his shopping on Saturday, why return Sunday?"

"Maybe he only wanted to see if we had what he wanted." A slight smile flickered on the boy's face. "A recon mission. Maybe he went home, made a list, and—"

Detective Hughes's solid poker face slipped. He eyed Li suspiciously. "Funny you should mention that ..." He produced an evidence bag with a slip of paper nestled inside it. He tossed it across the desk to Li. "We found this in the lining of Oscar's coat pocket. What do you make of it?"

Li bounced his gaze between the evidence and the detective, trying to sniff out a trap. Then, using the tips of his fingers, he pulled the bag toward him and examined its contents.

It was a list, written using a unique, personal form of abbreviation. The entries stretched down the slim shred of paper.

Milk

2dz. eggs

OJ

Apr. jelly

Hmbgr.

Rf. B.

Flr. Trtll.

Ch. Bst.

Tn. Flt.

G. W. P.

Wrctsr.

S. A. C.

Tom.

Potes.

Bans.

2h. L.

1000 I. D.

Sgr. 5lb.

"It's like it's written in code," Li replied, frowning at the stunted jumble of letters and numbers, "but I believe it's a list of groceries. What could he possibly want a thousand of?"

Detective Hughes favored the boy with a wide grin. "My partner believes that stands for Thousand Island salad dressing."

"Oh ... Ohhhhh!" Li rescanned the list. "That clears things up ... well, sort of. Still looks like gibberish sometimes." His gaze fell on the last entry, and his eyes ballooned. "Detective! Look here! I bet this last entry means 'sugar five lbs.' That could be why he was in aisle six!"

"Yes, it could, but I think you failed to see something more important."

Li's eyes dropped to the list, shifted to the window, back to the list, up to the detective. Was this some sort of test? A trap? A challenge? Was the detective egging him on? His eyebrows knitted together. "Where did you say you found this list?"

The grin stretched. "In the lining of his overcoat pocket."

"In the ... In the lining? You mean it was hidden under the actual pocket?"

"Essentially."

"Why on earth would anyone hide a list of groceries?"

"Aha." Something neighboring amusement danced across those dark brown eyes. "I thought you would have caught on to that sooner. Yes, it seems strange that a man would hide a list of groceries there. When my partner turned the coat pockets out, he discovered that one of the seams had been taped over with black electrical tape. Naturally, he was curious."

Li handed the evidence bag back to the detective. "But hiding a shopping list doesn't mean ... Wait ... Hold on ..." He raked a hand through his short crop of black hair. "This just got so much weirder."

"What is it?" The detective didn't sound so amused now.

"Where were his groceries?"

"Whose?"

Li leaned forward in his chair. "Oscar's. If he went grocery shopping tonight using this list, he would need a shopping cart or a basket. I didn't see a grocery-filled cart anywhere near Oscar when I found him. Did you?"

Detective Hughes stopped twirling his pencil and began tracing an invisible mustache with the eraser again. "Nothing at all. It appears Oscar wasn't here merely to shop for sustenance. Unless someone took his groceries after they killed him. But why would anyone do that?"

Li flopped against the back of the folding chair, slapping a hand against his forehead. "I'm an idiot. How could I miss that?"

"Would you mind enlightening me?"

"Something else is missing from the crime scene."

"Besides these imaginary groceries?"

"Oscar's cane!"

Detective Hughes stopped tracing and arched an eyebrow. "What cane?"

"Oscar carried this cane when he came in the store yesterday. Dark wood. Like ebony. A brass head. It seemed like he enjoyed using it for intimidation. He certainly made a point of sticking it in our faces." Li stood up and started to pace the little gray box like a tiger in its cage. His fingers continued to streak through his hair, causing cowlicks to erupt across his head. "I have a feeling that this cane was a trademark for him. He would have carried it everywhere. So where is it? It wasn't near his body. Could someone have taken it? Why would they do that?" He stopped pacing and rounded on Detective Hughes, his blue-gray eyes bright like new silver. "What if the cane was the murder weapon?"

Memories sparked in Li's mind. Disparate images. Old clues to a mystery at his last job. A hat. A ring. A bottle of sunscreen.

The pattern repeated itself. A list. A cane. A missing basket of groceries.

Detective Hughes stood and crossed over to the furiously pacing boy. He seized Li by the shoulder and steered him back to the folding chair. Li looked like he had been snatched from a trance.

The detective settled into his chair again. "You're getting ahead of yourself, kid. This is the first time I've heard of this mysterious cane. I can't make theories on facts I haven't proven yet. If there is a cane, he may have just left it at home."

"But why would he do that, Detective? That didn't seem like something he would do."

"Again, let me do the legwork before you jump headfirst into a theory. Besides, this isn't your concern. I'm the cop here, and you're the suspect."

Suspect. That word brought back all the horror. Li was involved in another murder. A violent murder. A murder in cold blood.

A murder his new friend might have committed.

Detective Hughes held the pencil eraser against his mouth and watched the boy. His face was unreadable, a veteran cop's face. Li squirmed in his seat and tried to loosen the collar of his shirt. Why did it feel like his collar shrank on him? Li tugged at his necktie, hoping that the detective couldn't read his thoughts. After all, Reuben's involvement in the murder was circumstantial at best. A look of black hate. Nothing more.

And his proximity to the crime scene.

And the fact he knew Oscar somehow.

Detective Hughes tilted the pencil so the eraser pointed at Li. "Uncomfortable?"

Li's heart skyrocketed into his nose. "Oh ... um ... no, I'm okay."

"You're fidgeting."

"My uniform is kind of itchy. I guess I need to use more fabric softener." His attempt at a laugh was depressing.

"You're holding something back. Something you're afraid of."

Li swallowed.

"A nervous swallow. Now I know you're keeping something from me. Do I have to remind you what obstruction of justice means? And you still haven't told me about your little snooping adventure. Does it have something to do with your very knowledgeable friend?"

Li wound his fingers into knots, fighting to keep the shakes out of them. What should he say? Should he admit that he was terrified about his friend being the murderer? Should he mention Reuben's hatred for the dead man? And what about the voices of Frank and Connie? He realized he was holding back more than he thought.

The veteran cop's eyes drilled into Li's face.

Li opted for a middle ground. He told half of the truth. At least for now.

"Well, while I was looking around, I heard these voices in aisle four. Two people. One named Frank. The other Connie."

"How do you know this?"

"That's what they called each other. I couldn't tell who they were. I never saw their faces." He told the detective about the conversation he overheard. "It sounds like they're ... covering something up. Something that involved Oscar Lindstrom."

The pencil twirled in the detective's dark chocolate fingers. "So you say."

"I swear that's what I heard, Detective. I'm not lying."

"Perhaps. Perhaps not. In this business, it's not wise to believe too much of what you're told. I have to check every fact in this case on my own. There's no proof that your story is genuine." His mouth quirked into a sly smile. "Besides, I have this feeling—call it police instinct, if you want—that you're still hiding something."

Li fought to keep from swallowing nervously again. That would be a dead giveaway. He couldn't sell out Reuben. Not until he was sure that ... nothing happened.

Detective Hughes let his smile collapse into a frown. "I think you've stopped being so forthcoming. Very well. I think I'm finished with you for now. I advise you not to leave town, or there will be a little gray cell in your future. You may wait down in the store until I release everyone for the night."

Li stood, but lingered by the chair. "Sir, you will check on everything I said, won't you?"

"Every last syllable. But I'm warning you ... it may turn up some answers you don't want to hear and some questions you don't want me to ask. Do you understand me, son?"

Li nodded slowly and turned toward the office door.

"Liam?"

Li turned back to the detective with the perfect poker face.

"I want the truth, Liam. And I'm going to get it."

Li listened to the gallop of raindrops on the cracked asphalt of the parking lot. Rain still hurtled to the ground as if furious with its existence. Li had hoped the storm would ease a little, a gallop to a trot at least. Wait ... Was that it? Was the rain finally—?

Thunder roared in the soot-black sky. God, Zeus, Thor, whoever was angry tonight.

There was nothing for it. The police kept all the witnesses late, so Li missed the last bus to his apartment. It would be a long, wet walk home. He plunged into the rain, soaked in nanoseconds. The water chilled his skin, brought to life goose bumps. Or was that a hangover from finding death where he worked again?

The dull *tha-wop* of his sodden shoes in gathering puddles seemed to echo the same word. *Murder. Murder. Murder.*

Rain blurred the glowing heads of the street lights pulsing through the black veil draped over Shorewood. The veil was so thick, so absolute that sound was the only clue to location and detail. The gallop of rain. The muffled bark of a dog followed by the rattle of a chain. The purr of an engine.

Li stepped into the puddle of light dribbling down from the street lamp. The engine snarled. Darting out of the darkness, a car, camouflaged by the night, swung toward the sidewalk. Tires screamed, kicking up waves of rainwater. Li launched backward, twisted, tripped, and splashed on his side in a giant puddle. Third strike for his elbow. At the last second, the car spun away from the curb without scraping it. Li lifted his head, coughing and spluttering, wet hair plastered to his forehead. The car sped into the shadows, lost except for the now distant, rain-fogged brake lights glaring at him like the red eyes of a huge black beast.

What the hell? That jerk could have killed me!

Li rose to his feet, shivering in his drenched clothes. He was going to drown in this damn storm. Still spluttering and rubbing his furious elbow, he started to shuffle away when another car, lazy compared to its cousin, slid up to the curb. The window rolled down.

"Li?" Reuben asked. "Are you okay? What happened?"

Li spat out a fat jot of rainwater. "Some jackass nearly ran me down. I fell in a puddle."

Reuben's eyes, still cold and dark, scanned Li. He sighed. "Get in. You're soaking wet. I'll drive you to your place."

Li hesitated. "Maybe I—"

"Just get your butt in the car."

Li shuffled over to the passenger's side and slipped into the seat. Water pooled onto the floor mats. "I'm sorry about the water."

"I'll clean it up later." Reuben sighed again, stretching and curling his fingers gripping the steering wheel. "To be honest, I didn't really want to pick you up. But then it was raining and you were lying in a puddle and my conscience got annoying, so here we are. I'm still really pissed at you."

Silence. Rain drummed on the car roof. The tension stretched taut between them.

"Reuben, I'm sorry," Li blurted out. "I shouldn't have said that about Noah. It was one of the stupidest things I've ever said. I ... I was mad at you and just wanted to take a cheap shot. I'm really really really sorry."

Reuben extended all his fingers while squeezing the wheel with his thumbs. He kept them that way. "It hurt, Li. I don't respond well when people use my boyfriend as ammo. Because that's a weapon that works too well. I don't want to hurt Noah in any way. I don't want to think about how he'd feel if ... if something happened to me. I'm already stressed about this stupid mess with Oscar." He turned hard, glassy eyes to his passenger. "I'm still your number one suspect, aren't I?"

"No, you're not. I was just scared. This whole disaster snowballed on me. First, I find Oscar murdered. Then, you catch me by surprise. Then, I remember how much you hated him." He leaned toward Reuben, his eyes like steel. "You did hate him, Reuben. A lot."

Reuben took a few deep, soul-settling breaths through his nose. His lips pushed out in a firm scowl. "I would see his face glare at me from his column in *The Gazette*. Do you have any clue what it's like to suffer every day? To have a constant reminder of your misery?"

Li's stress lines deepened on his wet skin, making him look forty. His chin thrust forward, his glare searing. "Do you see my eyes?"

"Is this going to get weird or—?"

"These are my dad's eyes. I inherited them from him. Every morning when I look in the mirror, I see my dad's eyes when he shriveled up and died in that stupid hospital. How sick he was. How bloodshot they were from hours of crying, crying he hid from us. Some days, I feel like ripping them out of my skull, because I can't bear to remember that look of agony. He suffered those last two years. And every morning, I see that suffering on my face. Every morning, I fight to keep from puking into my bathroom sink." Li crossed cold, wet arms over his chest. "So yes, I know a little something about suffering."

Reuben's eyes wavered. He deflated with another sigh. "He hurt my family, Li. That disgusting son of a bitch. He attacked us. The only thing I'm grateful for is that Noah wasn't there when it happened. If he was ..." His fingers strangled the steering wheel. "Oscar wouldn't be safe. No one hurts Noah if I'm around." His gaze flitted toward Li, then dropped to his lap. "Is that enough? Are you satisfied? I hate Oscar. He tried to destroy the people I love. Every time I saw his picture in the paper, it brought back all the terror ... the hate. I'm happy he's dead. Now I'm beyond done talking about him."

Silence again. The tension hummed in the air. Li wondered if this was the new norm for their budding friendship. Gone were the easy laughs and open generosity. Now there were long, tense silences broken only when one of them couldn't stand it anymore.

"So are we just going to sit here or are you going to tell me where you live, Li?"

Li mumbled his address. Reuben's car slipped into the Shorewood night, the headlights igniting the slanting rain into bolts of silver. For a long time, only the rain on the car roof and the squeaking wipers made conversation.

Reuben cleared his throat. "So, uh, do you want to stop at the police station to report that guy who almost hit you?"

Li started to shake his head, stopped, turned to stare into the black world outside of the window. That car. It could have hit him. If it wanted to. Swerving away from the sidewalk without even grazing the curb. Planned. Controlled. The car didn't want to hit him at all.

But the driver got close enough to get a good look at his face.

CHAPTER 6

Widows and Orphans

This was the worst part of the job. Widow-maker duty.

Detective Hughes lingered in his car, listening to the soft pitter-patter of rain on the roof. He made it a duet by drumming his thumbs on the steering wheel. His eyes swung over to the neon green numbers displayed on the stereo. Almost midnight. A bad time to get the news that someone murdered your husband.

Then again, what was a good time?

Detective Hughes glanced out of the driver's side window. Prichard Avenue was dark and lifeless. The rain dissolved into a fine mist, blurring the houses across the street. Oscar's house, vibrant as a tomb, should have been just a short jog across the asphalt, but the storm dulled these homes into inky smears against the starless night, all rendered anonymous by the rain. The detective thought he saw a light flickering in what he assumed was an upper story window. It made him think of haunted mansions.

He had not been surprised to learn that Oscar lived on Pricey Prichard. But he confessed to a slight surprise to learn that Oscar had a wife and son. He didn't look like a family man. His face, frozen in death, looked too angry and unpleasant to inspire love in a woman. You can never really tell with people, can you?

Knuckles tapped against the window. Detective Hughes opened the door to meet Adam, rain-soaked but professional, standing on the street.

"You okay, Tony?"

"Yeah, just hate this part of the gig. Did you bring Kleenex?"

"It's under my coat, sir."

"Good. Something tells me we'll be leaving the box here."

Detective Hughes pulled himself out of the safety of his car and slammed the door harder than he intended. A cloud of raindrops soaked him in a heartbeat. He and Adam jogged across the asphalt, their footsteps splashing through avenue-wide puddles. It was difficult to find the Lindstrom castle in this weather. All the lights were extinguished. Not even a porch light to guide a man home.

After a couple minutes of wandering through a fog of rain and darkness, the two men blundered up concrete steps and found shelter under a wooden porch.

"Think this is the place?" Adam asked.

Detective Hughes grimaced at his partner. "One of these days I'm going to have to talk to you about your mind-reading powers." He glanced at the silvery house number displayed next to the front door. "It's the right address. Here goes nothing." He lifted a fist and rapped on the door.

No answer.

"Maybe they all went to bed. Try the doorbell."

"I was getting to that."

He pressed the softly glowing button. Deep in the house, electronic bells echoed through the empty rooms. Diminuendo. Then crescendo. Like the classic chimes of a grandfather clock.

Detective Hughes felt his toes tingle. Waiting made him antsy.

The door glided open just a crack on well-oiled hinges, framing the half-sheltered figure of a beautiful woman. She peeked out like a shy but curious nymph. Her eyes, a deep, almost violet blue, were wide and scanned her visitors with immediate fear and distrust.

"Kathryn Lindstrom?"

"Yes."

Detective Hughes flashed his badge. "I'm Detective Antoine Hughes with the Shorewood Police Department. This is my partner, Officer Schafer-SchmiDetective We're here to . . . to . . ."

His words fumbled over his lips. Kathryn had opened the door fully, allowing him to take in all of her beauty at once. It was impossible to believe that this was Oscar's newly crowned widow. Nestled in an indigo-blue bathrobe, Kathryn Lindstrom existed with all the freshness of new violets, the coolness of spring rain, and the warmth of young love. Her thick brunette curls cascaded over one shoulder. Her violet eyes continued to search the faces of her guests for answers to silent questions.

Adam nudged his superior in the ribs.

Detective Hughes felt blessed that blushing didn't show on his skin. "Erm, yes, sorry ... I mean ... I am sorry to inform you that ... that your husband ..."

"Has something happened to Oscar?" Fear flushed all the color out of her peaches-and-milk complexion.

"I'm so sorry, Mrs. Lindstrom, but ... your husband was found dead at Esther's Family Grocery this evening."

Kathryn's heart-shaped lips parted with a gentle gasp. The lower one trembled. Soft tears poured over long eyelashes. She lifted a shaking hand to her lips and pulled away from the door. A sob, so tender it could have come from a heartbroken dove, broke through the muted horror and anguish caught on her lovely face.

Adam held out the box of Kleenex. Kathryn took one without question.

"Please," she said, her voice as hearty as a whisper, "come in. It's not good to stand out in the rain."

The Lindstrom house was already snuggled up for bed: curtains closed, lamps extinguished, feet muffled with slippers. Kathryn led her guests through the dark entryway and into a large room just to the right. A few floor lamps flickered on. A living room popped out of the darkness.

Although the design was obscured by the shadows clumped in the corners, the room was warmly furnished with showroom pieces upholstered and painted in varying shades of cream and gray. The scant flashes of wood were either dark ebony or coated in black lacquer. Cream trim framed pale gray walls. Detective Hughes wondered whether this case would be colored in a thousand shades of gray.

Kathryn wilted onto the arm of a white leather sofa, daubing her teary eyes with the tissue. Adam settled in an oversized gray corduroy club chair facing the sofa, discreetly resting an open notebook on his knee. Detective Hughes perched on the edge of the couch, close enough to breathe in Kathryn's soft natural scent. Like lilacs and lavender. The detective cleared his suddenly parched throat and forced himself to focus on his model-gorgeous,

Mensa-brilliant wife with her skin like Godiva chocolates and her inherent perfume of caramel and fresh brewed coffee.

Kathryn's low musical voice shattered his thoughts. "How ... How did Oscar ... die?"

Detective Hughes cleared his throat again. This was the part he really dreaded. "I'm afraid we believe he was ... murdered. Bludgeoned. I won't trouble you with the medical details."

Kathryn choked on her sobs. "M-murdered? But ... no! No, no, that's not possible ... Oscar ... My Oscar was a sweetheart. He was a good boy. No one would want to hurt him ..." Her words melted away.

"Mrs. Lindstrom, do you have any idea why your husband would be at Esther's Family Grocery?"

"I've never heard of the place. Is it far?"

"Actually, it's only a few blocks down Shorewood Avenue. You could walk there. Maybe take you fifteen minutes."

"Oh."

"Did he ever mention a trip to the grocery store tonight?"

"No. Never. In fact, he said he wanted to stay in tonight. He had a lot of work to do. He planned to stay in his office for the rest of the night after dinner."

"And did he?"

"I heard him go up to the office and lock the door."

"When was this?"

"Around six thirty. Just after dinner."

Detective Hughes lifted a pair of critical eyebrows. "And five and a half hours later, you aren't curious about his prolonged stay in his office?"

"Not at all. He always worked long hours. Sometimes, he'd be up there for ten hours straight. I never worried." Kathryn sucked up a thread of tears with the edge of her tissue. "He was a hard worker. Never lazy. Every success he had he slaved for."

Detective Hughes regarded the new widow with more suspicious eyes now. Could he really picture this tender, weeping angel of violets possessing the bloodthirsty strength to bludgeon a man? Did she hate her husband enough to crush his skull? His eyes roamed over the bright crystal tears trickling over pink cheeks. Murder didn't agree with the image of Kathryn Lindstrom.

"So you have no clue why your husband would be anywhere near that grocery store?"

Kathryn straightened her wilted shoulders, lifted her chin, and willed her tears to stop. She had the grim, unforgiving air of a Mother Superior defending her charges. "Absolutely none. We have never been there. We shopped at Whole Foods. We had absolutely no reason to ever go to that store. I suggest you look for the monster that lured my Oscar to that horrible place."

Duly reprimanded, Detective Hughes changed tactics. "I understand that your son is here."

"You must mean my stepson."

"Ah." The detective hesitated. "Then you aren't Jason Lindstrom's mother?"

"Of course not. Jason's mother died in childbirth. I'm Oscar's third wife."

"Interesting. Do you happen to know the names of Oscar's first and second wives?"

Kathryn lifted her shoulders in a delicate shrug. She sighed. "I never knew them. Jason's mother died like I said. And the second marriage was over years before I even came to Shorewood. I lived in Northern California most of my life. I've only been in Southern California for about six years."

"And how long have you been married to Mr. Lindstrom?"

A smile—cool, calm, definitely one a competent nanny would give when asked about her well-tended wards—touched those heart-shaped lips. "Six years."

A squeaky voice interrupted them. "Kathryn? What's going on? Who are these men?"

Detective Hughes aimed a glare at the intruder. His first impression was that of a stick figure scrawled in chalk on the blacktop. The young man stepped out from the darkened entryway. Mid-twenties, the detective surmised. His skin was anemic and tightly stretched over his bones. His dry, ash-blond hair was ruffled, and his amber-brown eyes darted among the three people seated in front of him. Glasses as thin as his body teetered on his nose. He looked like he fell into his pajamas.

"Who are you?" The man—more like a boy, Detective Hughes considered—directed his question at the senior officer. "What do you want with us?"

Kathryn Lindstrom rose from the arm of the sofa, the Kleenex strangled in her soft, clean hands. "Jason." Her voice came out stern and maternal. "This is Detective Hughes from the Shorewood Police Department. And this is Officer Schafer-SchmiDetective They're—"

"What do they want with us? We haven't done anything!"

"Don't interrupt, Jason. It's rude."

"Dad wouldn't allow anyone to come into his house at this time of night! He—"

Detective Hughes stood and crossed to Jason. The young man swallowed and jerked backward. Yes, he was frightened. And fear made the arrogant youngster bark at him. A high-pitched, trembling bark that had no force behind it. A puppy intimidated by the big dogs.

"You're Jason, Oscar Lindstrom's son?"

"What's it to you?"

"I'm afraid your father was found murdered at a local grocery store tonight."

Jason narrowed his amber-brown eyes. "How?"

"Bludgeoned. Not a pretty scene."

"You're sure of this?"

Detective Hughes let his frown deepen. "I'm not a man who calls any death a homicide just to have something to do. And I think it's my turn to ask questions. Do you know why your father went to Esther's Family Grocery tonight?"

"Rundown-looking store just off Shorewood Avenue? I have no idea. Dad wouldn't be caught—" He cleared his throat. "Anyway, Dad gave his proclamation tonight. He was spending the night in his office, working late. He was there since after dinner."

"This was usual for him?"

"Absolutely. He loved his office. He'd stay in there for days if he didn't have to eat. It was his private world in there. He'd lock his door and forget about the rest of us."

"You can confirm he was in there tonight?"

Jason tilted his colorless head to one side, a gesture both appraising and condescending. "No, Detective. I can't. He sent me to my room before he left the dining room. And my room is at the opposite end of the hall from his office. I never left it. I didn't see or hear anything. And since he wasn't found dead here, I'd assume someone lured him out of his precious castle. Although, let's be frank, not even the Apocalypse would force my dad to leave his house to go to some hole in the wall on a night like this."

"Jason!" Kathryn reprimanded. "Don't talk like that about your father."

Jason blushed, and his eyes dropped to his feet.

His *wet* feet.

Detective Hughes saw the beading of water on Jason's ankles. His face didn't change, but his eyes flicked up to the lifeless hair capping the young man's head. It was dry. Dry hair. Wet feet. Things just got interesting.

"So far as either of you know, Oscar planned to stay in his home office for the rest of the night. He had no plans to leave. He went up there at six thirty. You, Mr. Lindstrom, were in your room. May I ask where you were tonight, Mrs. Lindstrom?"

"Oh, come on!" Jason protested, "You can't really suggest that Kathryn—"

Detective Hughes stopped him with a stony look. "I'm thorough."

Kathryn nodded, whisking away a loose tear. "As he should be. He needs to catch the brute who ... who ..." She sniffed and dried her eyes again. "I was in between the kitchen and dining room at that time. Clearing up after dinner. Then I washed dishes until about eight o'clock. We had a roast duck and the roasting pan takes some time to clean properly. And from eight to when I went to bed at eleven, I was cleaning, doing laundry ... all the usual chores."

"Down here on the ground floor?"

"Yes."

"And neither of you heard Oscar leave this house?"

Both nodded.

"Sounds straightforward enough. Jason in his room. Kathryn in the kitchen. Neither of you know Oscar's movements after he locked himself in his office. And the fact he was found at Esther's Family Grocery is a complete mystery to both of you."

"He was *lured* there, Detective," Kathryn insisted. "Some monster did this to my Oscar."

Tears rained from her eyes. Adam handed the whole box of tissues to her.

"There's a lot left to determine. We're not in a position to form any theories at present. We just want information." His gaze drifted to the silver clock hung prominently over the electric fireplace with its white Carrera marble surround. Twelve twenty in the morning. His wife would be at home in bed, cuddling his pillow as a substitute to him being there. Another lost night. "I suggest we stop here for the night. I'll be back tomorrow with further questions."

"Of course, Detective," Kathryn said, slipping her tear-soaked tissue into the pocket of her robe. "We'll be here for you."

"Do either of you work?"

Jason snorted. "Dad worked. He was the much loved food critic expanding his empire. Kathryn was the perfect housewife. I was the dutiful, stay-at-home assistant."

The sarcasm in his voice was caustic. His meaning was clear. Oscar was the king, and Kathryn and Jason were his slaves. The son clearly felt his slavery. Was the wife so blinded by love that the domination of her life didn't touch her?

Detective Hughes smiled. "Then we'll all meet here tomorrow. Let's get moving, Adam."

He and his partner stepped into the entryway. In the soft light spilling from the living room, the detective spotted an umbrella stand next to the front door. Clustered among the unused umbrellas was an ebony cane with a brass head.

The cane that boy, Liam, said should have been at the crime scene.

He turned to Kathryn, who lingered in the opening to the living room. "Is that your husband's cane?"

Kathryn tiptoed around him. Her eyes swelled. "Yes, that's Oscar's. I don't understand ... He took it everywhere. He never left home without it." She wheeled around, her eyes intent and desperate on the dark, somber face of Detective Hughes. "What if Oscar was *kidnapped?*"

"We'll look into it, Mrs. Lindstrom. Do you mind if we borrowed the cane for analysis?"

"Yes, of course. Take anything you want. Just catch this monster."

Jason's face, hovering in the shadows, was carefully guarded. He didn't seem to share his stepmother's enthusiasm for justice.

Detective Hughes pulled a handkerchief out of his overcoat pocket and cupped the cane in his hand. It wouldn't hurt to check, right? He wasn't really listening to the suggestions of some snooping kid. But a murder weapon had to be found. Thanking the widow for her time, he and Adam strode into the rain and darkness again.

The senior officer tucked the cane under his coat to protect it from the rain. "Adam, why don't you go back to the store and see how the techs are doing? I want that whole store examined, even if you have to take every can, box, and bag off the shelves. If you find anything remotely valuable, bring it to my desk. I'll take this to the lab."

"Think it's the weapon?"

"Could be. Hopefully Rick can give us some results. The autopsy should be done later today. We'll come back here after we get those results."

Li writhed in his sleep, haunted and hunted by the evil possibilities birthed by his imagination. The images seemed to vibrate with light. Reuben's tan face flushed with blood and darkened with shadow. His eyes glittered like black pearls. A wide smile wrenched his lips, unveiling clean white teeth as keen as knives. He crept forward, keeping a man locked in his crosshairs. The man hid under a shaggy black pelt, the collar turned up to cloak his face. A yellowing bald spot peeking over the edge of the collar made the perfect target.

Reuben's face began to mutate. His tan melted into pale skin. His black-coffee eyes glowed silver and blue. Li's face. Li's features twisted by the lust to kill. There was something clutched in his trembling hands. He didn't know what it was, but he knew it was lethal. He lifted his weapon. His nostrils flared. He brought the nameless tool down on the man's fragile head. A geyser of blood.

Li bolted awake, his heart hammering against his ribs. Sweat glazed his forehead. His eyes searched the darkness for vestiges of his nightmare. Nothing. He leaned over and switched on his bedside lamp, chasing away the shadows suffocating him. He was in his studio apartment, tucked into bed. The clock on his nightstand reported that it was two thirty in the morning. This was the fifth time he woke from the nightmares since he flopped into bed.

It's just a stupid dream, he told himself. *Just forget about it.*

But he couldn't. The man in the dream was very dead. And he kept picturing Reuben, eyes gleaming, teeth bared, driving a weapon into Oscar's skull, squealing with delight at all the blood. Blood splotching his apron in bright red stains. And when Reuben's face melted into his own, Li worried whether that meant he wanted to kill Oscar too. Sure, the guy had been a jerk. But murder?

Unable to settle his brain, Li tossed back his blue plaid comforter, pried himself out of bed, and shuffled to the tiny bathroom. His nose crinkled up at the stale stench percolating inside the cramped room. He scrubbed his face with the water pouring out of a belching faucet. The light over the mirror blinked. Li looked up at his reflection.

A middle-aged man stared back at him.

He sprang backward and ran his fingers over his face, checking if it was really his. It was like looking into a sad future. He was a twenty-year-old man with a web of stress lines and premature wrinkles draped over his face. He was too young to look this old. In his stormy blue eyes, he saw the pain of his father, the agony that ate him alive. Then he saw the raw, wet eyes of his mother and sister at the memorial service. The hate and anger in Reuben's eyes. The sparkle of welcome in Noah's. The suspicion in Detective Hughes's. The dead, furious glare of Oscar Lindstrom. Eyes like Medusa. Eyes everywhere, staring at him, tracing the old age that crept into his face. Eyes. Eyes. *Eyes.*

Li's stomach lurched. He leaned over the edge of his sink.

When he was done, a terrible sense of purity washed over him. It was over. He fought it for so long. Now he had purged it, washed it out of his body. The drain could take all that crap from him. Maybe now he could enjoy an empty sleep, a mind cleaned of its sick memories.

He shoved out a sigh and gargled the funny, metallic-tasting water, trying to wash out the typical sour aftertaste. Then he could be clean and perfect again. A fresh start. No more old man in the mirror.

He glanced up, and there were even more lines in his face.

"Oh, screw you," he growled.

Li pawed at the towel and buffed away the frown pulling down his face. He smothered the white-hot anger sizzling under his skin. He hobbled out of the bathroom, crossed the clean but sparse layout of his studio, and collapsed face-first onto his bed. Nope. No good. The water woke him up, and his brain already started dissecting his dream. He kept reliving the murder, seeing it as the killer must have seen it. He hated his subconscious for constantly casting Reuben in that role. But this new twist—the killer mutating into Li—brought up another idea. The killer didn't have to be Reuben. He could be anyone who was there. And Reuben wasn't the only one who had issues with Oscar.

Li rolled onto his back and tried to summon answers from the ceiling. The weapon was a problem. He tried to remember whether his subconscious gave him a picture of it. Even just an idea, a suggestion, a possibility. Already the details were growing fuzzy. He felt that it was handheld. Portable. Easy to carry and use.

But that could lead to anything in the store. Oscar's cane. A basket. A can of soup. A box of Frosted Fizzle Bombs. It had to be inconspicuous. A killer wouldn't walk around a grocery store waving a hammer. Was it a weapon of opportunity? Was it planned beforehand? A headache crumpled his thoughts.

Amid the agonies of speculation, a new picture rose from the depths of his memories. Oscar's overcoat. Big, black, furry, and shapeless. The pelt of a Sasquatch. Li remembered how he hadn't been sure who the man was when he first found the body. The coat swallowed its owner.

Li launched forward, his eyes big and bright like searchlights. His hands, twitching, impulsive, started to rake through his hair. His subconscious *did* suggest something with that never-ending stream of nightmares. He could see the scene again, ignoring the killer. Oscar stood there, cloaked by his overcoat, *the collar turned up to hide his face.*

He combed his memories again. Yes. The collar had been turned up when he found Oscar. It cupped his face, some of his blood collecting in it like wine in a goblet. Whole worlds of suggestions whirled through Li's brain, making him dizzy. The missing cane. The missing groceries. The upturned collar. The fact no one in the store noticed Oscar's presence. The cloudy skies.

Oscar Lindstrom didn't want a soul in Shorewood to know he was at Esther's Family Grocery that night.

CHAPTER 7

Morning After

The clouds scuttled north, leaving the Monday skies a clear Tiffany blue. Detective Hughes watched the world strengthen in color and definition through the windows of the police station. The hours crawled by. He could see the geometric, eighties architecture of City Hall looming less than a block away. He wondered if Constance Henderson was there, marshaling her defense forces for a possible murder accusation.

He sighed, rubbed his weary eyes with the back of his hand, and dropped his gaze back to the reports stacked on his desk. Crime had so much paperwork. The blue skies trapped on the other side of the window panes served as the only break from the mass of black-and-white type. He drummed his fingers on the metal desktop, waiting for the call that was due—

The phone screamed. Detective Hughes allowed a little smile. Ten o'clock on the dot. Punctual as always.

"I've got a bone to pick with you," Dr. Reynolds growled on the other end.

"Isn't it a little early for anatomical humor, Rick?"

"I gave you the outline of a square weapon with rounded corners, and you give us something thin and cylindrical." The doctor snorted. "If you're expecting the results to match, then you need to get glasses, Tony."

"It was a lead, Rick. I had to check it out."

Dr. Reynolds grumbled. "It wasn't a good lead, Tony."

"Well, the kid said—"

"Kid? What kid?"

Detective Hughes could kick himself for that little slip. "Just some kid we interviewed last night. He told us that Oscar carried a cane, and that it should have been at the crime scene. The widow confirmed this. We found the cane in Oscar's house. Thought we would take a closer look."

"Hmph. And I suppose this kid is an expert of forensics? Where did he study? Let's see his qualifications."

"Lay off, Rick. I know you're annoyed."

Dr. Reynolds groused to himself for a moment. "All right ... All right ... I'm just bothered when people don't take my evidence seriously. The cane could not be the murder weapon in any way. Too fragile. Too thin. Too round. If someone hit Oscar with that, we'd find wood splinters in the wound. In my *professional* opinion, the cane was left behind when he went to the store."

"Wouldn't he need it to walk?"

"Nope. I didn't see anything wrong with his legs or back that would prompt him to use it. Probably used it for show."

"What about the rest of the autopsy?"

Dr. Reynolds cleared his throat. The annoyed bite finally worked out of his voice. "I'll save the jargon for the final report. Cause of death was that head wound. No doubt about it. Someone bashed his brains in. Oscar had a thin skull. In fact, the bruise covered up a more sinister problem. When that sugar bag hit him, it caused bleeding on the surface of the brain under the skull. Subdural hematoma. Probably would have killed him anyway. But someone definitely wasn't taking any chances and hit him. His skull was so thin that it cracked like an egg."

"Charming." The sarcasm was thick in the detective's throat. "Anything else?"

"Only wounds I saw were the skull fracture and the bruise. No defensive wounds. I don't think Oscar knew what happened to him until it was too late. The first blow to the head was enough to scramble his thoughts for a moment." Detective Hughes heard papers shuffling on the other end. "Heart was good. Stomach was a bit ulcerous, but nothing too bad. He definitely had a meal shortly before he died. The food was pretty intact in his system. Liver wasn't pretty. All that rich food and booze, you know? Other than that, he was pretty normal. We'll do some tests on his blood, but I don't really think we'll find anything out of the ordinary. I'll let you know if any bogeyman pops up."

"Let's get back to the major wound. Any changes there?"

"I still say it was a square weapon with rounded corners. But we did find some interesting particulate matter. Thick gray plastic and a piece of what might have been a liquid crystal display screen."

"In the wound?"

"Thereabouts."

"So what are we talking about? Someone smashed his skull with a cell phone?"

Dr. Reynolds snorted with laughter. "If they did, it would need to be a cell phone from the eighties. I was going with a tablet computer. Though I'm not sure if someone could wield one of those efficiently enough to kill someone. I want something with a handle."

Adam paused in the doorway to his superior's cubicle, wearing a wicked grin and holding up an evidence bag. "Found this stuffed into the toilet in the men's restroom at the store," he said quietly.

Detective Hughes eyed the contents, felt a smile spread across his face, and said into the receiver, "What about those handheld scanners they use in supermarkets?"

Dr. Reynolds sounded intrigued. "That'll work."

In the cold daylight, the Lindstrom house stood proud and pristine, not a flower out of line, nor a speck on its soul. There wasn't a whisper of the tragedy in those clean gray walls. Detective Hughes knew this was not a house of mourning. He could see that in the sidewalks empty of family, friends, and well-wishers. The house felt . . . relieved.

The detective rapped sharply on the front door. Jason pried it open. A faded sweatshirt, gray like the house, engulfed his thin frame, the sleeves so long that they covered his knuckles. He looked like a little kid trying to wear his dad's clothes. He peered over his glasses.

"Oh," he said, "it's you. More third degree?"

Detective Hughes held his poker face, but inside he scowled. "Yes, it is. Is Mrs. Lindstrom home?"

"Nope. Staci from across the street swept her up a few hours ago for a widow's breakfast and retail therapy." He shrugged his bony shoulders. "God knows when they'll get back."

"Then more time to talk to you."

Detective Hughes had to muscle his way inside the house. He could feel the waves of distrust ebbing off the young man. The detective settled in one of the club chairs. Jason perched himself on the arm of the sofa, his body tense and his eyes darting around the living room checking for escape routes.

"Now then, Mr. Lindstrom, do you have anything to add to your statement from last night?"

"Is that the polite way of asking if I want to change my story? The answer is no. I've told you everything I know about what happened last night."

Except for the cause of his wet feet. Detective Hughes kept that question tucked away for now. He wanted to pump as much information out of this hostile witness as possible. "And earlier that day? Anything of interest?"

"Nope. We stayed home. Dad seemed preoccupied, but he had a lot of work lately."

"Let's go back to Saturday. What happened?"

"Boring stuff. Errands. Paperwork. Dad hid in his office most of the day."

"What about Friday?"

A smile, sly as his father's, spread across Jason's colorless face. "So the stories are getting out, I see."

"Care to enlighten me, Mr. Lindstrom?"

Jason slid off the arm of the couch, smushed himself into the seat, and propped a skinny leg across his knee. He pretzeled his arms behind his head. "Dad resigned from *The Shorewood Gazette* on Friday afternoon. He told us at dinner. From what he hinted at, the resignation really pissed off his editor, Frank Dixon. Maybe even mad enough to leave a certain nasty package on our doorstep." There was a sadistic glow in those amber eyes.

Detective Hughes pulled his eyebrows together in a frown. Frank Dixon had been at Esther's Family Grocery last night.

Buying "party supplies," he said. He never mentioned Oscar's resignation. "What package?"

"Someone dumped a package on our doorstep early Friday afternoon. Not through mail. I never saw what was inside it. Kathryn opened it, showed Dad, and threw it away. You need to ask her what it was. But Dad scowled at it. Reminded me of the times kids dropped bags of dog crap on our porch." He leaned forward, his eyes bright. "I just remembered! Dad took a note out of the box. He never showed it to me, but he kept it. Might be in his office."

Detective Hughes tabled the package issue for the moment. "So your father resigned from the paper, did he? Odd decision to make in this economy. Especially if he was the sole breadwinner."

Jason snorted. He flopped back against the couch and drummed his fingers on the white leather arm. "You think *The Gazette* paid Dad enough to hold his interest? Dad wrote for them because he wanted a forum, an audience to listen to him. But he hated the way they edited his work. And he wanted to reach more people. That's why we started the blog, *Tough Bite to Swallow*. Now he could reach millions." He flicked a hand, tried to keep his tone casual. But there were ripples of resentment in his tone, a sudden tension in his jaw. Especially on the word "we."

The detective's eyes skimmed over the showroom pieces collected in the living room. "Then where does his money come from?"

"Royalties. Dad was a foodie his whole life. Went to culinary school, worked in restaurants, traveled the globe." Again, the ripples of resentment. "When he was twenty-six, he published a book of his adventures called *Full Plate*. First of the *Plate* saga. To this day, it's one of the most celebrated books in the food world. Chefs all over the world have a copy on their shelves. Wait one second . . ."

Jason jumped out of his seat, spry and catlike. He padded to the ebony bookcases flanking the fireplace. Long fingers lingered on the spine of a book. A minute or two passed. Then he pulled it off the shelf, flipped it over, frowned at the jacket photo, and handed it to Detective Hughes.

The detective allowed his eyebrows to rise. The photo came from an era before the weight piled on, the jaundice settled in, and the scowls weighed down the lips. A fresh, clean-shaven face with bold features, a summer glow, a wide, friendly smile, and an ambitious spark in his amber-brown eyes. The face of youth, health, and success—which meant middle age had been damn cruel to Oscar Lindstrom.

Detective Hughes flicked his gaze to Jason. There were the same bold features, but the skin was like chalk, the eyes, dead, dull, cowered behind glasses, and the small mouth must have found smiling foreign and uncomfortable. Total misery. A face like a haunted house—shuttered, silent, maybe a flicker or two quickly smothered. The son was a ghost of his father.

Jason snatched back the book. He fingered the pages as if too scared to turn them. "*Full Plate* is my favorite. I've read it so many times. Dreaming about—" He stopped, clearing his throat. "Dad . . . Dad was a different writer back then. Full of hope. He encouraged his readers to expand their tastes, get out of their comfort zones, explore the world. He wanted everyone to absorb the thousands of cultures, cuisines, and stories out there." Jason let the book fall open to a well-read page. "'The world is too big for one adventure.'" He delivered the quote like a eulogy.

Detective Hughes stroked his jawline. "But I take it that sentiment didn't last for long?"

Jason turned away, slipped the book back on the shelf, polished his glasses with his sweatshirt, rubbed his long sleeves as if he wanted to scratch his arms. His mouth twitched. Stalling. Chewing over his words.

"*Empty Plate*, the second book, came out shortly after I was born," he said, hedging the direct question. He caressed the other two books in the set but did not remove them. "Dad met Mom on his first book tour, and they traveled together. They got married in Singapore. Later, Mom died giving birth to me." His words bore sharp edges. His shoulders tensed. "Then the book was published. Not as loved as the first one. *Empty Plate* was just that— Dad emptying his plate of global cuisine and world travel. Much more somber and ... and final than his first book. His fans could sense that he was settling down. End of the Oscar Lindstrom, food explorer, era. He never stepped out of the country again."

Jason sank onto the arm of the couch again, twisting the bottom of his sweatshirt in his hands. Detective Hughes had to wonder why the kid wore it when it clearly didn't fit him. "Is that the end of the saga?"

Jason shook his head, keeping dull eyes locked on his hands. "Dad ... He became obsessed with perfection. Has been my whole life. He liked to say 'perfection can be perfected.' When I was in high school, Dad claimed to travel the country researching for his next book. He never did. He cheated and used his memories and his research. He called the book *Fill My Plate*." He rolled his eyes skyward. "You should have seen the publicity for this thing. Touting it as the great comeback for Oscar Lindstrom. Huge pre-sales." His voice rose in a farce of a jacket blurb. "'One man's nationwide search for the perfect dish.' Spoiler alert: He doesn't find it. Dad sounded bitter and frustrated throughout the book. He mutated from foodie to food critic. And not an impartial one. That's when he started making racial and ethnic slights against restaurants and chefs. Subtle ones. Like he was angry at the world he used to embrace. So he took a sour shot at every culture." He sighed. "It's been getting worse ever since. Dad was a monster."

A thorough recital, Detective Hughes noted. But the information was too easily given, an open book performance. There were undercurrents here. Secrets stuffed away like shut-ins. He tapped his finger against his leg, his dark eyes lasered on Oscar's son. He liked to let his suspects stew for a minute during interrogations. To gauge mood or temperament, to check for hesitation or evasion, to learn if the suspect or witness held something back. It worked on that boy, Liam. He had wriggled in his seat like a snake ready to shed. There was still a secret there.

And it was working right now. Already there were bouncing knees, wringing hands, eyes darting to the clock, to the door, back to the clock. When Jason opened his mouth, Detective Hughes cut him off. "So would you say your father had enemies?"

Jason's glasses magnified the flicker of scorn in his eyes. "Try reading the reviews on his blog. He was responsible for more restaurant closures than the health department. Anyone he shut down hated his guts." Then he flashed a knowing smile. "You want a good suspect? Look up Bauer. That place got a smear campaign with a couple of violent trimmings. Tasty, huh?"

Bauer. Detective Hughes knew the place. It had been connected to something that made the seasoned cop's blood boil. Hate crimes.

"What about his ex-wife? Your first stepmom?"

"I never really knew her. She sent me away to a private boarding school for a few years. All I know is that the marriage didn't last long. Divorce. Not like they loved each other or anything." Jason snorted. "Dad cheated on his wives. All the time. I bet he thought it was a secret. But I found out. Go look up 413 Helen Street. You'll learn something."

Again, openhanded with the information. Jason loved throwing his dad under a parade of buses. Detective Hughes stroked his jaw. "And what about the current Mrs. Lindstrom? What do you think of her?"

Jason's dry white cheeks glowed salmon pink. His fingers curled around the edge of his sweatshirt. His voice was raw, husky. "Kathryn wouldn't hurt someone like that."

Ah, so that's where the land lay. Boy loved his young, beautiful stepmom. Complicated home life. "And what about you? How did you feel about your father?"

Jason tensed. Muscles pulled against his neck like ropes. His fists trembled. "I don't know what you're trying to imply."

"It's a simple question, Mr. Lindstrom. How did you feel about him?"

"That has nothing to do with—"

Detective Hughes dived in anyway. It was time to turn the thumbscrews. Hard. "It seems like there was no love lost between you two."

Jason's cheeks blazed scarlet. He jerked one of his long sleeves up. Detective Hughes tensed, expecting to dodge an assault. Jason slammed his exposed arm on the arm of the couch. His amber eyes glowed like brush fire. His voice, high and angry, cracked like glass. "Would you love a father who did THIS to you?"

Burn scars. Old ones and newer ones pooling together across pale skin. Like he had been dipped in acid. These scars on the surface were healing, but the scars on Jason's soul cut down to the bone. Detective Hughes kept his face neutral, but his gaze continued to trace the terrible damage. "What did he do?"

"Oh no, I'm not going there. Let me keep some secrets, Sherlock." Jason yanked the sleeve down, hiding his shame from the world again. "I hated Dad, okay? And he hated me. He made me feel stupid and worthless and ugly. He abused me, torturing me for his own pleasure. I am so happy he's dead. I hope hell has enough room for his bloated ego."

"And you didn't try to escape? To live your own life?"

Jason's voice grew dark, murderous. "I couldn't. He trapped me. He had me trapped my whole life. I couldn't fight him. Honestly, you shouldn't even look for his killer, because that person is a saint to me. Saved my life."

"It's my job, Mr. Lindstrom. And I think you'll find that killers don't care who gets hurt when it comes to protecting themselves."

Jason just sat there, glaring at the detective, dark and fuming like a distant thunderhead.

Detective Hughes leveled his buckeye-hard eyes with Jason's. "I think you did try to escape, Mr. Lindstrom. A desperate attempt on the night your father was killed."

"I have no idea—"

"Something that would explain your curiously wet feet that night."

Jason's rage-red cheeks darkened to purple. He snarled. "Get out. I'm calling our lawyer. After the shit my dad said about people, you can BET he had a team of attorneys that would make the Supreme Court wince."

The witness was spent. It would take a cannonball of evidence to break through the stone walls, barbed wire, and machine guns Jason built around himself. Detective Hughes made the usual official murmurs and stood when the front door opened. Kathryn crossed the threshold, bringing the soft scent of violets into the house. Worry puckered her pretty face.

Detective Hughes turned his scrutiny to her. "Ah, Mrs. Lindstrom. I was hoping to have a word with you."

Kathryn jolted at his deep, smooth voice. "Oh ... Detective ... I didn't know you were here already. I'm sorry I wasn't here to greet you."

"Your stepson informed me of your whereabouts."

She nodded absently. "Yes, Detective, Staci, my neighbor, told me the strangest thing about Oscar. I think it's important that you talk to her."

"What did she say?"

"She said she saw Oscar in the house last night. All night. He never went to that grocery store."

CHAPTER 8

An Awkward Alibi

Crime scene tape. The flimsiest bulletproof wall.

Li grazed the gaudy yellow-and-black ribbon with his finger-tips. It cut off the double doors of Esther's Family Grocery. Great way to start a Monday afternoon at work.

"Store's closed," Leo said, making Li jump. The manager sat in a cloth folding chair tucked next to the doors and out of sight from the parking lot. A copy of *Maxim* lay open on his knee. His tone was sour, and he didn't look at his employee. "I'm here to let those of you without phones know the situation. Police in charge. Then we'll need special cleaners to come and deal with the blood. With all these blood-borne diseases, we can't be too careful. Probably lose a ton of our stock too. Who knows if we'll get the store opened again?" His voice grew ragged from annoyance. "Why couldn't that man have a nice, quiet death instead? Like a heart attack or something."

Li grimaced. "I don't think Oscar could choose how he died."

Leo flicked his eyes up at Li. They were bitter black pools. "Does it matter? None of us saw anything out of place. I think the cops are taking crazy pills. That man probably just stood up too fast and hit his head on a shelf. No murder."

And yet there were all those inconsistencies. The bag of sugar. The missing cane. The imaginary groceries. The list in the pocket. Oscar's multiple trips to the store. Li's brain spun at the mess it all made. "They seem pretty convinced."

"Bully for them. But I'm telling you that nothing out of the ordinary happened that night. It was a normal night for us. Except for the mess we have to clean off our floors."

A normal night. Interrupted by murder. No one noticed anything out of place. Definitely not a killer cloaked in shadows swinging impossible weapons. Did that mean—?

Leo dropped his gaze back to *Maxim*. "Why are you just standing there staring at the door? Go home, Liam."

Li shuffled into the bare parking lot. A lost day of pay. Fantastic. He kept his eyes glued to his trudging feet. He could always head home and work on his essay for English 102. Then again, he didn't really want to read or write about murder, domination, and frustrated escapism right now. He should have picked a different class.

"Oh dear . . . is the store closed?"

Li glanced up, and a warm blush crept up his neck. A woman hesitated next to a sleek silver Jag gleaming like a wet seal in the sunlight. Her hand lingered on the hood as if afraid to let it go. Her thick chocolate curls surged over one shoulder. Her eyes, the rich blue-violet of spring irises, grew wide and startled. Li cursed his hormones. The woman had to be in her thirties.

"D-do you work here?" Her voice stuttered softly. "Is the store closed?"

Li cleared his dry throat. "Sorry, ma'am . . . Yes, ma'am . . . We . . . uh . . . had a small . . . incident yesterday." Incident. What a nice, sweet gloss to put on a cold-blooded murder.

Tears bloomed in her eyes. "I . . . I heard. The police . . . They told me my husband was . . . was . . . He died here."

Li fought to keep from gaping. *This* was Oscar Lindstrom's *widow*? Uh-uh. No way. Does not compute. She had a fresh, peaceful beauty that didn't, couldn't, shouldn't harmonize with the sour aura around Oscar. Then Li yanked back on his feelings. This was clearly a grief-racked woman who lost the man she loved. "I'm so sorry, Mrs . . .?"

"Lindstrom. Call me Kathryn."

Well, that proved it. Oscar's widow. Li still had trouble fitting them together. "I'm sorry for your loss, Kathryn. Is there anything I could do to help?"

"I . . . I just wanted to see the place where he . . . he . . ." She opened her purse, fished out a Kleenex, and daubed her eyes with it.

"The police have taken custody of the store. I'm afraid you can't ..." He swallowed to moisten his throat. He didn't want to make her cry.

Kathryn nodded. "I understand. I just ... I wanted to see this place. I had never heard of it. We never shopped here. I-I just wondered why he would be found here of all places. I never heard him leave the house." Her eyes flickered with indecision. "He ... He was found here, wasn't he?"

"Unfortunately ... yes. He was. I ... I found him."

Kathryn's lips parted, her eyes spreading into huge, shocked windows. She abandoned the Jag, crossed to Li, and began brushing his bangs off his forehead like a mother prepping her child for the first day of school. "You poor boy. I just can't imagine ... That must have been terrible. And you're so young ..."

Last time a woman said things like that to Li, she ended up becoming someone he couldn't trust. Li took a half step backward. "I'm okay. Really."

Kathryn's maternal instincts would not be cooled. She stepped forward, straightening his tie, tidying his hair, brushing imaginary dust off his shoulders. "I just never believed this would happen. Oscar was such a good boy. He worked so hard all his life. No one would want to hurt him. I never believed those silly threats."

"Threats?"

Kathryn tugged at the end of her hair and bit her lip. "Oh ... They were just little pranks. Probably from old chef colleagues of his. Maybe it was an inside joke. Nothing serious."

Rationalizing, Li thought. "You never know."

"No! No one would hurt my Oscar! All they did was leave a package with a raw beef heart inside it on our doorstep. With a little note written on a page torn out of Oscar's first book. That's not the same thing as hurting someone! That's not a crime! That's not ... not ..."—her voice collapsed to a whisper—"... murder."

The word cracked her peaches-and-milk complexion. Tears raced over her cheeks. She fumbled in her purse for another Kleenex. Li reached out to pat her shoulder. His hand froze. His thoughts scrambled over the information she gave him. That "prank" did not play in the same playground as a ding-dong-ditch or even a bag of dog poop on a porch. Someone took the effort to buy a raw beef heart and wasted it by dumping it at Oscar's door. Then added a note scrawled on a page of Oscar's book, violating Oscar's work. It was action with real hate behind it. And some history too.

When he did pat her shoulder, the gesture was awkward, unfocused. "Don't worry, Kathryn. The police will catch the killer. They're professionals." His reassurances felt a little hollow to him.

Kathryn slipped the soiled tissue into her purse. "Everything is a mess. Nothing makes sense. Every detail the police tell me is confusing and out of place. A big muddle. What's going on? First, Oscar tells me that he's staying in his home office until late. Then, the police tell me he's been found dead in this grocery store I've never heard of. Then, my neighbor, Staci, tells me that Oscar never left the house. Now you're telling me Oscar *was* found here. I don't know if it'll ever get sorted out."

Li quirked an eyebrow. "What exactly did Staci see?"

Staci Belmont could not be a real person. Detective Hughes was glad of his iron poker face, because he might have laughed. Standing in the doorway of a house one across, two down from Oscar's, Staci looked plucked out of an eighties workout video. Jane Fonda would have coveted that body: thin, lithe, virtually breastless. This figure—what little there was—had been squeezed into an electric blue leotard and white tights flaunting good muscle in her legs. Clashing fuchsia leg warmers cozied up her calves. Her frizzy cloud of peroxide-blond hair looked at home clamped under a neon sweatband.

"Ooooo, you must be the police!"

Her voice, piercing as a whistle, buzzed in the detective's ears. He resisted the urge to cover them. He flashed his badge at her.

"Yes, of course!" she squealed. "You must be here about poor Kathy's husband. I told her I didn't know if what I saw would interest the police, but I see it must have. Please come in! Sorry for how I'm dressed. I was about to go to my aerobics class."

Stepping into the living room proved one thing: this house never had a woman's touch. Despite Staci being the charming hostess, she clearly never left so much as a skid mark on the place. Not a permanent fixture, Detective Hughes surmised. This was a house that wore cologne and aftershave, would never wear perfume. A bachelor pad.

The walls were paneled and trimmed in dark brown wood of vague origins. A choir of electronic singing bass filled the place of honor above the working wood fireplace's mantle. Fishing poles were racked against the far wall. A big screen TV—a studly sixty inches—dominated a corner by the front window. Detective Hughes and Adam elected to sit in the matching brown leather club chairs. Staci folded herself into a perfect lotus on the pool-table-green sofa. If she made any contribution to the room, it was probably insisting that there would be no neon signs advertising beer on the walls and maybe that pale blue throw slung over the back and arm of the sofa.

"Am I right, Detective?" Staci asked. "Are you here about Kathy Lindstrom's husband?"

Detective Hughes didn't think a woman like Kathryn deserved the truncated "Kathy," but he let it slide. "Yes, Miss Belmont. I understand you are friends with her."

"Oooooo, yes! Kathy and I have been friends about four months. Ever since I met my boo, Tommy, at Harper Lodge."

"And her husband? Were you friends with him?"

Staci tilted her head and scrunched up her face. "Ehhhh, not really. He wasn't the friendly type. Tommy knew him from work. We never saw much of him."

"I see. Miss Belmont, would you mind going over what you did Sunday evening?"

"Oh, of course, Detective. Well, Tommy and I went to see the Sea Lions/Scorpions game at Jordan Field at about two p.m. It ran a bit long so we didn't get home until six fifteen. I took a shower and then sat here on the couch while Tommy showered. You can see Kathy and Oscar's house from here. See?"

Detective Hughes glanced out of the window from this vantage point. He could clearly see the front flower beds of the Lindstrom house, two ice-white pools floating in the green sea of grass. A shard of the house itself was visible: a sliver of porch, a scrap of roof, and one unobstructed window.

"It was that window," Staci indicated. "I noticed it was lit when I sat down and I looked at it. Oscar was standing in the window. I could see his shadow."

"Pardon me, Miss Belmont," Detective Hughes said, "but how can you be sure it was him when all you saw was his silhouette?"

"I have seen him stand at that window many times since I started coming to Tommy's house. His silhouette is very distinct. That's his office window, by the way. Kathy told me he likes to spend long hours in it, and I have seen him myself, standing at that window like some general planning campaigns. I'm sure it was Oscar last night."

"Very well. Then what happened?"

"I read my magazine. Every so often, I'd look up at the window. Oscar was always there. When Tommy and I went to dinner, he was still staring down the world. He didn't move the entire time. We came back here at ten and he was still scowling at us through the window."

"Don't you think that's rather peculiar behavior?"

"Ooooo, not for Oscar. He did it all the time. He was like a statue up there."

Detective Hughes stared at Oscar's house as if the darkened window across the way held all the secrets to this mystery. Perhaps it did. "When did you and ... erm ... Tommy learn about Oscar's death?"

"Early this morning. Tommy's boss at *The Gazette*, Frank Dixon, called him and told him what happened. I decided to take Kathy for breakfast and shopping. I couldn't imagine how it must feel to lose your husband." Staci lifted her slim, bony shoulders in an unconcerned shrug. "Then again, I've never been married."

Frank Dixon. There he was again. A suspect with a reach as long as Constance Henderson's. "Tommy works at *The Shorewood Gazette?*"

"Oooooo, yes! Didn't I say? Oscar and Frank were colleagues. Oscar wrote the restaurant reviews. Tommy writes for sports. That's why we went to the ballgame."

A rumble in the driveway. The beep of an electronic car lock. Staci clapped her hands together and giggled. "Ooooo!" The detective thought his skull would split if he heard that squeal one more time. "Tommy's home!"

Based on Staci Belmont, Detective Hughes pulled up a rather scary image of the infamous "Tommy." A man with a Tom Selleck 'stache, a shirt featuring the set of *Hawaii Five-O* or *Miami Vice*, and a fat gold wristwatch that could be mistaken for rapper bling.

He was mistaken. "Tommy" was a tall, well-built man with wind-and-sea-swept curls of chestnut hair. His dark slacks and leather belt emphasized his lean waist while his white dress shirt—open at the collar and rolled at the sleeves—celebrated the admirable size of his shoulders. A perfect romance novel specimen of testosterone. His eyebrows arched high over his hazel eyes as he met his unexpected guests.

The detective and his partner stood and introduced themselves.

"Tom Delancey," Staci's boyfriend replied. "Sports writer for *The Gazette*. You're here about Oscar, I suspect."

Staci cooed. "Ooooo, yes, Tommy. I was telling them about last night."

Detective Hughes settled back in his club chair. "Yes. Could you tell us your version of what happened that night?"

Tom sat next to Staci, who rested her hand on his thigh. Adam turned to a fresh page in his notebook, scribbling his notes without even looking at the paper.

"I took Staci to Jordan Field to see a game. The Shorewood Sea Lions and the Cemetery Scorpions. I'm happy to report we trounced the Scorps six to five in extra innings. It ran long, but it was a great game. But you can learn about all the details in my article on Thursday."

"What happened after the game, Mr. Delancey?"

"Staci and I came back here. It was about a quarter after six when we got here. She took a quick shower, and we discussed having a late dinner. I took a shower and then worked on my article on the game for a couple of hours. I always like working on my pieces immediately after the games, so it's fresh in my mind. I think it was about eight thirty when we went to dinner at Page & Simon."

"Did you notice Oscar Lindstrom at any time?"

"I caught a glimpse of him in his office window when we left for dinner. I didn't really pay attention when we got back."

But Oscar was dead by eight thirty. So how could they see him?

Detective Hughes stowed that point away for the moment. He moved on. "I heard that Mr. Lindstrom was your colleague at *The Shorewood Gazette*, Mr. Delancey."

Tom gave the detective a smile that stretched across his face. "Emphasis on 'was,' Detective. He resigned on Friday."

"Were you surprised?"

Tom's brow furrowed, giving the question serious consideration. "A little, I guess. But Oscar did things on his own terms. He never let anyone tell him what to do or how to write. The editors weren't comfortable touching his articles. Oscar ... well ... he had a kind of holier-than-thou personality. He was king, and we were all peasants."

An attitude Detective Hughes felt in the Lindstrom house.

"How did the paper handle his resignation?"

"You'll have to ask Frank about that."

"And you? How close were you to Mr. Lindstrom? Were you friends?"

At this, Tom burst into laughter, a warm, young, untroubled sound. "Friends? Oscar Lindstrom did NOT have friends. He was a tyrant at times. I was his colleague. We weren't bosom buddies. I've had dinner with him and his wife a few times, but that wasn't a friendship. Oscar was a man who lived for himself."

Detective Hughes steepled his fingers and came back to the point that muddied this murder. "You must have heard that Oscar Lindstrom was found at Esther's Family Grocery."

Both Staci and Tom looked perplexed.

The detective elaborated. "It's a small grocery store found off Shorewood Avenue. Not very popular. It's about a fifteen-minute walk from here."

Tom frowned, eyes clouded with confusion. "I've never heard of it."

Staci bit her lip. "I think I have. Not fondly, if I remember. Some of the girls in my aerobics class complained about the terrible state of its organics. I definitely didn't shop there."

Not many people did, it seemed. The fact Oscar was found there at all became more and more outlandish. Why was he there?

Tom must have read the detective's thoughts. "Why would Oscar be found there, Detective? He wouldn't have known about it, and if he did, he would never take one step inside. He didn't leave the house when we were here. Like I said, we saw him in his office."

Once again, the man was locked into his office, the throne room of his imaginary empire. The endless back-and-forth in this case was making Detective Hughes dizzy. Where was Oscar and when did he get there? What happened?

He had to examine that office.

Picking a lock was a science and an art.

Charming the building manager had been easy. Finding the apartment building address had been effortless. Learning the name of his quarry had been child's play. The internet took all the struggle out of this work.

Morley was actually glad of the lock-picking. It let skills the internet hadn't been able to kill have a chance to stretch and grow.

He glanced over his shoulder to make sure the kid wasn't coming home too soon.

He felt the cheap lock give, and the door swung open. Now he had to be quick. He had a deadline, a usual experience for his past life as a reporter. The Lady wouldn't be happy if he dawdled. And he had no definite time when the kid would come home. He slipped inside, footsteps as light as a cat's shadow.

Morley pulled out his handheld tape recorder, an old friend from his newspaper days, and started it.

"Report on one, Liam Andrew Johnson. Age twenty. Birthday: March eleventh. Address: Apartment 317 in the Arcadian Estates building, 224 Allen Avenue. Prior addresses: Small apartment in Long Beach, family's home in Jefferson. Eldest child of Gene Johnson and Margaret Bailey. One sibling—sister, Annaleigh. Finances are shaky. Prior job was a waiter for the Howard Line of luxury cruise ships. Got tangled up in some interesting deaths there and was fired under unfriendly circumstances. Will investigate further."

He moved through the studio apartment like a machine, sifting, sorting, and replacing documents and files in the tiny space, continuing to record his report. The Lady wanted as much as possible. The Lady wanted to know everything about this kid, a kid, Morley thought, who wasn't worth the gum stuck to his shoe.

"Johnson takes a class at the Shorewood Community College. English 102. Apartment kept clean and organized. Furniture is third-hand at best." His sharp journalist eyes dropped to the foot of the bed. "Brand new sneakers though. Interesting." He moved to the closet to investigate the kid's clothes.

What did the Lady want? Morley swore under his breath as he thought about how he was sent on another goddamn rainbow chase. However, the Lady was in charge, the big boss, the numero uno, the biggest cheese of them all. She knew too much. It was how she got everything she wanted. She knew things. She liked knowing things.

Morley remembered that her ex-husband loved to know things too. Perhaps he still did.

She knew about Morley's little problem. His frequent nose bleeds and nights without sleep. She knew about his suspended license and the girl with the red sweater now buried under the Shorewood Memorial Lawn. She knew about his whiskey breath, his probation, and his dropped charge of manslaughter.

She knew that charge should have been murder. However, she knew she could use Morley, and she kept his leash tighter than a noose.

Morley rifled through the scant array of clothes hung neatly in the shoebox of a closet. "Very few personal belongings. The kid's nearly broke and starving. There was no food in his kitchen." He never added editorial comments to his reports, but felt compelled in this one case. "This kid's not a threat. He has nothing. This job is probably his last hope. Just let his situation take him down. He—"

Full stop. Morley's sensitive ears caught the minute jingle of keys on the other side of the door. The brittle clicks of the lock.

Morley dove into the closet and closed the door, leaving a hair of a crack open for observation. He managed to still his breathing, melting into the shadows, a sniper lining up a shot through his scope. He would wait and watch.

The quarry was home.

Waiting for the other end to answer their phone was a torture worse than looking into the self-satisfied sneer of Oscar Lindstrom, that face he made when he knew he had you cornered. The man wrung the corner of his brown apron in his quivering hands. Anxiety made a muscle twitch in his jaw. Damn this modern compulsion to text message everything. This was one conversation he didn't want to have a print record of.

"Hello."

"It's me. We have a problem. Have you seen the paper?"

"What about it?"

"Oscar's dead."

A pause. A *long* pause. "So?"

"You ... You didn't ... do anything, did you?"

"How could you ask me something like that?" Another pause. "Did *you* do anything?"

"Do you really think I'm ... I'm a killer?"

"Let's not fight about this. There's nothing we can do."

"But we did do something. And what if the police—?"

"No." The voice was hard, a flint-like sound that could spark a blaze of bad temper in half a second. "You will say nothing, got it? You don't know anything. We didn't do anything wrong, remember? *We did nothing wrong.*"

CHAPTER 9

Threats

"Back again, Detective?"

Jason's tone was just a shade off from being a sneer.

"Yes, Mr. Lindstrom. I'd like to examine your father's office, if I may."

Jason prickled like a porcupine, his nostrils flared, his shoulder hiked up to his ears. "Where's your warrant?"

Kathryn swept—literally—from the dining room, clad in her gingham apron and wielding her broom. She looked up, frowning at the interruption in her chore schedule, and then warming into her charming hostess role. "They don't need a warrant, Jason. We want to help them catch your father's killer. Now why don't you be polite and go show them where it is?"

Jason turned a splotchy red and his head drooped, chin buried in his shrunken chest. Tears threaded his eyelashes. He rubbed his secret scarred arms under his baggy sweatshirt.

Poor kid, Detective Hughes thought. *Loathes his father so much. Thought he was the Devil incarnate. Only to be told to support him by the stepmother he secretly loves. His life must be hell. He looks physically sick with hatred.*

Jason looked up again, his jawline rigid, his eyes cold behind his glasses. "Follow me."

As the son led them up the entry stairs with its dark ebony banister and glacier-white spindles, Detective Hughes took the opportunity to survey the design of the house again. Every couch, every rug, every clock, every knickknack was magazine-flawless. The house was a move-in ready showroom model. The detective could just catch the scent of furniture polish and cleaning solution. A sterile stink.

There were no family photographs. Oscar wasn't one for preserving memories, it seemed. Detective Hughes recalled, when his son was born, he and his wife cluttered the walls with his pictures, finger paintings, and drawings. Photos of his family warmed up his desk at work. But the Lindstrom residence was not a place to celebrate family. All this gray, cream, silver, mirror, and glass made this house a modern ice palace. Sunlight reflected off the finishes here in hard white bands as opposed to the dappled gold that flowed through the windows in the detective's home. To live in this sterile showroom box without an atom of love displayed anywhere had to be like living in a chic padded cell. Jason looked ready to snap. How did Kathryn stand it?

Jason brought them to a white door about midway down the second-floor landing. He stood by it, his emaciated arms knotted over his chest, his face stiff. "This is it."

Detective Hughes rattled the knob. "It's locked."

"Exactly. Dad locked it. Dad always locks it. Dad locked it the night he died."

"Do you have a key?"

Jason snorted. "You really think my father trusted me? He thought I was stupid."

"Then where is the key?"

"Beats me. Hidden on his person somewhere. I think he liked to hide it in his shoe when he left the house."

"And what do you suggest we should do?"

Jason glared at the detective, breathing heavily. Jason's hands shook with effort as he popped the lock out of place with brute force. The door slid open. Jason Lindstrom was stronger than he looked.

Strong enough to drive a scanner into his father's skull?

Detective Hughes kept his face guarded. "Thank you, Mr. Lindstrom."

Oscar's office. The king's private chambers. Detective Hughes hoped this room—Oscar's inner sanctum—would give him clues to Oscar's character when he was alone. He had a lot of testimony regarding Oscar's public persona. What was the man like when he was by himself? What ideas and memories did he cherish in his solitary hours? What tokens of his globe-trekking past did he celebrate in his secret world?

His hopes fizzled. The office matched the rest of the house: luxuriously furnished, meticulously maintained, and chromatically austere. No photographs. No souvenirs. No treasures. There was no personality in this house.

He spoke over his shoulder. "Were you allowed in this room, Mr. Lindstrom?"

"At times," Jason replied. "And only when he wanted me here. I was his tech guy for the blog. He didn't have the patience to learn how to work a computer. So he'd let me in here to work on it."

"And anyone else?"

"Kathryn cleans it every day. But Dad was a neat freak, so there wasn't much to do. And he's had colleagues and his boss, Frank Dixon, over a few times. Again, only when he wanted them there. I feel bound to add that he could easily keep us out when he didn't want anyone to disturb him."

Detective Hughes's eyes roamed around the room. Ebony bookcases matching the ones downstairs stretched across the two walls to his left and right. They were stuffed with books and reference material. Straight ahead was a large window, so spotless it was like a hole cut into the wall. This was the window easily viewed from the neighbors and the street below. Oscar's royal perch. Angled in front of the window, its chair facing the door, was a slick glass desk topped with tidy, docketed files and the latest computer model money could buy. The office lights were burning bright, lights left lit from the night before.

It was the window that fixed everyone's attention. Part of the view was muffled by creamy linen sheers. Behind these sheers was a dark blot. A human-sized blot.

All three men strode forward. Detective Hughes, after slipping on gloves, slid back the curtain and frowned at what he saw. As if there weren't *enough* weird complications in this case.

A human silhouette cut out of plywood and painted black. Detective Hughes cautiously tilted the silhouette back to reveal that a large poster of Oscar Lindstrom, scowling as always, had been cut to fit the plywood backing.

"Interesting," Detective Hughes said. "Follow my train of thought, Adam. The office lights are on. This silhouette is placed in the window with a photograph of Oscar on it. If anyone on the street looks up, they'd see what they'd expect to see: a shadowy Oscar Lindstrom looking out his office window. Nobody gave this more than a cursory glance."

"Instant alibi," Adam replied.

"But why? Why form an alibi for your own death?"

Jason stared at the silhouette of his father in mute disbelief. "Oh God . . . is that what he was doing up here?"

Detective Hughes rounded on him. "Did you suspect he was doing something else?"

Jason retreated, his pale brown eyes wider than the windows, all his hate and hostility shattering. He was now the frightened and trembling boy underneath his flimsy pretense. "I . . . I-I sometimes heard Dad messing around up here. It sounded like he was fussing with the window. I . . . I-I just w-wondered . . ."

". . . what he was doing? Yes, we wonder that as well. And I wonder what you were doing when you were listening to him."

Terror scuttled into the boy's face. His fingers throttled the hem of his floppy sweatshirt. "I-I . . . I . . ."

Detective Hughes's tone softened but his eyes stayed firm. "You were listening to see how occupied your father was before you escaped the house, weren't you? You listened to make sure he was busy before you left. Am I close?"

The naked fear in Jason's eyes told Detective Hughes everything he needed to know.

"Did you hear anything in here the night your father died, Mr. Lindstrom?"

Jason's head wilted, his complexion gray and his lips strained. His voice had collapsed to a monotone. "Yes. Not . . . Not long after he went into the office, I listened at the door. He was working on something. There were bumps and scuffles. I . . . I thought he was working at the window. I was going to leave the house, but then I heard his footsteps move toward the office door while I was listening outside it. I panicked and fled to my room. I decided to wait it out for an hour or two before trying to leave."

"Why did you want to escape?"

Jason's head snapped up, narrow stripes of red inflaming his cheeks, tears threatening to spill. His voice quavered, but stayed low and controlled. "*Wouldn't you?*"

Before Detective Hughes could ask anything else, Jason fled.

There was nothing else to do but search the office.

Detective Hughes rummaged through the neat files on the desk. "Interesting. It seems Oscar recently bought a house in the LA area. Plans to move? And look at this—he sent his résumé to the *LA Times* to be their restaurant critic. He was definitely making plans to leave Shorewood. That explains his resignation from *The Gazette*."

Adam, sifting through the wastebasket like an archaeologist, excavated an important bit of evidence. "Sir? Look at this. I think this was the note found in that package with the beef heart Mrs. Lindstrom told us about."

Detective Hughes took the note from his partner. It was a page torn out of a book. Probably a hardcover, given the size of the page. The title at the top of the page said *Full Plate*. Oscar's first book. Blood from the beef heart smeared the paper, and it had been crumpled into a ball. Two words had been scrawled shakily across the page in vivid red marker.

FIRST WARNING.

This was a desecration.

"Someone certainly was a critic of Oscar's work"

Adam, for once, looked a bit awkward. "Sir, I know you might not want to hear any theories, but ... um ..."

"Theories are cheap, Adam. It never hurts to share your ideas."

"Well, sir, I think this feels like an act based on betrayal."

Detective Hughes bent his head and cocked an eyebrow. "Why would you think that?"

Adam brushed a hand over his dishwater-blond hair, smoothing its already smooth texture. "The note came from Oscar's first book. Someone who was very angry at Oscar had a copy of it on their shelves. I believe this person must have respected Oscar once. He or she bought this book because they were a fan. Now they felt betrayed by something Oscar did to them, so they betrayed *him* by defiling his work."

A brief nod. "Not a bad thought. It's definitely a point to clear up. Check out these notes here, will you? I want to examine these bills."

Adam flipped through a legal pad packed with microscopic handwriting. "Looks like he was working on a new book. No title yet. There's a weird note here: Discuss with Miranda. Got any ideas who that could be, Tony?"

A small smile curled the detective's lips. "I think she may have something to do with this. Bills and invoices for roses, jewelry, fancy dinners ... the works for an extramarital affair. But the big red flag—hell, it's a red billboard at this point—is that Oscar paid the mortgage on a house in town, a house that wasn't his own. Address is 413 Helen Street. Sound familiar?"

413 Helen Street. What did Jason Lindstrom say about it?

You'll learn something.

Morley pressed his body into the meager wardrobe inside the closet, silent as death, watching with the intensity of a bird of prey. The shadows closed over him like a cloak of invisibility. He didn't dare to breathe. He watched his quarry enter the apartment and take off his chocolate-colored apron, part of the uniform of that hole-in-the-wall grocery store where he worked. Morley, his hawk eyes tracing the stress and strain in every line and untimely wrinkle in his quarry's face, could tell that the kid had a lot on his mind. He moved through the apartment in that dreamy, hazy, floating way of a mind on autopilot. If the kid went to the bathroom, Morley could slip out undetected.

Luck did not favor him. The kid started shuffling toward the closet to hang up his apron.

Morley's hand, blind in the shadows, swam through the darkness to find something to use. His long, agile fingers stroked something wooden. He tried to divine its shape and form with nothing but his fingertips, keeping his eyes fastened on the kid's movements.

A baseball bat. The kid kept a bat in his closet. For protection or for sport? For Morley, it would be used for the former.

The kid's hand lifted to grasp the closet doorknob.

Morley, a cornered panther, pounced out of the closet, swung the bat, and slammed it into the kid's head. The boy, stunned by the speed and efficiency of the blow, spun on his toes before crumbling to the floor into deep unconsciousness. He lay on the floor like a used rag, crumpled and tossed aside. He could have been dead for all Morley cared.

Morley dumped the baseball bat by the kid's body. His face when he stared at the prone figure was as immovable as the Rock of Gibraltar. It wasn't his fault if the damn kid showed up too early.

He left the apartment to deliver his report to the Lady.

CHAPTER 10

Clean Plate

413 Helen Street.

Altogether, a good impression. A cozy bungalow painted the exact shade of a key lime pie with tufts of ornamental white trim to mimic the meringue. The garden was a well-loved jubilee of color, a stark contrast to the fiercely maintained rings of nondescript white at the Lindstrom house. Sandstone pavers serpentined through the trimmed lawn in a path leading to the sky-blue front door. Somewhere in the distant trees, songbirds trilled. So might a cottage in a fairy tale would have looked.

This was the home of Miranda Raglietti.

Detective Hughes knocked on the door, his buckeye-brown eyes taking in the vibrant red-and-yellow welcome mat cheerfully inviting visitors to COME ON IN! He doubted if that request would ever truly be welcome.

A boy, probably no older than four or five, pulled open the door. He regarded the two men standing at the doorstep with a mature, rather calculating expression. "Are you my new daddies? Mom is always bringing home new daddies."

Detective Hughes and Adam exchanged a look.

Detective Hughes crouched so he would be on the same level as the boy. "We're the police," he said, his tone friendly. "Is your mom around?"

The boy's eyes lit up like twin Jumbotrons. "The police! Cool! Can I see your badge?"

Detective Hughes indulged him. The boy bellowed over his shoulder. "HEY, MOM! THE POLICE ARE HERE!" He turned back to the detective, his face eager. "Do you guys have the car with the big lights on it?"

A woman's voice, sharp and cutting, shouted back at him. "For God's sake, Trevor! How many times do I have to tell you not to shout? Do you even listen to me?"

Trevor howled even louder. "THE POLICE ARE HERE!"

The woman, grumbling, emerged from the small hallway balancing a tiny laundry basket on her hip and a glass of what smelled like scotch. She was a young mother, mid- to late-twenties. She wore a floppy tank top that laughed at the idea of covering her body and shorts hiked to her upper thigh. Her bottle-blonde hair, yanked into a high ponytail, needed a root touch-up. She faltered when she saw the two policemen at her doorstep, one of whom was holding up his badge for inspection.

"What do you want?" she asked, suspicion and fear making a potent cocktail in her cognac-colored eyes.

"Miranda Raglietti?" At her nod, he continued. "Detective Hughes and Officer Schafer-Schmidt, ma'am. We'd like to talk to you about Oscar Lindstrom."

A double shot of fear to those eyes. Miranda shooed her son into his bedroom to play with his Legos, despite his protests that he wanted to see "the police car with the big lights." Once Trevor was safely ensconced, she invited her guests into her small but pleasant living room. They declined her offer of a cocktail.

She flopped on the flower-print armchair and sucked down her scotch. "What do you want to know about Oscar?"

The two men sat on the sofa slipcovered in robin's egg blue. "You've heard about his death, I take it?" Detective Hughes asked.

She nodded, keeping her expression wary and shuttered.

"He was murdered."

"So I gathered from the paper. How did you find out about me?"

Detective Hughes casually mentioned the bills and the invoices.

Miranda unfurled a sly smile. "Men can be astonishingly stupid, can't they?" She pushed out a sigh, more from resignation than exasperation. The fear fled her face, leaving it remote, almost bored with the proceedings. "Yes, I had an affair with Oscar. Yes, I knew he was married. No, I didn't care. No, I didn't love him. No, I didn't want to marry him. No, I didn't kill him."

Beneath the pretty, cozy presentation, there was a blunt edge of ruthlessness.

"You don't seem to care much that he died."

Miranda's slim shoulders lifted in an apathetic shrug. "It was an affair, not a marriage. I'm more emotionally attached to my area rugs than I was to Oscar Lindstrom."

"Your son—Trevor, I believe his name was—made references to various 'daddies' you brought home."

A coy smile teased the tips of her rose-lacquered lips. "Don't sound so disapproving, Detective. You make it sound like I was comparison shopping. I'm not in the market for a new father for Trevor. Think of it like ... window shopping. Just because I'm a single mother doesn't mean I have to behave like a nun."

Detective Hughes cleared his throat. "Could you tell me more about your relationship with Oscar Lindstrom? Where, for instance, did you meet?"

"At the grocery store, if you can believe it. He had some pretty critical things to say about my groceries. But he was always like that. About *everything*. A critic to his soul."

That was the second time Detective Hughes heard that phrase. Once from Liam, the second from Oscar's mistress. Being a critic appeared to be one of the pillars of his personality.

Was it also a driving force behind his death?

Miranda continued. "Despite the critiques, I could tell he was interested. And I thought, 'What the hell?' It would be an experience. Life is short anyway." The mischievous light in her eyes faded into that remote stare again. "He was boring and typical and old-fashioned. Antiquated, even. Like his views on women. He expected me to act like his docile wife and be a nursemaid to him. Fat chance! One child in my life is plenty, please and thank you. I think Kathryn spoiled him rotten." She waved a dismissive hand. "The flowers, the jewelry, the champagne ... Those weren't acts of affection. Oscar felt he had to do it, like it was tradition or expected of him. I'd have been happier with Lakers tickets. He was very conventional. And he acted like these gifts were reminders that I owed him or something. That his 'affection' was conditional. Quid pro quo. A business transaction. And I bet you already know that Oscar paid my mortgage last month. Let me tell you something: I didn't ask him to do it nor did I need him. He did it on his own. Another 'little reminder.' He wanted to control me. Wasn't going to happen. Our affair was a long battle for power." A flicker of pleasure. "Of course, that could be fun too. It's certainly been fun with the lawyer I'm currently seeing. *He* knows who's really on top in this game . . ."

Detective Hughes slid a finger along his jawline, a thinking gesture. He kept his tone conversational. "What did you two like to talk about?"

Miranda smothered her laugh into a snort. "Talking was not one of our preferred pastimes, Detective. Mostly he talked. About Kathryn and how perfect she was and how he could never find anything wrong with her. About Jason, which turned into a tirade of hate and disgust and disappointment. I think, really, he loathed his son. Don't ask me why. He'd preen about all the restaurants he closed. Stuff like that. He spent most of our time criticizing people."

Criticizing. A critic to his soul. "Any person or business he particularly bragged about?"

The phantom of a smile. "He did gloat about Bauer a few times."

"Tell me about that."

Her ponytail swung wildly as she snapped her head to him, eyes suspicious. "Don't tell me you missed it. It was everywhere. A huge scandal. You must have heard all about it."

"Humor me."

Again the I-could-care-less shrug, the aloof stare. Did this blunt ruthlessness disguise a more sharply felt passion? Detective Hughes could not say for sure. Even the decor in her home felt calculated, designed, as it had, to make a good first impression.

Miranda was nobody's fool, would change for no one, and played her own game. Was this ruthlessness the thing that attracted Oscar in the first place?

"Oscar took his wife to dinner at Bauer when he went to review the place," she said. "Bauer and its chef/owner, Felix Bauer, were already becoming enormously popular in town. Diners flocked to his restaurant, went on pilgrimages just to nab a seat at one of his tables. The press started dubbing Chef Felix 'the Joël Robuchon of

Germanic cuisine.' The chefs working there were on the fast track to sterling careers. So what Oscar did was nothing less than mass murder."

"You remember quite a bit."

A glimmer of amusement. "I pay attention to things." Without turning her head and still with that ghost of an amused smile hovering on her face, she raised her voice. "Trevor! Put those cookies back on the plate! Those are for after dinner."

A rumble of little footsteps. A hearty protest.

Miranda was unyielding.

With Trevor, master cookie thief, once again in his room, she returned to the interrogation. "His bedroom door squeaks, and he's been eyeing those cookies since I mixed the batter. If he happens to think I'm a super-mom with X-ray vision, supersonic hearing, and a built-in lie detector, so much the better. Now getting back to Bauer ..."

It was clear who was the boss of this questioning.

"I don't think Oscar went into the restaurant with any favorable intentions. He was already bitter about the Robuchon comparison, because he wasn't the one to make it. So he went to Bauer to find the fatal flaw. And he brought witnesses."

"And what happened, Miss Raglietti?"

"His wife got sick from the food."

The death knell for any restaurant. The detective could hear it echo across time and in the hearts of the chefs who worked so passionately on building Bauer into a great restaurant.

Through one man, their dreams imploded.

Miranda drummed her fingers on the floral arm of her chair, all her fingers moving as one unit, the piston for the finely tuned machine of her brain. Her eyes stayed as glassy and hard as full bottles of brandy. "Oscar *crucified* them. If you thought his column was harsh, the blog post made the column look like a testimonial. It was a masterpiece of hate speech. He held nothing back. It was like dumping an ocean of acid on the restaurant and anyone who came within breathing distance of it. But that wasn't the end of it.

You see, Oscar brought race into his review, and the propaganda sparked riots at home with the worst ethnic cleansings in history."

Detective Hughes remembered. Too well. They had been horrible nights. Chefs and their families cowering in their homes. Fire. Blood. A massive flood of hate. It had been all hands at the department. There were fears that these incidents would ignite citywide explosions.

He glanced at Adam, saw the kid's eyes cloud over and his forehead crease, and knew that he recalled those nights as well.

Miranda's fingers paused, then curled into a fist, her close-clipped nails scratching and clawing the flowers printed on the upholstery. "The riots were the nail in the coffin for Bauer. *No one* wanted to be associated with it. They were frightened. What if these lunatics attacked them? People were afraid for their families, afraid for their *lives*. Bauer became a bad omen, a disaster zone. The pilgrimages for a seat stopped cold. Diners dried up. Chef Felix went bankrupt and left town. And those young, eager, passionate chefs were ruined. No restaurant would hire them with the name Bauer on their résumés. I wouldn't be surprised if we found these talented boys and girls working at Happy Burger and dreaming about tearing Oscar limb from limb. Their careers were destroyed."

The sad history of one of Shorewood's premier restaurants definitely opened new vistas for Detective Hughes. Hot-blooded, furious, wounded chefs who dreamed of success, who wore their fingers down to bone for the opportunity, who had that dream pulverized by one bad review. People angry enough to kill the man responsible for their destruction.

When he returned to the police station, he would try to locate a list of the people who once worked at the ill-fated Bauer.

"I hope you see where this leads you, Detective."

"You've certainly given us plenty to think about, Miss Raglietti."

"There are certainly better suspects for Oscar's murder than me."

Detective Hughes chose not to deign that summation with a response. "Did Oscar mention any plans he had for the future? Did he discuss anything with you?"

Miranda frowned in concentration. That look of unconcerned boredom was gone again. She was giving this question serious thought.

"I did get the impression Oscar had something up his sleeve. He was excited, elated at times, but he fought to keep it hidden. It was in his eyes. They were practically shining. He didn't tell me any details. He did mention that changes were on the way." The frown cleared, and she thumped her fist on the arm of the chair. "It might have been his new book he was working on. Sometimes, he talked about it with me. It was in very early stages. The return of Oscar Lindstrom, food expert of the world. He even had a title for it, even though he hadn't written a single word yet."

"And what was this title?"

Miranda unveiled the only true smile of the entire interview. Her white teeth gleamed like a necklace of polished pearls.

"*Clean Plate.*"

Adam's cell phone jangled. With the speed of an Olympic sprinter, he got up, answered it, and excused himself to the foyer.

Detective Hughes sensed a disturbance. He could chalk it up to police instinct, but he knew Adam wouldn't accept a personal call during an interview. News from the station?

The detective thanked his hostess for her time and mentioned that they may return with more questions. Miranda studied him, furnace fire burning in her eyes as she tried to divine the truth of this interruption from the veteran cop's immovable expression. Their goodbyes were formal. Detective Hughes stepped into the foyer.

Adam hung up his phone, his face alert and wary, a wolf on the scent of something big and dangerous. Detective Hughes caught the scent of something serious as well. The two policemen moved outside onto the porch.

"What is it, Adam?"

"There's been a report of a burglary and assault in an apartment on Allen Avenue, sir."

"And this pertains to our investigation?"

"It's the home of one of the suspects, Tony. Liam Johnson. That boy who found Oscar's body."

It seemed all roads—the highways, byways, and dirt alleys—led back to this mysterious Liam Johnson. The boy who knew too much. The boy who knew more than he shared.

"Li? Li! Can you hear me?"

That voice, strident and agitated, seemed to pulse behind the fiery, furious supernova of pain raging in front of him. Li wanted to sink into the cool darkness surrounding his body. He didn't want to return to the searing light where pain and fear waited for him. Oblivion. That was the ticket. Dark, cool oblivion.

"Li, wake up! Please!"

A moan gurgled in his throat. Reluctantly, Li wrenched open an eye.

Noah's face hovered over him. His skin was gruel gray, his Amazon-green eyes bulging in terror, and his mouth puckered in a worried frown. Even his golden hair lost its shine. A huge sigh escaped him.

"Oh thank God . . . I thought you were dead."

"Noah?"

"I already called the cops, and they'll be here soon. Here you go." Noah pressed a bag of frozen peas onto Li's head, making the boy hiss and groan. When Noah pulled the peas back, a flower of blood stained the bag.

The room spun gently, and Li had to fight his sudden urge to get sick. "W-what happened?"

"You tell me. I came by to visit, found your door open, and saw you lying on the floor with a head wound and a bloody baseball bat."

"I . . . I don't really know . . . I wasn't paying much attention. I had a lot on my mind." He scrunched up his eyes and grimaced, trying to think through the adamant throb of his skull. "I . . . I came home early because the store was closed. I walked in my apartment. This is where it gets fuzzy." He squeezed his eyes shut. "The ... The closet. I-I went to the closet to hang up my work apron. Something jumped out at me." He relaxed. "That's all I know."

Noah pressed the bag of peas back on Li's wound. Li gasped at the cold. "It sounds like someone hid in the closet and attacked you. But that also sounds crazy."

"I know. I don't know anyone who would do that to me. I'm no threat." He recalled the shadowy sedan that missed him by a hair on a rain-soaked night. "Why would someone hunt me like this?"

A voice from the doorway. "That's a question I ask myself."

Detective Hughes and his shadow, Adam, sauntered in, followed by paramedics. The procedure turned formal as the meds carefully examined and bandaged Li's wound. Adam handled most of the questioning. Detective Hughes let his eyes wander over the whole of Li's tiny apartment, absorbing all the details. Li tried to focus on the questions, but his eyes kept darting toward Detective Hughes, wondering what details he spotted, what conclusions he reached. He wasn't sure if his matchbox of a studio could hold this many people.

Detective Hughes cut in with a question. "You're certain you never saw this man's face? You didn't recognize him?"

"I can't be sure it was a 'him.' It happened so fast. I didn't see the face."

"Can you think of anyone who might have a reason to attack you?"

Li's memory raced back to the night Oscar died. Frank. Connie. The argument in a neighboring aisle.

Detective Hughes aimed his unsentimental frown right on Li's face. "You've thought of something, haven't you?"

Li gulped. Was he really that transparent?

"Liam?" First warning.

Li told the story of the psycho car in the storm and added: "Maybe Frank or Connie heard that I spilled the beans, more or less, and is after me to shut me up."

It wasn't a comforting thought, but at least it was some sort of theory.

Detective Hughes crouched down to Li's eye level, his glare skewering the boy's heart. "Are you absolutely certain you've told us everything?"

I haven't. The words bubbled in Li's stomach, rising higher and higher like a lake of magma in the mouth of an active volcano. He was getting better at hiding his nervous tics, but his self-discipline was eroding. The truth boiled in his throat, burned his tongue. Those two words were practically rubbing against his clamped teeth. *I haven't. I haven't. I haven't.*

Reuben. His hatred. His desire to bash Oscar's head in. The suspicions of murder.

The insubstantial evidence. The hasty conclusion. The likelihood that Li talking could ruin a wonderful relationship between Reuben and Noah.

Li said nothing. Perhaps for the last time.

Detective Hughes straightened, his expression immovable and intangible. "The truth will out, Liam. A hackneyed expression, but always relevant. Truth hates to be contained under pressure. One day, it will get out."

A few more routine questions, then the authorities left his apartment.

Li's whole body sagged, his stress lines cutting huge canyons in his face. Energy drained through his fingertips. It had taken all his reserves not to crumble before the detective.

"I couldn't do it." His voice was low, dead. "I couldn't hurt you and Reuben like that. Not after everything you have done for me."

Noah rested a hesitant hand on Li's shoulder. "Li? You okay?"

"Why did you come here anyway, Noah? Is everything all right?"

Noah gestured to a pile of bagged groceries congregating on Li's counter. "I bought groceries for you. Reuben suspected you must be nearly out of food, and we don't want you to starve. So I brought a few provisions to tide you over until your paychecks start coming in."

"See, this is why I can't tell Detective Hughes anything! You two are the nicest people I've ever met!" His voice started to crack. "How could you two be mixed up in a mess like this? I can't picture either of you hurting anyone! And yet, I can! I keep picturing it! My brain won't shut up! It's driving me insane!" He clawed at his temples. "Why did Reuben have to loathe Oscar?"

Noah's eyes widened. "So that's it. You think Reuben might have killed Oscar Lindstrom."

Li's wrinkles gouged deeper into his skin and a frown dragged down his face. "I don't want to. I can't help it. He makes an excellent suspect. He hated Oscar. He even said he wanted 'to bash Oscar's head in.'"

Noah blew out a sigh and hauled Li to his feet. "I wish Reuben would think before he spoke. It gets him in trouble sometimes."

"You ... You're not angry?"

"No, of course not. You're right. He makes an excellent suspect. He hated Oscar with the intensity of a million nuclear reactors. He could have killed him."

Li gaped at his new friend. "How ... How can you say that with a straight face? He's your boyfriend. I barely know you guys, and it's been robbing me of sleep."

"Because it's the truth, Li. Look, I love Reuben. I know him better than anyone else, including his own family. I know he wouldn't hurt a soul, but that doesn't cancel out the bare facts that he *did* hate Oscar and he *was* there the night Oscar died. So yes, he's a suspect. That doesn't equal killer."

"Then you know why he hated Oscar so much."

Noah's mouth tensed into a frown. "Yes, I do. But I'm not going to betray his confidence. He was bawling that day. I had never seen him like that, and it scared the hell out of me. All I can say is that Oscar had a hand in hurting the Rodriguez family very badly. I've been trying to help Reuben heal, but these past few days have been a nightmare. It's not my place to tell you what he went through. It's Reuben's. It's his choice." His sigh was heavy. "But I'll see if I can talk some sense into him. I think you want to help. That's why this whole thing is tearing you apart. You want to help Reuben, but you can't deny the facts. And I wouldn't want you to."

Li shuffled his feet. "I—is he still angry at me?"

"He's upset. But mostly, I think he's frightened. Oscar's death scared him." Worry stole into Noah's eyes. "And now he's starting to be evasive with me. Something's making him nervous. I think he's terrified that you will mention something to the police. Don't tell him I said this, but his greatest fear in life is losing me. And he might be terrified that the police will take him away from me forever."

That was a major reason Li stayed quiet. He had no concrete proof. Just fears. If he let himself get carried away by the currents of his fears, he could hurt two innocent people. Maybe even more. Violent death did that, sent out ripples of terror and suspicion in all directions, without prejudice to those who get swallowed by its riptide. Oscar's murder affected everyone from those as close as his widow to as distant as Li himself.

"I'm sorry, Noah. I don't want to hurt you or Reuben. You're the only friends I have in town."

"It's okay, Li. We'll weather through this. But instead of being opposite sides, let's try working together for a change." Noah clapped Li on the shoulder. "Let's put the groceries away and forget about all this for now. Also, if your head's up for it, I wanted to teach you this simple recipe so you won't go hungry on us. I believe you should learn how to cook, especially living on your own."

Li's answer was distracted. "Yeah . . . sounds good to me."

He couldn't shut off the engine in his mind, despite the never-ending throb on the crown of his skull. He couldn't shake the idea he gave to Detective Hughes that someone was after him, someone who didn't mind hurting him.

A car. A baseball bat. What next?

"The report's incomplete. I'm afraid he showed up at the wrong time."

Morley slid the tape recorder across the table to his employer.

The Lady tapped the recorder with a manicured nail. "It's satisfactory. As you say, he's not much of a threat. But I don't like loose ends. Or loose lips." Her tapping nail sounded like a ticking bomb in the silence around them. "I assume you've dealt with him, Morley."

"He never knew what hit him. I'm certain."

"Is he dead?"

"That I can't say. I gave him a good smack, but not at full power. He'll be seeing stars for a while. Shall I go back and—?"

"Let's not get ahead of ourselves. I want to know what he knows."

Morley cleared his throat. "May I interject something, ma'am?"

The ticking time bomb halted. A pause. "I suppose."

"The kid can't hurt us. He's new in town. He doesn't even have the resources to feed himself properly. The amount of firepower he has wouldn't be enough to fuel a sneeze."

Another pause, this one stretching longer. The Lady spoke quietly, but her words were rimmed in steel teeth. "You don't understand, Morley. It's not who he is that I worry about. It's what he knows. He blabbed to the cops about my conversation with your former boss. That I can't allow. How much did he hear? How much has he figured out? Information can kill as effectively as a gunshot. A knife in the heart. A thimble of poison." Her voice curdled with irony. "A baseball bat to the skull. Information in the wrong quarters is lethal. I have to eliminate the problem."

Morley swallowed hard. He had never heard The Lady sound so cold.

The Lady tapped her finger. The return of the time bomb, tick-tick-ticking its countdown clock. "Perhaps it would be best to invite the young man to tea."

CHAPTER 11

Long Shadows

"Hi, Li."

Never before had two little words sounded so defeated and unwilling.

Li froze mid-scan of the can of soup in his hand. Now what was going to happen? After that eventful Monday (the pain in his head had reduced to a dim hum), Li shuddered at the prospects of Tuesday when the employees of Esther's Family Grocery were allowed to return to work.

Reuben twisted the corner of his apron in his hands, and he had trouble making eye contact with Li. "My boyfriend would like me to invite you to have dinner with us tonight after work. Seven o'clock. If you can make it."

Li paused, slowly lowering the scanner. "Do you . . . want me there?"

"I . . . Noah asked me to invite you. And . . . And we did offer to lend you the computer for your essay if you still need it. It's due tomorrow, isn't it?"

Li nodded. Actually, he had started to stress about his paper since this weekend had proved to be more thrilling than Li wanted. However, this invitation still felt like tiptoeing across no-man's-land into an enemy camp.

Reuben inhaled deeply and drilled his stare into Li's eyes. "Then come. Your education is important. And I don't welch on a promise. Noah . . . *We* would like you to come."

"Um . . . thank you. I'll be there."

"Just one thing." Reuben stepped forward, his eyes starting to heat up. A frown pushed out his bottom lip. "You won't mention him at all tonight. Understand? I've been miserable all weekend and it's starting to affect Noah, which I can't allow. So don't bring him up. For once, I'd like to not think about it."

"I promise, Reuben. Really."

"Good. Great. See you then."

With that cheery finish, Reuben slumped off to continue his work. Li could read in the carriage of his shoulders that the burden of the universe perched on Reuben's back, making the once buoyant man drag his feet as if wading through slime. Slime left behind by the malice of Oscar Lindstrom. Misery, thy name is Reuben Rodriguez.

How am I going to help him?

Li returned to scanning the soups. The repetitive activity would help clear his mind, letting him dissect the problem. He remembered that being the case when he washed dishes on the cruise ship. An out-of-body experience where his hands worked in a routine while his brain organized one heck of a murderous mess.

Back and forth and back and forth. That's the direction Oscar kept going on his last night on Earth. Oscar in his home. Oscar at the store. Oscar in his office. Oscar in the spice aisle. Would they ever clear up this tangle in his travels?

Where was he going? What was he doing?

"Enjoying your day at work, Liam?"

Li flinched. Dammit, couldn't Detective Hughes just stop being everywhere? "Is this a courtesy call, Detective?"

The detective was alone today and looked—in his own veteran policeman way—kind of friendly. He wore a dark sweater and slacks emphasizing the lean cut of his figure, and carried a basket with a bag of coffee in it. He—and Li was flabbergasted that this was possible—even smiled at him, his teeth sparkling against his dark skin. Li could almost forget there was a murder investigation. Almost. "I am wondering where you suddenly picked up some sass. I didn't expect it from you. I'm here buying coffee for the station coffee maker before I head in for work."

"I'm sorry. Is there anything I can help you with?"

The smile relaxed, eased into something more pensive. He nodded at the scanner in Li's hand. "I wondered if you could tell me something about those scanners."

Li arched a brow, glanced at the scanner, frowned, and glanced back at Detective Hughes. "The scanners? But why—?" His eyes ballooned to an unnatural size. Double take. He stared at the thing in his hands as though it morphed into a cobra.

Handheld. Portable. Easy to carry and use.

The gorge rose in his throat. He fought to keep it in place.

"Oh my God." His words were raw and horrified. "This killed Oscar."

Detective Hughes gripped his shoulder. "Easy does it, kid. Don't get sick. That's not the one that did it. And I would appreciate it if you would keep this to yourself, okay?"

Li nodded and gingerly rested the scanner on the shelf. His cheeks were green.

"Okay there, Liam?" The answering nod was dazed. "Then is there anything you can tell me about this equipment?"

Despite the nausea, Li worked to keep his words even. "We don't hand them to customers, if that's what you're thinking. We're supposed to keep them locked up. But ..." He tossed a glance over his shoulder, hunting for his boss with the thousand-watt smile. "... I have noticed that Leo has a bad tendency to leave them lying around. Like on shelves or on carts. The rest of the employees have to clean up after him."

"Making it very easy for the murderer to find his weapon. A nice weapon of opportunity. Did you see anyone with a scanner who shouldn't have had one?"

"No. I don't think so. It would be pretty noticeable."

"The one we believe is responsible for the murder was found in the public men's room toilet. Do you recall seeing anyone near there that night? Anyone suspicious? Anyone who seemed out of the ordinary?"

"No, I'm sorry. I wasn't over there most of the time. And I hate to say it, but other than Oscar's death, it was a normal night. Nothing seemed out of place."

"Can you account for any of the scanners on the night Oscar died?"

Li winced. His memory just punched him with a cruel one. He had had a scanner that night. And before he had found Oscar's body, he had placed the scanner right in Reuben's hand.

So many black marks against his would-be friend.

"Liam?"

Li couldn't lie. Detective Hughes would sniff it out. That would end disastrously. "Only one, sir. I had it. My training partner, Reuben Rodriguez, and I were doing price changes on oatmeal that night. He was teaching me how to use it. Then our boss split us up. I swept the floors while Reuben did price changes on the canned pasta." Now for the part that knotted his stomach. "I . . . I handed Reuben the scanner I used."

Detective Hughes tilted his head, studied him like a brand-new artifact in a museum. "You know, this might be the first time you were completely honest with me." A faint tinge of approval warmed his voice. "You're coming around, son. Thank you."

Li felt lower than the dirt sub-floor of the bottom level of a 200-story underground hotel. And he had a shovel to dig himself deeper. "But, Detective, that still doesn't sort out how Oscar could be in two places at the same time."

Detective Hughes's smile dropped into a frown. Li could almost hear the iron thud it made when it hit his chin. "Now I wonder where you would get that idea, young man?"

Li gulped. Well, he was on this honesty kick. Besides, he didn't like that you-have-the-right-to-remain-silent look on the detective's face. "Kathryn Lindstrom came to the store on Monday. I was headed home after finding out the store was closed for the day. I met Mrs. Lindstrom in the parking lot. She told me about her neighbors seeing Oscar in his office that night."

"Oh? And I suppose you might have a theory on how to solve that little paradox?"

"Since there's no question that Oscar came here because we found his body, the Oscar they saw couldn't be the real one. It might have been a silhouette, a dummy, or even somebody else posing as him. Almost like an alibi for Oscar."

The you-have-the-right-to-remain-silent look morphed into the-electric-chair-is-down-the-hall look. Li had a feeling he had nailed the target on that theory. "And why would Mr. Lindstrom or whoever do that?"

"Oscar Lindstrom didn't want anyone in Shorewood to know he was going to Esther's Family Grocery." Li advanced the conjectures about the upturned coat collar and the stormy night.

The glare diminished, but not by much. "You've given this case a lot of thought, Liam. Is there anything else you and Kathryn Lindstrom discussed?"

"Well, she did mention the package with the beef heart dumped on Oscar's doorstep."

"Did she now? Seems like you're becoming a crack investigator, aren't you?"

Li glared back. After all, he couldn't be arrested for glaring. "I didn't ask for this to happen, Detective. It just does. I've got rotten luck. I can't help it if all this stuff gets thrown in my lap."

He wondered if Detective Hughes believed him. Hell, he wondered if he believed himself. Why *did* murder and misfortune haunt his footsteps?

Detective Hughes's face molded itself back into the immobile mask of the police, a face that gave nothing away. "You've certainly given me a lot to think about, Liam. And next time you learn something interesting, I would appreciate it if you would deliver this information to me as soon as possible. I'm a little concerned where these enterprising efforts of yours will lead. And Liam . . ." He leaned forward, his voice dipping an octave. He was so close that Li could see a few golden flakes in the detective's brown eyes. "*Keep your nose clean.* Killers are dangerous. I don't need more kids hurting themselves thinking they're invincible." The hard eyes softened a bit. "You're somebody's son, somebody's pride and joy. I can't allow you to get killed trying to do my job. Just a reminder."

Li didn't need reminding. After the cruise, it had taken a week for the finger-shaped bruises on his throat to disappear.

"Be safe, Liam." With that, Detective Hughes took off for the checkout stands, not turning back once.

A coil of tension slinked its way around Li's exposed throat, a residual memory of the man who tried to squeeze the life out of Li's body. Now there was the car in the rain. The bat to the skull. Someone was after him, someone with deadly intentions. How would his mother and sister react if these lunatics finished the job? Only three scant years after losing a loving husband and father, could they survive losing a son and brother? Could anyone? Could he really let himself rip another huge hole in their hearts?

Li settled it. He would not discuss, investigate, or even think about Oscar anymore. It was over and done. It was an episode of his life he wanted to bury deeper than the tombs of ancient Egyptians. He wanted to live to see his next birthday, his sister's birthday, the engagement announcement of his new friends . . .

He hoped that resolution lasted longer than those made at New Year's.

Detective Hughes loaded the coffee maker and set the cardinal-red box of croissants on the counter. Around him, the police force of Shorewood was a peaceful hive of activity. Phones blared, quickly answered. Officers flitted in and out of their cubicles and offices, bees on the honeycomb. There was a sedate buzz in the air, the surface atmosphere calm and cool, but underneath brains hummed furiously as they dissected and resolved the problems of the city.

Adam materialized next to his case partner, flipped open the box, and teased out a flaky, buttery croissant. "Ruby makes a pretty good croissant, but you haven't lived until you've tried mine, Tony." Nonetheless, he tore off a huge bite and guzzled coffee.

Detective Hughes studied Adam's eyes, which were turning an incandescent red like the box from Ruby's Bakery. "Did you get any sleep last night?"

"Couple hours."

"Kid, don't kill yourself just for a promotion. I know you really want it, and heaven knows you've earned it, but don't hurt yourself for a title. We risk our lives as it is."

"It's not that, Tony." His red-rimmed gaze dropped to the ground. "Well, not all of it." A glaze slid over his eyes, suggesting his thoughts had turned to distant memories far from the murder of Oscar Lindstrom. "It was a horrible night, wasn't it?"

"Adam?"

Adam squared his shoulders and thrust his chin forward, but it didn't quite erase the glazed gloom in his face. "We've got the information on Bauer and ... and Hate Night. It's on your desk, Tony."

"Thank you." Detective Hughes moved to his little slice of the station. He scanned the crowd of photographs milling about on his desktop. All showed his beautiful, brilliant wife and the light of his life, his two-year-old son. The detective's eyes softened.

I hope you'll understand one day why I work so much, son. I want this city to be a safe place to grow up.

The files were neatly bundled on the desk, so innocuous, so without menace. No clue as to the horror nestled within that manila folder.

A list of the one-time employees of Bauer restaurant whose dreams were incinerated by Oscar Lindstrom.

A dossier on Chef Felix Bauer, his career, and his whereabouts since Hate Night.

A collection of Oscar's restaurant reviews.

A printout of the infamous blog post that sparked the riots.

A list and a map of addresses attacked on Hate Night, forming a distinct and unwelcome pattern.

Police reports. Witness statements. Articles.

Could a murderous truth lie within these documents?

Hate Night. That was the name of it at the station. A furnace of a night fed by hate and terror. Detective Hughes would never forget the fear, the fire, the blood. No one at the department would forget the hurricane pulse of the station, the screaming phones, the sharp orders to protect the innocent citizens who were terrorized. Shorewood was on red alert. And when motives were uncovered, the police worked even harder, throats scraped raw and fingers whittled to bone, to save their city.

A group of twenty or so men had held them all hostage that night. They infected the streets, dividing into hostile, cancerous cells and targeting specific houses. These men sprayed graffiti, burned effigies on the lawns, hollered obscenities, and threw smoke bombs, balloons filled with pig blood, and even lit torches into people's homes. Houses burned. Families cowered. Sirens howled through the night. First responders raced to evacuate people from neighborhoods, stop the spreading fires, catch the lunatics.

The only small blessing was that these terrorists weren't armed. However, on Hate Night, no one knew for sure and spent those tense hours clutching their loved ones close to their hearts, waiting for the darkness to end.

The houses formed a pattern. They were homes of the chefs who worked at Bauer when the place shut down. Oscar's blog post incited lunatic men to enact a horrifying ethnic cleansing, swarming the streets like rabid beasts, desiring a holocaust. Hate Night was a hate crime of natural disaster proportions.

"I was just a beat cop that night."

Detective Hughes, reliving the nightmare through the reports, glanced up to see Adam leaning on the visitor's chair. Adam's face was old and his eyes haunted. He slumped into the seat. "It was my worst night as a cop. I still have nightmares sometimes. Felix was a family friend. We were so proud of all his hard work. He raised his chefs to be superstars. And that kitchen was spotless. I had a buddy in the health department who said he would eat off Bauer's floors. Felix and his staff took the business seriously. Everything was clean and fresh and handled with laser precision. So whatever Kathryn Lindstrom got sick from, it definitely wasn't food poisoning. I've been trying to find out what it was, but no dice so far." His eyes hardened. "It wasn't Felix. It wasn't his team. None of them deserved that torture. I was partnered with Bianca at the time. When the call came in, she recognized one of the addresses as her fiancé's brother's house. I remember getting there when those insane assholes lit the house on fire. We helped the family escape. As the mother carried her baby out the back door, one of the terrorists hiding in the bushes hit her baby with a blood balloon. The baby screamed. I don't mean cried. *Screamed.* And soaked in blood. The memory is burned on my brain forever."

There were dozens of stories like this. Hate Night challenged the strength and character of every woman and man. Many left town afterwards, unable to feel safe. Chef Felix, accused by the terrorists of being a Nazi due to his German heritage and losing his home and restaurant to fire, abandoned California. Current whereabouts listed as Massachusetts. And he never again worked as a chef of any stripe.

Detective Hughes had called his wife two dozen times that night, always assuring the safety of his own family. He hadn't known how thorough the lunatics intended to be.

The madmen were subdued, arrested, and carted to prison for a long stay. No one died on Hate Night, an enormous blessing. But the scars ran deep. You couldn't stay a rookie after that night. Detective Hughes and his colleagues all had the war-weary eyes of battle-scarred veterans.

Adam reached out a hand and stroked the edge of a framed photograph with his finger. Was he thinking of his own family waiting by the phone that night to hear whether or not he died on duty? "It was the only night where I questioned being a policeman. It was ugly. And my friends and colleagues were hurt. *Gott im Himmel,* I wondered if I would survive this job. But if someone doesn't fight for what's right, who will?" He jerked to his feet, again trying to mask the pain of the memory with the firm, professional set of his face. "I'm going to see if I can trace that package Oscar received. We need to resolve some of these mysteries."

"Sounds good. I'll look over these documents. And Adam ... you're going to be a great detective. You care about people. You care about the team. We couldn't do this without you." Detective Hughes grinned. "Don't worry, Wolf. We'll figure this out."

At the sound of his nickname, Adam smiled. "Thanks, Tony. Couldn't do this without you either." With a gleam of renewed determination in his eyes, he left the cubicle.

Detective Hughes began examining the list of former Bauer employees. His eyebrow arched. That was a familiar name. He grabbed the witness statements taken at Esther's Family Grocery. Yes, there was the name again. But it was a common name. No definitive connection, but it did open a line of inquiry. He felt he was edging closer to the heart of Liam Johnson's secret, the knowledge he was withholding.

A frown creased the space between his eyes. Who *was* Liam? Detective Hughes had faced off with many an amateur detective in his time, but this kid was beyond all of them. He knew far more than he told. He always seemed to be up-to-date with information and had access to suspects that made the back of the detective's neck prickle. And there was the look in Liam's eyes, unconscious probably, of suffering and grief. Perhaps the reason Detective Hughes cared so much about this boy was that he was someone's child, lost and lonely. He could see the potent pain that scarred the kid's face with wrinkles and lines.

But still ... Liam was a suspect. An extremely bright suspect with an ability to collect and process information. A suspect with backstory. Adam said something about Oscar Lindstrom not being the kid's first body. Could it be? Detective Hughes called Leilani, the station's internet and tech guru, and asked for a background check on one Liam Andrew Johnson.

Adam stuck his head back into the cubicle, breaking the reverie. "Hey, Tony. Staci Belmont, the Lindstroms' neighbor, just phoned in a statement. She heard from Kathryn Lindstrom about the package left on Oscar's doorstep, and said she saw the person who dropped it off." He gave Staci's description of the man.

Detective Hughes' eyes gleamed. Very familiar indeed. Particularly the description of the uniform. Yes ... Now he was certain they were reaching the heart of a secret.

Liam's secret.

Ugh. Dumpster duty. Worst part of any job, along with cleaning public restrooms. After finishing the latter (where he concluded that the toilet would be the only reasonable place for the murderer to hide the fatal scanner), Li hauled two huge, stuffed trash bags down the hallway past the restrooms, through their receiving area, and out the back doors. The alley behind the supermarket was drab. Slums in Victorian England had more charm. Rainwater from the storm stagnated in muddy pools threaded down the center of the alley. Graffiti screamed obscenities on the back walls of businesses like hieroglyphics of hate. A withered alley cat with matted orange fur made a bed for itself out of a crumpled, choc-olate-brown apron, one probably balled up and tossed aside by a disgruntled employee of Esther's Family Grocery.

Li dragged his payload to the dented dumpster. The perfume of rotted food coming from it, mixing with the odor of fresh mud, forcibly reminded him of the scent of spices and blood on the night Oscar died. Details from the scene flared in his head, big bright spotlights on each one. The bag of sugar lying in a pool of blood. The clatter of the dropped broom. The dead, angry stare. Eyes staring. Eyes like Medusa. Turning, stumbling, slipping on that patch of water . . .

Wait. *Water.* Li stopped mid-toss, the weight of the garbage bag nearly hurtling him to the muddy ground. What was water doing in the aisle that night? Oscar came into the store before the rain started. So had the night shift employees. And no one mopped the aisles yet. So why was there a puddle of water in the aisle where Oscar died?

An unwanted memory teased him. Reuben mopped the pasta aisle. Li saw him with that Wet Floor sign. But hold on . . . why would Reuben suddenly decide to mop the spice aisle? He had to do the pasta aisle because that stoner smashed a can of spaghetti with his boot. There was no need to mop the spice aisle.

Unless he wanted an excuse to get close to Oscar.

Li let out a growl as he heaved the trash bag into the dump-ster, wishing the burden on his mind was as easily disposed as that burden had been. Why couldn't his brain just—?

"Shut up, Reuben."

The whisper Li heard was sharp, like the sudden release of high-pressure air. Li ducked behind the dumpster, acting on instinct. The whisperer sounded angry. And scared out of his wits.

Li saw two figures emerge from the back doors of Esther's Family Grocery. One was Reuben, twisting and knotting the corner of his apron, his round face drawn tight over the bones of his skull. The other was taller, thinner, and older than Reuben, but there was a faint resemblance in the cut and line of his features. A rose tattoo with curling vines wound its way up the man's biceps.

Reuben's hands trembled as they squeezed the apron. Li had to lean closer to catch the weak, warbling words. "Fern, you're not listening to me!"

"Maybe I don't want to! Maybe I want to forget it!"

"Fern, this is serious!"

"It didn't have to be!" Fern rubbed the back of his neck with a huge hand, making the rose on his biceps pulsate. "It ... It was a joke!"

"No, it wasn't. It really wasn't. We were furious. Angelo always said that would get us in trouble." Reuben swallowed. "And now it has. Oh God, what are going to do?"

"Pipe down! Do you know how to whisper or not?" Fern tossed a glance over each shoulder. For a split second, Li could see the terror of a hunted animal in his eyes.

Reuben pulled Fern back. "There's no one here except Bill."

"Bill?"

"That orange cat. He's a stray I feed sometimes. Whenever I can. He won't rat us out."

"Dammit, Reuben! You're making it sound like we broke the law!"

"But Fern, Oscar's dead."

"I know, I know. You told me. This has turned into a big mess. You haven't told anyone, have you?"

Reuben's eyes dropped to his shoes. "Fern, I can't keep this up. I'm going crazy. I never hide things from Noah. He knows I'm not telling him something. And there's this new guy at work who scares me. He ... He asks things I wish he wouldn't ask. He asks all the right questions. He's suspicious too. I'm starting to crack, Fern. I'm not built for the third degree."

"Well, find a way to hold out longer, bro. It's got to blow over sometime, right?"

"Can't we just confess?"

Fern shook his head wildly. "No! Never! I don't want to risk it!"

Reuben's eyes widened and his expression softened. "You're worried about Sarah, aren't you?"

A shadow crossed Fern's face, his mouth tightening. "She's got enough on her mind with all those treatments. So we did something stupid. We've come too far now. I ... I can't get taken away from her right now. I just can't. I can't hurt her like that. She needs me." There was a glassy glint in his eyes. "Just hold out a little longer. It'll be okay. It *has* to be okay. It has to ..."

Eyes uncertain, faces strained, the two men slipped back inside the supermarket.

Li slid out from his impromptu hiding spot, staring at the doors where two frightened souls had passed through, staring at them as if he was alive and had watched two people slip through the threshold between life and death. His silver-softened baby blues fell to the sleeping orange ball nuzzled inside the soiled apron. Bill. A poor creature kept alive through Reuben's actions. How had he looked when Reuben found him? Skeletal? Starving? Cold? Lonely? Just as Li had been. Li had been a stray saved by Reuben Rodriguez.

Whatever Reuben and the mysterious "Fern" did, it was backfiring. And Li could sense the first glimmers of what that secret could be.

"We can't rat them out, can we, Bill?" Li said to the fuzzy orange ball.

The cat purred.

It was well past quitting time. The keyboards were silent. The computers were dark. The phones slept. But in the office of the editor-in-chief, a light still burned, and Frank Dixon sliced wide swathes in the floor with his nervous pacing.

What are we going to do? What am I going to do?

What could he do? Oscar was dead. Very, very, very dead. Murdered. Frank had covered dozens of murders in his career, his emotions detached from them, each one treated as a curiosity or a statistic. But this one . . . this one plunged right into the core of his soul. He could picture—sometimes even feel—his hands molded around the handle of the weapon. That thought always opened a cold vacuum in his stomach.

Because he knew the victim. Because he wanted him dead.

The more he paced, the deeper the lines around his eyes and mouth sank.

Was it too late to back out? To give up the threadbare charade? Yes. Oh yes, it was *way* too late now. Frank could wallpaper *The Gazette*'s parking garage with bills, overdraft notices, demands for raises, and resignations. Maryann was spending more and more time on the phone with her sister and had left a brochure for a marriage counselor on his side of the bed. And he could feel the large ears, long nose, and curious fingers of law enforcement creep and crawl closer and closer toward him. Like dogs sniffing in places they shouldn't, digging for bones buried in the basement.

Frank tugged at his shirt collar. It was suddenly boiling in that room.

He wondered vaguely if suicide was a resolution. But he remembered he feared the frigid, sterile vacuum on the other side of the veil as much as he feared the one in his stomach. And as his thoughts careened down spiraling roads, always crashing into dead ends, he realized that empty feeling in his stomach was growing larger and larger, a tumor of terror.

Should he wait for further instructions? Was there anything any of them could accomplish now? Would it all just fade away in time?

He felt like laughing in hysterics and sobbing in a corner at the same time.

His rage, balking at the doom and depression, spiked. He seized one of the glass paperweights and smashed it on the floor. A perfect metaphor for his life. Death. Waste. Destruction. He felt no better, just more exhausted.

What am I going to do?

Frank tore off his necktie, wishing it didn't feel so much like a noose.

"Domination? Bondage? Escapism? What kind of English class are you taking anyway?"

Li jumped, his train of thought derailed. His flinching fingers struck the keyboard haphazardly, adding an articulate "dfsarew" to the sentence "Mrs. Boynton's style of mental domination and torture included examples of free will subversion, isolation techniques, and—".

Reuben stepped back. "Whoa. Didn't mean to scare you. I was just curious. I didn't realize you were so jumpy."

Li's cheeks burned pink. "Sorry. I kind of lose myself when I write. It's like I forget where I am."

"Ah. In the zone. I get it."

Silence. Dead, awkward silence. The bubbling of the soup stock in the kitchen behind them rose to an ominous volume. Like hearing the gurgle of a bog just before you stepped in it and drowned.

Li deleted his creative spelling. "So, um, did you need the computer?"

Now Reuben blushed. "No, no, I was just ... trying to make conversation."

More silence. Noah's regimented carrot chopping, the firm patter of blade to cutting board, became the never-ending slicing of a guillotine. *Thop thop thop.* Off with their heads.

"How's your class?"

"It's okay." *This is insanity! We're both too afraid to say anything! I don't know what's worse. The silences or the struggling conversation.*

Reuben knotted his fingers together, and a bulge that must have been his tongue bowed out his cheek. Like he was tasting his words before he spoke them. "So ... erm ... What are you writing about? Looks ... very different."

Li tried to relax. This was a safe topic. He wouldn't talk about work. He wouldn't talk about Oscar. He wouldn't mention the scene he saw at the dumpster. And Reuben was trying, so Li could try too. He didn't want to lose the few friends he had. "I've got Mallowan for English 102. The theme of our class is emotional bondage, domination, escapism, and the illusions of freedom. Not especially cheery, but it does force us to think critically. Mallowan likes to use popular genre fiction along with classics in his courses." Li turned back to the computer and typed "financial control" to cap off the sentence. "We're writing an essay explaining our interpretation of this quote from Agatha Christie's *Appointment with Death*: 'He knew that no race, no country, and no individual could be described as free. But he also knew that there were different degrees of bondage.'"

Reuben let out a low whistle. "Deep stuff. What line are you taking?"

Li felt the tension knots in his shoulders start to untie themselves. Maybe this would turn out okay. Maybe they could put this Oscar fiasco behind them. "Emotional bondage, especially that caused by mental abuse. I guess you can say I was inspired from my time as a waiter on the Howard Line." He fingered the escape key. "But it's a sensitive topic. Someone in my class is writing something similar, and I think it's extremely personal. Not a happy home life."

Reuben tugged at the sleeve of his shirt, his eyes suddenly very interested in the apartment floor. "Yeah, probably. You're . . . You're very perceptive, aren't you?"

Uh-oh. Dangerous waters. Li, perceptive as he was, could sense the explosives deeply submerged, dormant but not dead. "It's not something I relish. Not anymore."

"Anymore?"

"My dad used to be really proud of it. He liked that I was curious and asked a bunch of questions. Now it just gets me in trouble. It's like I don't know how to stay out of people's business."

"I noticed." Reuben's eyes shot up, and he bit his lip. "I'm sorry. That was a bit harsh. I meant . . . well . . . you are really invested in people." A tattered sigh pushed through his lips. "Man, I suck at this. I meant . . . ugh, I don't know what I mean. I guess I see a lot of myself in you. An interest in other people. I personally can't stand it if someone is in pain or suffering. I have to find a way to help them."

Li watched Reuben's face. There didn't seem to be any spark of anger. Just sadness. "I understand. Noah ... Noah has an idea that that's why I pester you so much. You're suffering, and I want to help."

A whisper of a smile. "Noah always knows best. He's more practical than me when it comes to emotions. I take things personally. I once brought home a stray cat I found in the alley behind the store. He looked like a skeleton in fur. I couldn't bear to watch him starve. I fed him and gave him a place to sleep. I ... I grew to care about him. After two months, he ran away." Reuben hung his head. "I know he was just a cat, but it felt like betrayal. It hurt. It was like he took advantage of me. It was silly to think like that, but I took it to heart."

Li knew it was potentially explosive, but tested the waters anyway. "And I remind you of this cat?"

Reuben's cheeks reddened to that warm cinnamon shade. "You were starving and suffering when I met you. You are way too skinny, and I can see how badly you want to go home. You couldn't even stop the tears at the slightest mention of your family. How could I not help you? How could I walk by and pretend that you didn't need at least some kind of human compassion? But then you kept asking and asking and asking about Oscar." Reuben's eyes darkened. Li retreated an inch. "It started to feel like you were deliberately trying to hurt me. Maybe you were just trying to understand what I'm going through, but I want you to understand that I take things to heart really easily. What Oscar did was tantamount to murder. He hurt me with fear and panic and horror and ... and all sorts of emotions I couldn't control. I'm struggling to let it all go, so that I don't end up destroying the most important relationships in my life."

Li saw Reuben's eyes drift over to Noah in the kitchen. The look of agony and longing was almost too much to stomach. This secret *was* starting to tear them apart. And Reuben was at a loss over what to do to fix it.

Li took one more hazardous dip. "You think you're hurting Noah?"

Reuben's brown eyes swung to Li. In their gaze was a deep, dark abyss of misery and the tiniest flicker—maybe an appeal, a desperate cry for any kind of help. "The Rodriguez boys will *never* hurt the ones they love."

Noah's voice, a dash hesitant, called out from the kitchen. "Everything okay over there?"

Reuben sniffed abruptly and rubbed his eyes with his forearm. "Yeah, everything's fine, babe. Better than fine." He forced a weak, trembling, unconvincing smile.

Three swift, soft knocks. A trio of faces turned to the apartment door. None of them moved, perhaps in a united worry about finding the police on the other side. The knocking came again, swifter, sharper. Noah crossed to the door.

It wasn't the police. It was a young, pale stick figure of a man with mousy hair, an oversized sweatshirt, and thin glasses. He wrung his long fingers together. "Is ... Is there a Liam Johnson here?"

Li craned his neck to get a better look. "Jason? What's wrong? What are you doing here?"

Noah glanced at him. "You know him, Li?"

"He's in my English class. He sits next to me. Jason, what's going on?"

Jason Lindstrom stuttered forward. "Li, my dad has been murdered, and I don't know what do!"

CHAPTER 12

Unexpected Guests

Noah, ever the host, invited their unexpected guest for dinner.

The revelation that he was, in fact, Oscar Lindstrom's son sat rather less comfortably with the others. Reuben seemed to curl in on himself, withdrawing from conversations and answering only in monosyllables. His eyes were dark. Noah played defense between his boyfriend and Jason, a few stripes of strain pulling at his usually easy smile.

Li was silent, watching, thinking.

Jason lifted a spoonful of soup and let the broth drizzle back into the bowl without tasting it. "This has to be extremely awkward for all of you." His thin, high voice played out like a dirge from a reed flute. "I didn't know what else to do. I ... I remembered Li. He's been a good listener when it comes to my problems at home with Dad. I needed help. I, um, I followed him here and spent most of the time in the hallway trying to muster the courage to knock."

Li remembered Jason talking to him from the adjacent desk, always couching his stories and anecdotes in "a friend of a friend has a problem." When it was something really personal—and really painful—the relation to this person became more and more nebulous: "my stepmother's uncle's cousin's dentist's podiatrist's daughter's teacher's dog walker." Any wonder why Li started to believe the problems were Jason's? He just never knew that Oscar was Jason's father. Until now.

Jason doled out more soup, sipped, poured the rest back in the bowl. "It feels like the police are crawling all over the place. They know I left the house. They ... I think they suspect ... They won't leave me alone! I'm scared. I've been scared since before Dad died. I-I tried to talk to Li earlier. It ... It was the night Dad ... was murdered. You see ..." He twisted his fingers together, forming bizarre Gordian knots. "... I had to escape from him. I've always had to. He kept me a prisoner. He wouldn't let me go to college. I was to be his assistant, his slave. I've been his slave since I was a kid. I . . . I just had to get out!" His voice cracked.

Li employed the same tone he used before on Jason in class—soothing, even, very gently probing. Force didn't work here. Finesse was key. "So our class on Wednesdays was your ticket to freedom."

Jason nodded. "I snuck out of the house every Wednesday night and caught the bus to Shorewood Community College. I couldn't stay trapped with Dad. He was depriving me of a future. My Dad's second wife sent me to a private boarding school. It was amazing. Not necessarily the school itself, but being on my own, being away from him. I actually had friends! But then Dad got divorced and I was shipped back home. Back to prison."

"You typically snuck out of your house on Wednesdays. But your father died Sunday night. So why did you leave the house that night?" The question was mild—a nudge, not a shove.

"I needed to talk to someone. I thought about you, Li. You were always willing to listen. So I snuck out and went to your apartment, but you weren't home."

That's because Li was working one deadly evening shift. "Why did you want to see me? Was everything okay?"

"Things . . . Things at home were looking serious. Dad resigned from *The Shorewood Gazette* on Saturday. I never thought he would do something like that. He loved having an audience. He loved being in control. And when I'd sneak into his office to work on my English papers, I'd find all sorts of weird stuff. An application to the *LA Times* to be a food critic. House listings down there. Change of address forms. You see, my dad could be criminally vain and didn't think twice about leaving all sorts of incriminating stuff around. He thought no one was as observant or clever as him. That's how I learned about the dozens of mistresses he had. By him leaving receipts for flowers and jewelry or awful love letters around. So when I saw the stuff about LA, I knew Dad was planning something big. Only it hadn't happened yet. He didn't tell us about moving. In any way. It . . . It was like there was still one more step he had to do before we could know about his plans. Whatever they were."

So Oscar did resign from the newspaper. Just like the unknown Frank had said. Could it be ... ? "Did your father know anyone named Frank by any chance?"

If Jason found the inquiry odd, it didn't show. "I think just Frank Dixon, his former boss at *The Gazette*. He's the editor-in-chief of the paper." A shadow passed over his ghostly face. "Come to think of it, things at the paper were weird lately too. Dad ... Dad treated it like a conquest. I mean, he treated the whole world like it was his personal property, but I got the feeling he had some sort of coup at *The Gazette*. He'd brag about it in vague terms, like 'Frank is soon going to eat his words' and 'He should have thought twice before firing Juliana.' Then he'd make these oblique references about the mayor and his wife, like 'They won't be on their high horse for long' and 'The Hendersons should watch their words.' But he'd never come out and say anything definite. Just hints."

Sounds like he was holding something over their heads. Could this be the connection between Frank and Connie? Were they Frank Dixon and Constance Henderson? Did Oscar blackmail them? That would be a powerful motive for murder. "Who's Juliana?"

Jason's bony shoulders jerked into a shrug, one of indifference rather than ignorance. "Used to be a reporter colleague of his. Juliana Esposito. I think she worked politics. Mostly front page stuff. Dad did have dinner with her a few times after she lost her job. But he entertained a lot of his colleagues. Luanne Clemmons from lifestyle, Tom Delancey from sports, Paul Taggert and Jessie Molina from the front page, Keith Bryers from obits, Sheila Davenport from book reviews, and even Frank Dixon. We saw a lot of Frank."

Li took a few healthy slurps of his soup, keeping his face peaceful and his voice nonchalant. But he wanted this next bit of information badly. It was like Jason had started the ignition to Li's machine of a brain, now incapable of shutting down until every last fact was absorbed, itemized, and stored. "Your dad didn't have many friends, did he? He viewed these people as colleagues, right?"

Jason snorted. "If you think my father viewed anybody as an equal, then you need to get an MRI on your skull. Oh sure, he'd make an effort to play along, just to keep some of them quiet. Some of his colleagues would stop by the house or they'd go out to dinner at a fancy place. I was never allowed to be seen, of course. But nobody was fooled. He had no friends. Not that he wanted any. He'd just criticize them, find everything that was wrong with them. The only one he thought was perfect was my latest stepmom, Kathryn."

Li lifted an eyebrow at the sourness that tinged Jason's voice. Jealousy? Hatred? Before he could ask something else, Noah cut in. "Was he a perfectionist?"

Everyone at the table stared at Noah, whose face matched the tomato sauce on the second course: spaghetti and meatballs.

The calm Li had settled over the proceedings shattered. Jason snapped back to the reality of the dinner, the strangers around him. His pale, somber face flushed scarlet, and he tried to hide his sudden tears by staring into his untouched soup. "I don't want to talk about it."

"Agreed." Reuben spoke up, his face hacked from the hardest stone, his eyes mutinous. "Let's just eat and call it a night."

The next few minutes of slurping, chewing, and silence made Thanksgiving with your worst enemies look like a celebration.

Jason didn't eat. He continued to stare into the soup. It was some time before they realized he was salting it with his tears.

"Jason?" Li asked, concern rising.

Oscar's son strangled the spoon handle in his fist. "He was a monster."

"You don't have to talk about it if—"

"He was a cold, mean, heartless, abusive, lying, cruel son of a BITCH!"

Jason's shout, loud enough to set off a car alarm, made them all jump. Spoons clattered. Chairs squawked. Jason's breathing deepened, and his magnified eyes glowed with venom. An emotional time bomb just exploded, and they were all going to feel its wrath.

"He never loved me! He hated me! He thought I was stupid! He thought, because my mom died in labor, that I killed her! He blamed me! He tortured me! All my life! Perfectionist? HA! He was a LUNATIC! 'Perfection can be perfected,' he'd tell me! Over and over and over and OVER! I was going crazy! He was Satan to me! The worst human being ever created! He was a sadist! I constantly prayed that someone would kill him! But NO! All I got in return was THIS!"

Jason yanked up the huge sleeve on his two-sizes-too-big sweatshirt and slammed his arm on the dining table, making the bowls and silverware bounce and soup flood the tabletop. His burn scars stood out sharply against his colorless skin. The other three gaped at them, triple looks of worry and fear in their eyes.

Jason's screeching voice withered into wet, ugly sobs. "He used to dump lye or bleach or whatever kind of chemicals into the tub and make me take a bath in it. It burned every inch of my body. And no one would stop it. He liked to say it was a cleansing experience for me. I think he just wanted to watch me burn, watch me suffer, listen to me howl and scream. He would just LAUGH at me!" Swift as a blink, Jason launched away from the table and his stunned companions, buried his face in his hands, and bawled.

Li was the first to move. He tiptoed toward his classmate. His voice returned to the placid, placating tone he favored. "Jason? Come sit down. You're with friends now. It's all over. No one will hurt you like that ever again. I promise."

Jason's sobs dissolved into hiccups.

Li placed a light hand on Jason's upper arm, not squeezing, just supporting. "Take deep, easy breaths. There you go. You're safe here."

Reuben and Noah gawked at them, watching Li handle Jason with the competence of a well-trained nursemaid.

"Easy does it. It's okay. No one will hurt you." Li maneuvered the calming man back to his seat.

"He hurt me. My own father."

"And he won't hurt you ever again. We're here for you, Jason."

Jason hiccuped and wiped away his tears. "I-I-I'm sorry. I lost it. Dad . . . he . . . I . . ."

"It's okay. We understand. You needed this. Talk only when you want to."

Jason's breathing settled, but there were two florid spots of color high on his cheekbones. His eyes looked like a violent sunset, burning amber amid blood red. "It's been hell. For a long time. Probably ever since the crap that happened at Bauer."

Li heard a sharp intake of breath. An angry hiss. A strong reaction to that name. *Who or what is Bauer?*

Jason plowed forward. "But even in death, my father had to make things difficult. I don't know what's going on, and it terrifies me. Things are so backwards and confused." In stuttering words, Jason described the police findings in the office, especially what the neighbors knew and that silhouette of Oscar Lindstrom. "It doesn't make any sense! What did Dad do? And who killed him?"

Li looked Jason square in the face. "Do you have any ideas who did it?"

Jason paused, then shook his head. "No, I don't. I just know I didn't do it. As much as I wanted to. He made so many people angry that it could be the entire city banded together to bump him off, for all I know. Do *you* have any ideas who did it, Li?"

Li hesitated and sized up each word before he spoke. "Well . . . if I had to hazard a guess . . . I'd have to say his wife was involved somehow."

"Kathryn?" The reed flute in his throat shrieked, a pitch that was almost exclusive to dogs and bats. "Murder? No way! That's not how she would hurt someone! Ever!"

Li had to wonder how Kathryn *would* hurt someone. "It's practically a cliché. Wives murdering husbands, husbands murdering wives. As his wife, Kathryn Lindstrom has an obvious motive. I'm sure his money would go to her, particularly if he was so disparaging toward you, Jason. Maybe she didn't want to be married to an abusive man anymore. Also, there are ways of being involved other than just holding the weapon."

And Li's ears caught, just barely, the sound of someone swallowing hard. A nervous gulp?

Jason shook his head even harder than all the other times. "Never. Kathryn wouldn't kill Dad. In any way. She adored him. She babied him. She acted more like his mother than his wife. And Dad could find no fault in her. She was the perfect everything, the text-book by which the rest of us mere mortals should live by. Kathryn was his queen." His voice dropped as low as it could. "Maybe even more so than my mother." He shoved himself away from the table, fingers locking together in weird knots again. He avoided all eye contact. "I-I'm so sorry. I-I've totally ruined the evening. I should go home. Kathryn will be . . . I should just get home right now." As an afterthought: "Thanks."

Li jolted to his feet. "Jas—?"

Jason bolted from the apartment, the door banging shut behind him.

No one had any appetite after all that.

"Quite a night, huh?"

Reuben grunted, grabbed a book from the nightstand, and plopped into bed.

Noah slid in next to him. "I'm not sure if I'll be able to make that soup again for a while." He glanced at his boyfriend, searching, waiting.

Reuben said nothing. He stared at the open book, his mouth fixed in a firm line.

Noah sighed and opened his own book.

Five minutes passed.

"I was thinking of trying out this recipe for a cobbler my grand-mother sent me. Sound good?"

No response.

Three minutes passed.

"Reuben, I think we should sell the apartment and start living on the streets."

Still no response.

One minute later.

Noah frowned. "Babe, I'm sleeping with your lesbian cousin, Julia."

Reuben's eyes narrowed, showing only the thinnest slit of dark abyss.

"Reuben!"

"Why won't he let it go?"

Noah watched him, brow creased, eyes wide and wondering. It was the first time Reuben spoke all night. It was then he realized that Reuben hadn't turned the pages of his book since he got in bed.

Reuben's words were raw and rough around the edges. Like unsanded stone. "He won't stop. He won't let it go. He just can't help himself. He just keeps poking and prying, and I can't take it anymore."

"Honey?"

"Why won't he stop? He promised. He said he wouldn't. And he practically weaseled all that stuff out of that kid. What's wrong with him? Why does he do this?"

"Reuben, talk to me."

"Does he know? He can't know. He just can't. What would he do if he found out?"

Noah touched his boyfriend's hand. Reuben yelped, as if Noah's fingertips carried an electric shock. He flung his book away from him. The stone mask chipped, cracked, and crumbled away, allowing the terror and misery to come fully alive on Reuben's face. Reuben turned to Noah, eyes desperate and watering.

Noah held his hand, squeezing it. He couldn't explain it, but he felt an urgent sense of now-or-never. "Reuben, you have to tell me what's wrong. Please don't keep me out of this. I love you. I want to help you. Please."

A thick tear oozed down Reuben's cheek. "I'm scared. I'm really scared. We didn't do anything wrong. Fern and I were just angry. We weren't going to hurt him. I swear." His lip quivered, jarring another tear. "I can't stop thinking about Desireé."

In the dream, Jason was seven years old. In the dream, the monster had acid-green skin, yellow snake eyes, oily remnants of hair, a forked tongue, and a smile glinting with bear trap teeth. The Monster he called "Dad."

The bath was ready. Always ready. Jason never knew what sinister potions the monster mixed into the water, making it look as clouded as an eye with cataracts. The smooth porcelain walls of the tub became walls of unblemished ice, slippery surfaces without any handholds to escape from the corrosive geothermal spring they shielded. Jason knew if the water was white, it would be a bad night.

The monster, chuckling, said it was time for Jason's nightly session in hydrotherapy.

The acid ate into his skin. Liquid fire singed and surged over his arms and legs, chewing and burning the sensitive bits. Little Jason screamed, the squeal of slaughtered pigs. How could anyone sleep through that? Why wouldn't anyone come and save him? His squeals ripped open the night.

The monster stood there. The Monster laughed. The Monster shoved Jason's thrashing head into the liquid fire, bellowing with laughter as he watched the water eat into the boy's eyes, watched screams turn into bubbles. The bubbles shrank ... slowed ... stopped.

The world continued to sleep.

Jason, at twenty-five, didn't know he got out of bed and stood in the bathroom, gazing as the bathtub filled with water, water cleaner than any conscience on Earth. But to Jason, it would always be cloudy. Water of death.

Was he sleepwalking? Was he acting out his dream?

The tub gurgled when it finished filling. Jason, blind and deaf to the outside world, slid out of his baggy pajamas. He stuck a leg into the water, wincing at the imaginary burn. Skinny as a sea serpent, he slithered into the tub, water rising up to his chin. He hissed at the heat, picturing the vat of acid.

What was he going to do? The monster owned him. The monster controlled his every breath. Someone had slain the monster, leaving Jason to starve. What could he do? How was he going to survive? He knew next to nothing about the world beyond this icy prison.

Forgive me, Monster, for I have sinned. I must seek penance.

Jason dipped his head under the water. He opened his mouth to drown.

Li shambled into his tiny studio apartment. His eyes swung to his alarm clock. Ten p.m. Well, this day had taken a bizarre turn. Several bizarre turns, in fact. Weapons, eavesdropping, unexpected guests, huge emotional scars. Groaning, Li realized he hadn't even worked at Esther's Family Grocery for a week. With all this drama, maybe he had to rethink his career choices.

Right now, he just wanted to kick off his sneakers and crumple into bed. No dreams. No ideas. Just emptiness.

Li set his finished, printed essay on the kitchen counter and forced his thoughts from the dead to the living. What was he going to do about Jason? His soul had been scraped raw by his father's actions. He was a wounded animal. And wounded animals could be the most dangerous. What could Li do to help Jason move past this point, to start sweeping up the storm debris and rebuilding his life? But how could Li be any assistance when he himself hadn't come to terms with his dad's death three years ago? And there was the headache again, back to scatter his loosely strung thoughts.

The healing wound on the back of Li's head was a sharp reminder, however. Anxiety trickled from his brain to his quickening heartbeat. He shuffled to the closet, flung it open, and peered into his emaciated wardrobe. Nothing. No twitching shadows. No phantom men swinging baseball bats. For an extra measure, he checked behind the door. Not even a stray dust mote. Good.

Leave it alone for now. You're going to pass out. See that bed? Use it.

The hairs on the back of his neck tingled. He could feel the air pressure change in the room, a sudden density to the atmosphere. The sense of extra bodies. He felt the intruder before he heard the sandpapery voice.

He had forgotten to check under the bed, that place where monsters dwell.

"Hello, Liam. The Lady wants to invite you to tea."

Lights out.

CHAPTER 13

Tea Time

Fade from black.

A groan wormed between his lips. Why was he always getting hurt? He was far too aware of the way his blood pounded through his body. His head throbbed, reawakening the dormant wound from Monday. He should really invest in a bubble wrap suit of armor at this point.

"Lapsang souchong, dear?"

Li lifted his aching head to see Mrs. Mayor, The First Lady of Shorewood herself, Constance Henderson pouring him a cup of steaming tea.

What the—?

Li tried to stand, but a rough, unfriendly hand shoved him back into his seat. His eyes searched the room, but it was kept dark, a cellar of shadows, a black void. The only things there were Li, Constance, the table they sat at, a tea set, and a disembodied hand acting as a bodyguard. A lamp on the table provided a soft glow, but seemed to accentuate the shadows rather than cut through them.

Constance nudged the full teacup toward him. A black business suit draped around her figure and melted, along with her mostly black hair, into the darkness. The lamplight caught the bolts of silver in her hair, giving them an electric glimmer like distant lightning. A wide, smooth, faultless smile—the easy grin of a politician—glided across her face.

"Hello, Liam. I was hoping to talk to you."

Li glanced at the cup, but did not pick it up. "Mrs. Henderson?"

She laughed lightly, but there were too many shadows to reveal the truth of her eyes. "It's been so long since someone has called me that. Do you care for sugar? Milk? Cream?" She decanted tea into her own china cup. The design on it was a swirl of black roses. "I am glad you do know who I am. It saves on introductions."

"Why am I here? Why did you kidnap me?"

Constance enjoyed a slow sip of her tea.

"What's going on?"

She took extra care to reunite the cup and saucer.

"Have you been the one trying to kill me?"

"You like to strike right at the heart of a situation, don't you?" Her voice reminded him of a cello concert he heard once: deep, rich, velvety notes. "Getting straight to business, asking blunt questions, down to brass tacks. It's an unconventional way to make friends, isn't it? You hack and chop and slice your way to the roots without appreciating the curves of the branches. What happened to nuance, subtlety, finesse?" She stirred a grain of sugar into her tea. "I do so want to be your friend, Liam."

Or you'd make one hell of an enemy. Li pulled his tea toward him and sniffed it. Though how was he supposed to know what poison smelled like? "Friends?"

Her smile, already dominating her face, widened a degree. "Yes. Friends make things so much better, don't they? I do believe in making friends the old-fashioned way. Really getting to know the person." She leaned forward, the light washing over her eyes. Li saw a tiger sizing up a field mouse. "Let's play a game. A game of questions. We'll alternate asking each other something. We have to answer every single one honestly. This way we'll get to know all about each other. Sounds like fun?"

Li thought playing tag with a scorpion sounded more fun. And less dangerous. "I suppose."

"Now we have to tell the truth, and only one question at a time. We must play fair. You might win a game of chess by swiping your hand across the board and knocking off all the pieces, but you'll learn nothing from the experience. Do you understand?"

So Mrs. Mayor wanted to play a round of chess, eh? "Yes." Li was about to ask a question when Constance cut him short.

"I'm sorry, but when you came here, you asked four questions right off the bat. We'll address those questions of yours first."

Li felt the bottom of his stomach drop. Constance played a mean game.

Her dark eyes glittered, the tiger playing with its food. "We'll let you go first. Why are you here? Simply put, I wanted to talk to you. Now my question." She cleared her throat with a petite cough, a nice dramatic pause. Li wasn't fooled. "Why did you decide to move to Shorewood?"

"I lost my last job and wanted to live closer to my family."

"Very well. Your next question: Why were you kidnapped? Well, I'm afraid Morley has rather unconventional invitations to my tea parties, don't you, Morley?"

The disembodied hand gave a hard squeeze on Li's shoulder. Li gulped.

Constance sipped her tea. "My next question: How did you get the money to move here? It's rather expensive these days."

"I . . . I got a check from a friend I helped out at my last job."

The hungry gleam in her eyes told Li she already knew what happened during that final cruise. "Let's see. Your next query was 'What's going on?' I believe we're playing a game of questions. Isn't this fun?"

Li scowled. "Your next question, Mrs. Henderson?"

Constance cooled that spark of greedy satisfaction. "How did you get your job at Esther's Family Grocery?"

Li told her the story as quickly and unemotionally as possible.

"You're a lucky boy, Liam. Your fourth question, I believe, was if I'm the one trying to kill you. Now of course I can't speak for others, but I know *I* am not. Last I checked murder is still illegal. Now as to a few incidents . . ." Her politically perfect smile shone on her face, a beacon of honesty and righteousness and down-right hooey. "You were never in any danger with the car. I am an excellent driver. And I cannot account for Morley's behavior. He acts as he sees fit. And now . . . what do you know about Oscar Lindstrom's death?"

Ah, they were reaching the nucleus of this strange meeting. Li decided he had no secrets and outlined everything he knew. He watched Constance's intelligent face grow still and remote, down-loading all the information he gave her into that computer brain of hers. When he finished, he saw her smile spread in slow inches across her features again. It wasn't her glib politician's grin. It was sly.

Li knew he had to play smart. This was chess. You didn't ask what the opponent planned to do or how they figured things out. You had to know. You had to think ahead. He had to out-strategize a woman whose clout could rename Saturday to Constanceday.

Constance watched him, the tiger growing tired of its toy. She was peckish for a Li-sized snack. "Your question, Liam?"

Li unleashed his own smile, deadly as a dagger aimed at a beating heart. "What do you know about Bauer?"

This, he knew, she never expected, never calculated. The measliest flicker of unease flitted across her face. "Bauer was a fine restaurant. Germanic cuisine. Chef Felix Bauer was a genius at taking these simple, homey dishes and making Michelin stars out of them. He had to close when Oscar Lindstrom wrote a negative review after his latest wife got sick from the food. It was a huge scandal. I take it that explains your interest in it." She studied his expression, hunting for cracks. "My turn. What did you overhear on the night Oscar died?"

Li needed no more confirmation that "Connie" was Constance. "An interesting discussion between Connie and Frank about Oscar, his resignation, and how they followed him there. Maybe they wanted to reason with him. Maybe they just wanted to see what he was doing. I got the impression Oscar was holding a secret over their heads."

Constance's eyes tightened into scratches on her clear skin. "I see. And what do you think that secret is?"

"Uh-uh-uh, Mrs. Henderson. It's my turn to ask something. We have to play fair, remember?"

Her nostrils flared.

Li's eyes glinted like swords raised for a charge on an enemy camp. "My question: What can you tell me about your time as Oscar's second wife?"

It was one heck of a long shot. Like pole vaulting over Everest long. But Li had a feeling Constance knew Oscar far more intimately than she expressed.

He caught her off guard. There was an instant, swift as a shutter release, of surprise in her face. Then her features softened and warmed into a smile far friendlier than her running-for-office grin. The question must have amused her, and he hoped she would humor him.

"That's ancient history. Not many people remember me as Mrs. Lindstrom. I'd like to keep it that way." She settled further into her chair, taking deep, satisfying sips of her tea. Everything—from the line of her shoulders to the intensity of her eyes—seemed to relax. These memories must not have held any danger for her. They were far removed from murder. "Oscar was a man with ambition and drive, two things I rather enjoy. He also had early success with his first two books, *Full Plate* and *Empty Plate*, so he certainly piqued my curiosity. I like a man who's going somewhere, making a name for himself. I can't abide obscurity." Her tone became reflective. "I met him several years after his first wife died. He was angry at the world, angry and hurt. He blamed everyone for killing his beloved Nancy. But I could see he was a gifted food writer who had one ruling passion above all others: finding absolute perfection in the world of haute cuisine. I became his assistant and helped him return to the world of food writing. I like to think his highly successful third book, *Fill My Plate*, was largely my idea." She tittered. "Naturally, we got married."

Li had to phrase this carefully. Not a question. A statement. "Jason Lindstrom must have been excited to have a new mother."

Constance smirked. She must have noticed his cautious phrasing. "I wouldn't put it like that. I didn't really have the patience to be his mother. And Oscar blamed him most of all for Nancy's death. I could see that Jason needed to get away from his father, or the damage would be irreparable. I arranged for him to go to one of the finest boarding schools in the country as far from California as I could manage. I also arranged that his visits home were few and far between. Most probably thought this was callous, but Jason needed to be independent from his father. Oscar wanted to dominate his son, and the school gave Jason an opportunity to develop outside of Oscar's influence. I think it did him a world of good."

"Too bad it didn't last forever."

Constance's shoulders rose in an unconcerned shrug. "Nothing does. Oscar had rather antiquated views on women, probably stemming from some abandonment complex he suffered after Nancy died. He wanted his wives to stay at home and be 'the women behind the man.' That I can't allow. I was not his subordinate. I would never be subordinate to a man. And it became clear that Oscar had become settled in his position on *The Gazette.* Divorce was only natural, as natural as when we got married. We saw our marriage through to its conclusion. There were better prospects out there." She poured herself more tea. "Irreconcilable differences. That was the official verdict. Of course, I knew he had been cheating on me throughout our marriage. Always chasing the ideal of perfection whether it was Peking duck or partners in life. I wonder if his latest model knows about his little side projects. She's just one in a long line of women. Fidelity isn't important to a man in constant pursuit of perfection."

"But why would—?"

The political grin returned. "You've already asked your rather detailed question, Liam. Remember the rules. Let's see . . . How do you know Oscar Lindstrom?"

Li told the story about the grocery store visits. "That's basically it. He was a customer. I know his son because we're in the same English class. However, I didn't know Jason was Oscar's son until tonight." He jumped to his question without giving her time to react. "What do you know about *The Shorewood Gazette?*"

Her expression became withdrawn, shuttered—the face of access denied, of need-to-know basis. "*The Gazette* is an institution in Shorewood. Been around nearly as long as the city. A fair and just publication. Frank Dixon, the current editor, runs a tight ship. Next question: You mentioned a secret Oscar knew. What do you think that secret is?"

"I have no idea."

"You swore to tell the truth, Liam."

"I am. I have no idea what secrets he might have known. My turn. Since it's clear you and Frank Dixon were at Esther's Family Grocery that night, did either of you see or hear anything that you can recall that was suspicious or out of place?"

Constance, now a tiger at rest, stirred her tea with a spoon, but did not drink it. Her black eyes bored into Li's face. "I can't speak for anyone else. I had nothing to do with it. The only suspicious thing I noticed was a young man with a bad habit of sticking his nose into private business."

Morley's hand clapped Li hard on the shoulder, pinning him in place.

The sly smile curled her long lips. "You play a good game, Liam, but you haven't had the years of practice that I have. I suggest you learn to forget all about tonight. Move on with your life. It can be very difficult keeping a job in Shorewood. *Very* difficult." She drained the tea from her black rose cup. "I'm satisfied with his answers. Thank you, Morley."

The lights went out again.

Sunlight sliced through the window blinds.

Li moaned, the only sign he was still alive. Blindly, his hands clawed at his surroundings. Soft. Plush. Fabric. He wrestled open an eye. He was in his bed. Fully clothed. Flung face-first. He didn't sleep so much as enjoyed unconsciousness.

He flopped onto his back and watched his apartment ceiling undulate until his stomach protested. He pinched his eyelids shut, fighting the battery of blood against the knot on his skull. When he managed to conquer his seasickness, he turned to his alarm clock. Ten a.m. Wednesday morning. Twelve hours since his abrupt invitation to tea with the Queen of Shorewood. Had it only been twelve hours? Come to think of it, had it only been five days since he was hired at the supermarket? Li shoved his face into the meat of his pillow and screamed. This was just the first week. Could he survive any more?

It was at least his official day off. Maybe he could sleep until class tonight. Then sleep in class. Sleep forever. Just until this damn headache disappeared.

But as his headache mutated into a brain-eating migraine, robbing any chance at rest he had, Li heaved himself out of bed. Maybe caffeine would help, given how his whole head throbbed. He stood, and the room spun. That was when he noticed his shoes.

His brand-new sneakers, gifts from his new friends.

His currently slashed and shredded sneakers, victims of an enthusiastic blade, with a note pinned on them. One word. REMEMBER.

Li would never forget.

Why did she let him go? Why did she let him walk away with his knowledge? How did he escape with his life? He racked his brain, trying to jar the memory loose. What did she say at the end? "I'm satisfied with his answers." Satisfied with his station in town. Satisfied that he didn't know her secret. Satisfied with her ability to silence him. That mad tea party served as a test, a chance for Constance Henderson to sum up his character.

He passed. Just barely.

But that didn't mean he was out of danger yet.

Because he wanted to know that secret. It was a secret that could possibly save Reuben. There were dark motives at work here. And he felt he had opportunities Constance didn't consider. Opportunities to learn certain information.

One: She, much like Oscar, hardly cared for Jason Lindstrom and didn't realize the young man saw, heard, and understood many things without people knowing.

Two: Per their agreement, she stayed away from Frank Dixon and he from her.

Three: Whoever this mysterious Juliana Esposito was.

Li had opportunities. The question was how to best employ them.

Frantic knocking exploded on his apartment door, a noise that gnawed into Li's howling head wound. A voice, shrill, panicked, burst from the other side.

"Li? It's Noah! I need your help! It's an emergency! Please open up!"

Li stumbled to the door. His hand had no more touched the doorknob when Noah rushed into Li's apartment. Noah's eyes were huge and red, his skin ashen, and his golden hair mussed. His panic filled the air with a volatile electricity.

"Li! The police arrested Reuben!"

CHAPTER 14

Day of Wrath

"Oh, it's you again."

Detective Hughes frowned as he saw Li march into his cubicle at the police station. The expression on Li's face—grim, firmly set eyes flashing—was more suited for a man astride a horse tearing into a bloody battle.

"Yes, it's me again. I'd like to know why you arrested Reuben Rodriguez."

"First things first, we did not arrest him. He and his brother, Fernando Rodriguez, are being held as material witnesses pending further questioning. We've learned that they were responsible for leaving the threatening package on Oscar's doorstep. They've confessed to it." He glared at the young man. "Second, you do not have the authority to demand information from me. In fact, I have a feeling this has been the secret you were holding back, and I have half a mind to toss you in a cell with them."

Li thrust his chin forward, his eyes defiant. "Fine. I confess. I thought it was possible that Reuben could have killed Oscar Lindstrom. He loathed Oscar, but he wouldn't tell me why. It's been ripping me in half all this time. I had no proof. All I knew is that Reuben was hiding something from me. And if this is what he was hiding, any other accusation falls flat."

"That may be your biased belief, but I don't work like that. Now unless you want to make a statement, find someone else to harass."

Li yanked out the visitor's chair and plopped in it. "Yeah, I'll make a statement. No more secrets. I'll tell you everything I know and think. Better get out your notebook, Detective. We'll be here awhile."

Detective Hughes scowled. His glare transmitted a desire to lock Li in jail until the Rapture. He pulled out a notebook and slid into his seat. "I'm not fond of this attitude, Liam."

"I'm not fond of losing the few friends I have."

"Very well." Detective Hughes poised a pen over the blank page, hostile eyes drilling into the angry eyes of his witness. "You have my attention. Make it count."

And Li did. In spades. Starting from his suspicions on Sunday to waking up after the kidnapping tea party this morning, Li outlined everything he could. He talked about his meetings with Kathryn and Jason, what he learned about Reuben, the game of verbal chess with Constance. Everything. As he listened, Detective Hughes seemed to shift between three settings: the impervious police mask, quiet contemplation, and downright fury.

"After I woke up with this headache that is still bothering me, I found my new shoes slashed with a note on them. It was one word: REMEMBER. I think it was a final threat from this guy Morley, the guy who broke into my apartment." Li lifted a foot to display the damaged sneaker. Bits of his sock peeped through the fraying gashes. He pulled the note out his jeans pocket and pushed it toward the detective. "Then Reuben's boyfriend, Noah, stopped at my place in a panic, because the police hauled Reuben in for questioning. I came straight here. And that's *everything*."

Detective Hughes shut the now full-to-bursting notebook. "Thorough."

Li snorted like a pissed-off bull. "Thorough? Is that all?"

"I'll have to check on every claim you made. It's a lot to shovel through." His eyes became needle-thin slits. "I don't know what to make of you, Liam. Are you a good guy or a bad guy? Are you telling me the truth at last? Or are you spinning a wild fairy tale to try and get your friend off the hook? You are the mystery that's driving me the craziest."

"Detective ... I'm sorry for withholding information. I didn't know what to believe about Reuben. But when Noah told me that Reuben had been 'arrested,' I realized how stupid I was. I went off my fears, my insecurities, my own personal issues. I withheld information because I couldn't resolve the issues in my head. I'm over it now. You need to catch Oscar's killer, whoever it is. I'll help however I can."

Detective Hughes took to twirling his pen between his fingers, but his eyes were cold. "A pretty speech. But who are you, Liam Johnson?" He pulled a file folder out of his desk and dropped it in front of his guest. "What have you been up to?"

Li didn't need to be psychic to predict what lay within that folder. A background check.

"It says here that you were peripherally involved in at least three deaths at your last job, which you left under a thundercloud, if I'm not mistaken. Now you come to my city and, in less than a week at your new job, a citizen is murdered. Exactly what am I supposed to make of this, Liam? What kind of things are you involved in?"

Li gritted his teeth. "I have rotten luck. None of this is my fault."

"Rotten luck doesn't explain half of it. It seems wherever you go, death follows. You are lucky in the sense there is no evidence to tie you directly to any of these deaths."

Li's scowl tore across his face. Then the glower relaxed, and his thoughts turned away from the police station and the nebulous accusations. Three deaths then. One death now.

Detective Hughes scrutinized that faraway expression. "I know that look. You've thought of something."

"Detective, don't you find it odd that there's been only one murder?"

A hint of horror tinged the detective's tone. "Exactly how many do you want, kid?"

"I just realized that Oscar was the only one killed. No one else. There have been a lot witnesses, and I've basically stuck my finger into everyone's business, but no one else has been murdered. Surely someone must have seen something and could be a danger to the killer. But that hasn't surfaced. So either the murderer doesn't know about all of this, or he felt he had accomplished all he needed to do when he killed Oscar. Like Oscar's death was the end of the problem, not the start of new ones."

"I think you've theorized enough for one day." Detective Hughes stood, a silent dismissal. "I don't have evidence to hold you other than your suspicious habit of being everywhere I don't want you to be. And I am not a man who 'hauls people in' unless I have solid evidence. If there's nothing else—"

"There is." Li launched to his feet, the same laser determination in his eyes. He had a scrappiness today, a terrier ready to dig up a dinosaur bone. "I'd like to see Reuben, please."

Shock practically jettisoned Detective Hughes's eyebrows off his forehead. "You must be out of your mind."

"Detective, I'm going to talk to him. You said yourself that you're just holding him as a witness. Unless you're fully prepared to charge him with murder, you're going to have to release him eventually. Wouldn't you rather hear what I'm going to say to him rather than let me do it in private? You are totally welcome to listen in. Heck, stand in the room with me if you're so worried." Li didn't flinch before the detective's stony gaze this time. "I have nothing to hide anymore. And I have nothing to lose."

Detective Hughes grumbled under his breath, but Li was able to snatch the words "completely insane" and "disregard for authority."

"Fine," he barked. "Ten minutes. No more. An officer will be outside the room, and I'll be listening. If I see you even *thinking* about doing something funny, you're out of there." He walked to the entrance of his cubicle. "Officer Flores? Could you escort this young man to interrogation room two? Ten minutes only. And whatever you do"— he skewered Li with his basilisk glare— "don't let him out of your sight for a millisecond."

The interrogation room reminded Li of Leo's shabby office at the grocery store. Everything in a thousand tints and shades of gray. The long mirror against one wall seemed to double the size of the cold chamber, but Li could feel the detective's eyes incinerate him through the glass. Plunked at the metal table were two people who had all the energy and spirit sucked out of them.

Reuben's eyes were as red as his boyfriend's. His face sagged like a deflated balloon; the fight sapped out of his whole body. His brother, the mysterious Fernando Rodriguez, was twitchy, wringing his hands and fidgeting in the rigid metal chair. His face, much like Reuben's, reflected his Latino heritage, and closer inspection revealed the vines on his rose tattoo were actually letters that spelled the name Sarah.

They both looked up when Li walked in, Fernando confused, Reuben mortified.

The introductions were awkward, stilted. Neither brother was in the mood for conversation.

Reuben made a tentative step forward, asking a question that Li believed plagued him ever since he had been taken to the station. "How ... H-how's Noah?"

Li paused. "He's ... upset." Hysterical was more like it. Li had to get Noah to stop hyperventilating in his apartment. But he thought Reuben had suffered enough.

Reuben plunged his face in his hands, muffling his words. "I screwed up. I just ruined the best thing that's ever happened to me. Oh God, Noah! I'm so sorry!"

Fernando placed a hand on his brother's shoulder. His face strained. "Take it easy, little bro. I shouldn't have asked you to do this. It was my problem, not yours. I put you up to it."

"But I hated him too. I hated him so much. I wanted to hurt him. And now I might never see Noah again!"

Li's voice, calm, rational, sliced through their grief. "Reuben ... we'll figure this out. The police just want to get the facts straight. If you come clean, put everything on the table, it might turn out better than you think. You're both in a lot of pain. Let me help you." He closed his hand on Reuben's arm, gave it a supportive squeeze. "I will not let them take you away from Noah. I promise."

Reuben's bloodshot eye peeked out between his fingers through a glaze of tears.

Li kept his tone even and cool. "Tell me what happened, please. How did you feel?"

Reuben unearthed his face, sniffed, and smeared away his tears with his forearm. His lip quivered. "Fern was a chef at Bauer when Oscar came and tore the place apart. Fern ... Fern always wanted to be a chef. He loved it. He worked really hard and graduated top of his class at culinary school. And working at Bauer was a dream come true for him."

Fernando's voice was heavy, and his dark brown eyes were shiny with the memory. "Chef Felix was the best man I ever worked for. He believed in us. He gave us a chance. He hired women and minorities and let anyone with a passion for food learn in his kitchen. He was the first one to look at me and say 'chef' instead of 'dishwasher' because of my Mexican heritage. Do you know how important that was to me? I finally got to do the job I loved. And I was able to plan a life for my girlfriend and me. Especially once we learned about the breast cancer." A spasm of pain broke his composure.

Reuben took up the tale. "Then Oscar came. His wife got sick, but no one knew how."

"It wasn't us!" Fernando's voice cracked, and his eyes blazed like lit coals. "Felix was strict on cleanliness. I personally handled their meal, and I can tell you that nothing was wrong. Our service staff checked for food allergies like they were supposed to. Our suppliers were dumbfounded. No one had any clue! Not even Oscar! He turned it into a witch hunt!"

"The review came out, which wasn't great. But his blog post was disgusting. You met Oscar, Li. You knew he was a racist. Well, he basically dumped a truckload of manure on Bauer and aimed a nuclear warhead at it. It was vile. Nothing but hate speech. And Shorewood is one of the most ethnically diverse cities in the state. Just look around the police station! People of all types! I don't know how Oscar thought he could get away with it."

"But a bunch of these white supremacists got together and decided to riot and attack us for 'trying to kill them.' They went after Bauer's staff with their torches."

Reuben's eyes darkened to that familiar color of molten tar. "It was a horrible night. It was family game night, and all of us were there. My four brothers and me. Noah was, thankfully, at work. My parents were there. My nephews and nieces. My sisters-in-law. My *abuela*. Big, happy family. Then those lunatics attacked. It was like the end of the world. They threw bricks through our windows, burned Mexican flags on our lawn, screamed at us to leave the country, set off things that sounded like gunfire. We huddled in the corner, too frightened to move. I thought they were going to slaughter us. We heard sirens and screaming and suddenly one of the crazies threw a flaming torch and smoke bombs in the house. The house was on fire! My ... My oldest brother, Angelo, ran to the kitchen to get water to put it out. His son was just six years old and didn't understand why people were attacking us. He tore away from his mom to reach his dad, screaming for Daddy because he thought he'd lose him. Those monsters threw a balloon filled with pig's blood at him. It hit him right in the face." Reuben's face crumpled, and tears welled against his eyelids. "Can you imagine what it sounds like to hear your little nephew wail as if his soul got ripped out? We didn't know what happened at first. We thought they shot him. All we saw was Devin standing there drenched in blood and howling for the daddy he thought was going to die." Reuben shuddered. "I'll never forget it. That wail. That absolute certainty that you were going to die. That blood all over Devin's face. I was near my youngest brother, Miguel, during the whole thing. He was home from college and I remember him muttering in Latin, which was a class he took at the time. It sounded like 'Desireé.' He said it so deeply, and his voice shook. I don't know why, but that's how I remember that night. As Desireé."

Li, numb with horror, said under his breath, "*Dies irae.* The day of wrath."

Fernando's jaw hardened, his eyes dark and flashing. "Oscar was, if not responsible for the attacks, at least the catalyst to them. He *approved* of them. His blog practically congratulated those terrorists. I loathed him from then on. He used to be something of a hero in the food community. His books inspired so many chefs and foodies. But that ... That was murder. Even though no one died, Oscar destroyed everything we built and devastated innocent families. I hated him with all my heart."

Li saw the same hardening of Reuben's jaw. The two brothers got along very well because of their similar temperaments. Both were powerfully devoted to the ones they loved and had swift, fiery tempers. "So why the beef heart?"

Now shame and embarrassment washed away the fury. Fernando cleared his throat. "We ... *I* wasn't thinking all that clearly. I saw a recent review he gave and I could smell the ethnic slights in it, just like he did with Bauer. He was going to do it again. What if there were more riots? What if someone got killed? I ... I couldn't take it anymore. I just lost it. I wanted to make him afraid, afraid like we had been. It was stupid, but I couldn't stop myself. I got a beef heart from one of my suppliers." A cinnamon flush spead over his cheeks. "I ... I run a taco stand on Clark Street, and I said I was using it for beef heart tacos. Actually, that doesn't sound too bad ..."

Li nudged him back on track. "The beef heart symbolized your heart, right? And the hearts of your friends and family and any other chef victimized by Oscar Lindstrom?"

Fernando's nod was slow, reluctant. "Yeah ... I guess. I chopped it up and planned to drop it off on his doorstep. At the last second, I ... I saw his first book still in my kitchen, the book I admired so much. I tore out a few pages before writing a stupid note on one and wrapping it with the heart. It said FIRST WARNING. It was melodramatic, but I wanted to scare him. And ... And I wasn't really rational at the time. My temper is ugly sometimes."

"That's where I came in," Reuben said. "Fern told me about his plan, and I agreed with him. Oscar had a hand in that nightmare. I wanted to get back at him. All I did was drop the package off on my way to work. He lived on Pricey Pritchard, pretty damn close to the store. 218 Pritchard Avenue. I was there and gone in no time."

Li's tone was pensive. "And the very next day after your threat, someone kills Oscar."

The brothers shouted in unison. "We didn't do it!"

Reuben became frantic, spitting out words faster than he could think about them. "We didn't want to kill him! Well, I mean maybe, but we didn't! We were angry! But we wouldn't actually hurt anyone! There's been enough pain! We just wanted to scare him, to make him think twice before he destroyed more people! We didn't know what else to do!"

"Reuben, breathe." Reuben gulped air, color returning to his cheeks. Li continued to share his ideas. "So I'm going to see if I understand what happened next. You were both frightened when you learned Oscar had been murdered. You had threatened him the previous day. Despite your intentions, it was still a threat. You resolved to keep quiet about it, hoping it would go away. I made things worse, didn't I, Reuben? I knew you were hiding something. My constant questions and suspicions frayed your nerves. You were miserable. Above all, you've both been afraid of hurting the ones you love most in the entire universe."

Misery scored the faces of the Rodriguez boys.

Fernando's voice softened, wet with subdued tears. "Sarah is my world. She . . . She's going through chemotherapy right now. I need to be there for her. I love her so much."

A similar emotion colored Reuben's expression. His eyes were damp and distant. No doubt his thoughts were on Noah.

Li sensed his ten minutes were drying up. "Listen, I don't have much time left to talk, so I need to make this quick. Fernando, do you recall the dish you made for Kathryn Lindstrom that night?"

Fern's face stiffened. "I'll never forget it. It was for a table of three. Her dish was a perfectly roasted beef tenderloin with a white pepper sauce and homemade spaetzle using Chef Felix's grandmother's recipe. There was nothing wrong with it."

I believe you. "Reuben, did you see or hear anything while you were in the pasta aisle that night?"

"I've thought about it over and over, and I can't think of anything. Nothing seemed off! I think Oscar might have been dead before I even got to the pasta aisle."

Officer Bianca Flores opened the door. Li stood, his eyes intent on their terrified faces.

"Don't give up. I will make sure you both are back home in no time. I swear on my father's grave."

Pricey Pritchard. It was Li's first glimpse into how the fancier half of Shorewood lived. Homes of good, expensive quality lined the street, not mansions per se, but homes with enough square footage to price themselves far out of reach of Li's minimum wage scraps. Every lawn was trimmed, every wall razor-straight, every window polished.

Li found 218 Pritchard quickly, aided by the sight of Kathryn Lindstrom tending to the pools of white mums circling the trees in front of the gray-and-white house. Her rich brown curls were tamed into a braid and, despite the activity, she looked fresh and clean as if dirt couldn't bear the idea of sullying her. She glanced up at Li's approach. Her violet eyes glimmered, and she mopped up a nonexistent sheen of sweat from her brow.

"Oh hello. You're that boy from the grocery store, right?"

"Yes, I am. Hello, Kathryn."

Kathryn brushed off some imaginary dirt and stood, trowel in her gloved hand. "I was just tidying up the flower beds. Would you like to come inside for some lemonade? I made cookies yesterday."

Li wondered about her generous nature. Her spoonfuls of sugar were more like dump trucks. Was that how she hurt people? Not by a lack of sweetness, but an inconsideration toward uglier emotions, toward suffering, toward pain.

"Is everything okay?"

She reminded him, very sharply, of his own mother. A dagger twisted in his heart, and he forced his body to swallow the memory. "That'd be really nice, Kathryn. My name's Li, by the way. Li Johnson. I'm actually a friend of Jason's. Is he home?"

A little cloud hovered over her face. "Jason? Yes, he is. He . . . He didn't tell me he had friends. We would have had you over sooner. Well, come on inside."

She led the way into the Lindstrom palace. Li took note of the crystal sheen, the designer furnishings, the surgically fine execution of the decor. A showroom house. Style over sensitivity. As he sipped his lemonade, he heard Kathryn call up the stairs. "Jason! One of your friends has come to visit!" He noticed the slight lilt on the word "friends." A foreign word to associate with Oscar's son.

Li felt a stab of sympathy for Jason, the boy who was a prisoner all his life.

Jason, his amber eyes bewildered, crept into the kitchen, shoulders hunched as if waiting for the blow of a sinister prank. His eyes quadrupled in size when he saw his visitor. "Li? What are you doing here?"

"It's my day off. Thought you could use some company."

Jason scanned Li. "Really?"

"Yes, of course. You want some cookies? Your stepmom made them."

Jason shoved the plate aside. "Not really hungry."

"Then let's go for a walk. It's a nice day outside. You can show me around the neighborhood."

"I . . . I don't . . . I . . . well . . ."

"Come on, it'll be fun." He took a hold of Jason's arm and steered him toward the door. He steered him because Jason seemed incapable of moving his feet on his own. Only when they got to the sidewalk did Jason control his footsteps again. His eyes kept darting back to the loveless gray house.

Li's voice was gentle. "Jason, you're not a prisoner. You're free. You can do whatever you want. And I promise I'm not pulling a joke on you."

A hot, red blush flooded Jason's pale face. "I'm sorry. I'm not used to this. I keep waiting for the punchline." He kicked at the dust on the concrete. "I tried to kill myself last night."

"What? Jason, what happened?"

Jason shuffled down the street with Li in tow. "I . . . I wasn't really aware of what I was doing. I had a nightmare where Dad made me take another of his evil baths. This time, he shoved my head under the water. I didn't realize I was sleepwalking and had actually made a bath. I got in and tried to drown myself." His shoulders hiked to his ears. "Kathryn heard the water running and got there in time to pull me out. I swear she must have permanent blinders glued on her face or something. She thought I fell asleep while having a bath. But I . . . I realized what truly happened."

"Jason . . . do you need to talk to someone?"

"I-I don't know. I . . . I feel so lost. Dad controlled everything I did. When I ate, when I slept, when I breathed. How am I going to survive? What am I going to do?" His expression was pleading, pathetic, pained.

Li could sense he wanted someone—anyone—to tell him what to do. To manage his life. Jason grew up without freedom, and freedom was something he both craved and feared.

"What do you want to do, Jason?"

Fear, surprise, confusion all collided on that wan face. "W-what?"

"What do you want to do? It's not my place to say. It's no one's."

"Y-you don't understand! I don't know!"

"It's still not my business to *tell* you what you should do. That's just as damaging as your father keeping you prisoner. This might be the scariest moment of your life, the moment where *you* have to make the choices and take the steps. Is it any scarier than sneaking out to take a class? It's *your* choice." Li clapped both hands on Jason's shoulders and looked squarely into those fearful amber eyes poorly concealed behind hair-thin glasses. "What do *you* want to do?"

Jason nearly swallowed his bottom lip. "I . . . I do like to write. I-is that good?"

"It's not for me to say."

Jason's expression started to crumble.

Li stood firm. "Jason, I am not in charge of you. No one is. You are free to go out and explore and make mistakes and find triumph and take that adventure you've always wanted. If you want to write, write! If you want to open a store, go for it! If you want to travel the world, nothing is stopping you! It's *your* life now. Whatever you decide, I hope you are following your heart and that you are happy. That's the most important thing. Your happiness is now in your hands."

Jason stared at him, speechless. Then a small, fragile smile tweaked his lips.

"Thank you, Li. For everything."

They walked on in silence for a bit. With each step, Jason grew a little more sure of it, and the small smile strengthened. He didn't look as drained and colorless as he once did.

Jason broke the silence after they crossed the street and started walking down the opposite side. "Don't take this the wrong way, Li, but I have a feeling you have more you want to ask me about than just my welfare."

"I'm that transparent, am I?"

"A little bit. But I do appreciate you being here. At least someone cares. I thought Kathryn's eyes were going to shoot out of her head when she said I had a friend over for a visit." He sighed, but it wasn't a melancholy sound. More like the release of pent-up tension. "So what's on your mind? Do they have any more information about Dad's murder?"

Li went into the story Reuben told him. "And now he and his brother are at the station as material witnesses. But I don't think they killed your father. Just the threat alone nearly sent them to the madhouse. I can't imagine what keeping the secret of a murder would do to them."

Jason crammed his fists in his pockets, and his eyes were somber. "Aw damn . . . I told my dad a thousand times not to publish that stuff about Bauer. It was wrong. Most of it was outright lies. I wasn't there when it happened, but I gathered that it was an accident, a fluke. No one, least of all Kathryn, saw it coming. He was just jealous that the place was popular without his having a hand in any of it. But he would never listen to me." His reedy voice dropped as low as it could. "I'm so so so sorry that happened to their family. To all those families. No one deserves that. No one."

"I don't believe Reuben and Fernando are murderers. I think they made a mistake because they were angry, but I don't think they hurt anyone." Urgency stole into Li's voice. "That's why I have to figure this out. I have to know the truth. The longer they sit there uncertain, the longer they wonder 'What if?,' the longer they brood over their mistakes—it can do disastrous damage to their relationships. The uncertainty and fear and regret could kill them.

I can't let that happen. Like Reuben said, there's been enough pain. So I need your help, Jason. We need to know the truth."

"Whatever you need, I'm here to help."

The serpent that had coiled around Li's torso, a band of anxiety squeezing his lungs, eased a bit. "Thank you so much. First of all, do you know of anyone who would have access to your father's office?"

"Mostly just Kathryn and me. Sometimes he'd have colleagues over, but he had the only key."

"Did your father ever write in a special ... code?"

"Code?" Jason looked at Li like he had announced his candidacy for emperor of all eggplants. "What kind of code?"

"Mainly abbreviations." Li told him about the list of groceries secreted in Oscar's pocket, giving him a few of the entries he could remember.

Jason's eyebrows scrunched together. "Hmmm ... He sometimes abbreviated his entries when he took notes. I think some of those can be worked out. *T-n F-l-t* could be tuna filets. *W-r-c-t-s-r* could be Worcestershire sauce. *S-A-C* could be sliced American cheese. But I'm no expert. What else?"

"When Oscar reviewed Bauer, did he receive any media backlash?"

"Nope. Freedom of press and all that. *The Gazette* is really gun-shy. They like to water down bad news."

Not a great attribute for a newspaper. "You mentioned your father's resignation. Did he give any impression on how his boss took it?"

"From what I gathered, Frank was livid. Dad never played fair. He rubbed it in Frank's face. Made Frank want to kill him." His eyes widened, and he cleared his throat.

Li ignored the awkwardness. "And this business with Juliana Esposito? What happened with her?"

"I don't know much about it. Just that Dad suspected something was off. And that she was fired from *The Gazette*. I think he hinted at some article she wrote too."

"When you left the house Sunday night, did you notice anything suspicious? Did you maybe see someone walking home from the grocery store? Any trace of your dad?"

Jason shook his head. "Sorry. I saw nothing. It was a dark, quiet night."

"What about the neighbors who saw that silhouette of Oscar? Where do they live?"

"We're standing in front of it."

One across and two down from the Lindstrom abode, the house was a two-story picture in warm earth browns and forest greens, the colors equally applied to the wilderness or a pool table. The lawn was as flat as a football field, totally bare of flower beds or any other attempt at gardening. A large uncurtained window faced the street.

Jason gestured at it. "If you're hoping to talk to Staci Belmont, think again. Tom and Staci broke up. Then again, this was never her house. It's Tom Delancey's. Tom and my dad had one thing in common: They weren't 'one-woman' men. But while my dad cheated on his wives, Tom never married. He's the perpetual bachelor. We're talking singing-bass, fishing-pole-art, novelty-beer-sign kind of bachelor. Many of his girlfriends come from the fishing and hiking lodges he frequents. Outdoorsy types."

Li turned to face Oscar's house. He could see Kathryn working in her flower beds and had a good view of a second-story window. "I take it that's the office window?"

"Yes, it is."

Very thorough job, Oscar. Placing a silhouette in that window was the perfect vantage point to get at least one witness to "Oscar" never leaving his house. He must have planned it all with extreme clinical care, the kind a bomb technician would employ. He felt the puzzle pieces starting to fit together, forming a design from the tangle and mess.

Li started walking again, the gears and sprockets spinning in his skull. "Jason, you said you felt your dad had something big planned, right?"

Jason followed. "Yeah, I did."

"Do you have any idea what that something could have been?"

"No, I don't."

But Li was going to find out. An upcoming destination on his truth tour was a vital and hopefully illuminating job interview.

Li wanted to make a stop before his interview. A very important stop.

He stood outside the apartment door of Juliana Esposito. He knocked twice.

A redhead with a quick glare and a strong chin opened the door with a brusque jerk. She sized up her visitor in one sweep of her ice-blue eyes. "I'm not buying anything." She moved to slam the door.

"I'm not selling. My name is Li Johnson. I wanted to ask you about your time at *The Shorewood Gazette*."

The door stopped. Her cold eyes roved over his face, a general inspecting the enemy fortress for a weakness. "Reporter?"

"Justice seeker."

She snorted. "What are you? A superhero? This isn't playtime, kid."

"You are Juliana Esposito, right? Former political reporter for *The Gazette*?"

She exaggerated the arch of one swooping eyebrow. "I haven't decided whether you deserve to know."

"I'm here to ask about the article you wrote about Marshall Henderson, the mayor."

"Is this a threat?"

"This is justice." Li's blue-gray eyes gleamed like the shine of a new sword. "You were fired because of what you wrote, weren't you? Because you knew something about the Hendersons they didn't want revealed. And Oscar Lindstrom found out. This secret, whatever it is, might have killed him. You heard about the murder, right? Well, whatever this secret is has also come after me. I've been attacked and kidnapped by the agents of Constance Henderson herself. And now I want to know why."

Juliana's eyes narrowed. "So what you're saying is that I must know something about our so-called loving and open-minded mayor and that this something might have killed one of my former colleagues?"

"Exactly."

"And how would this be justice, Mr. Superhero?"

"Because if there was a major cover-up, you can get the story out there. You have the chance to expose all their corruption." He gave her a confident, knowing grin. "You could have any reporter job you wanted."

Li could see Juliana weighing her options by the intensity and faraway glaze of her icy stare. Like she was seeing him and seeing right through him. He crossed his fingers behind his back.

A savvy smile spread across her lips. "I suppose I can spare a few minutes. Work is slow. And I'm intrigued by this murder and kidnapping story. Come in. But no funny business. You haven't met Attila, my Great Dane, yet."

Li stepped into her apartment, positive he was going to have a clear, concise chat that answered a lot of lingering questions. Then he'd be off for his interview.

At *The Shorewood Gazette.*

CHAPTER 15

When Words Hurt

"So you can see, Liam, *The Gazette* offices are full of high-profile professionals with a combined experience of 120 years in the news business."

Li glanced around the active office, the reporters hunched like goblins over their treasured articles, the reception desk abuzz with cantankerous phones whose calls were quickly shuttled to the appropriate desks. Not a single face turned to them; *The Gazette* was absorbed in the activity of Thursday's paper.

Li shifted his scrutiny to Frank Dixon, who had gestured with a wide arc of his arm over the office space. Like an acne-scarred Ozymandias. "Look on my works, ye Mighty, and despair!" But Li recalled the next part of that poem. "Nothing beside remain." The secret Li learned from Juliana could devastate Dixon's petty empire, reduce it to dust and ashes.

Frank nudged Li with a hand on his back. "Let's continue the interview in my office." His toothy smile stretched across his pock-marked skin, but a web of stress lines ringed his eyes.

Li inspected Frank's office. Walnut paneling clad three of the four walls, the fourth occupied by windows looking out on the cityscape. The only artwork was framed front pages of past issues of *The Gazette*, highlighting its top stories in its eighty-year existence. Frank Dixon's personality had been confined to his desk, a huge mahogany monster decorated with little paperweights and family pictures. The editor-in-chief's office, no matter who held the position, had been designed to be stern, stolid, and stark, a fortress of respectability and truth.

Truth. The hallmark of journalism.

But did that tradition of truth-telling reflect on *The Gazette's* current editor?

As Li settled into the visitor's chair, he recalled the moment of his arrival: the split-second terror in Frank's face, the way he talked too loud, the insistence that he'd personally give Li a tour of the offices. Frank was anxious to accommodate him. Probably because when Li booked this appointment with *The Gazette*'s editor, he said, "Constance Henderson suggested I take a look around your offices."

If there was one person Frank wanted to please, it was Constance.

Whoever Frank believed Li to actually be, it seemed Frank wasn't privy to Mrs. Mayor's espionage and had zero background on his enigmatic applicant. "So Liam, do you have any questions?"

"Yes. What sort of experience does your staff have?"

Frank propelled into a celebration of the staff's credentials. "From all over the world of publishing and broadcasting. Jessie Molina runs her own radio program here in the city. Luanne Clemmons worked as a contributor and later editor for *Shire Magazine*. Tom Delancey is a nationally syndicated sports columnist who had quite a successful run at *The San Francisco Chronicle* before coming down here. Sheila Davenport had stints at both Simon and Schuster and *Publishers Weekly*. And our previous restaurant critic had three global best sellers in the food world. Years of diverse experience." His smile strained at the corners.

"Sterling careers. It must be a coup to have them all here working for the local paper."

"Well, we all come to Shorewood for different reasons. Some wanted to change the focus of their careers. Others had spouses who acquired jobs in the area. Still others wanted to move closer to their families." Frank's fingers had trouble staying still. They flitted about his desk, straightening this, moving that. Li's eyes fell on a brass paperweight on the desktop. A football paperweight that had been dented somehow.

Sign of a violent temper?

Frank cleared his throat. Loudly. "Did you have a specific position you were interested in filling?"

Li applied for the only vacancy. "I was curious about the post of restaurant critic."

Frank's right eye winced. "Ah. Yes. Well, we do ask our applicants to submit a five hundred-word sample of their writing—"

"Which I have right here." Li handed Frank a single sheet of paper. He thought it would come to this and needed an opening gambit. And he thought of a doozy.

Frank examined the sample. His face emptied of all color, his old acne scars making his cheeks look like twin golf balls. His eyes swelled, and the hand holding the sample started to tremble. His jaw slackened.

The sample was only four words.

I know your secret.

An old device, but Li believed it would work. He remembered how frightened and submissive Frank's voice had been on the night Oscar died. And when Li saw the rampant anxiety scuttling through Frank's body, he was even more certain of its success. He wanted to get a reaction. He wanted to spur the truth.

He got it. "W-what is this? Who are you?"

"Constance Henderson sent me."

"But . . . But why? We weren't supposed to be communicating!"

"She felt she was uncertain about your end of the bargain."

Frank's jittery hands knocked over a picture of his wife. "I did everything she told me! I fired Juliana! I changed the article! I published what she wanted!"

"You were there at the grocery store when Oscar was killed. Things change when it comes to murder."

"I didn't do it! I just followed him to find out what he was up to, I swear! He was scheming again. I could smell it. His resignation scared the hell out of me. I wondered if he wanted to devastate *The Gazette* completely. I was shocked when I found out Connie had followed him there too."

"Did you tell the police what you knew?"

"I told them what I was supposed to tell them. Connie handled that. Connie handled everything. Don't you know that?"

"She's not sure she's satisfied. What exactly did you see?"

Frank flinched. His eyes darted around the room as if calculating whether he could take the risk to rush for the exit. "I . . . I saw nothing. I . . . I spent all my time in seafood. Connie knows that! I never left!"

"I find that hard to believe." Li steepled his fingers, hoping his portrayal of an agent of Constance Henderson was convincing. "Mrs. Mayor was there to survey the surroundings, to ascertain why the *grocery store* was important to Oscar." Li didn't know this for certain, but it had a nice ring to it. In any case, it was tightening a noose around the fidgeting Frank Dixon. "*You* went there specifically to find Oscar, to follow him, to learn what *he* was doing. Did you?"

Frank bumped the desktop with his agitated hands, making more things fall. His face was the exact shade of newsprint.

Li's memories roared into life. Frank Dixon in seafood. Staring at a dead fish. In a yellow rain slicker dripping water on the floor.

Water on the floor. Water in the spice aisle. *Water.*

Li wasn't aware that he started speaking his thoughts. "You *did* see Oscar that night. You found his body. There was a puddle of water in the spice aisle where his body was. The store didn't mop yet. But you came in after the rain started, and your slicker dripped rainwater onto the floor. I slipped in it. So you must have hunted down Oscar and found him dead. Probably not long before I did. You panicked. You had a motive for wanting him dead, because he knew your secret. And now he *was* dead. So you slipped out of the aisle towards the back of the store, unaware that you left behind a trail of water. When you got toward seafood, you spotted the eyes of a dead fish in the counter, and it must have forcibly reminded you of your discovery. Oscar's lifeless glare. So misery and horror washed over you, and you were paralyzed by the shock."

Frank's voice was brittle. "All right, yes! I found him! I didn't know what else to do, so I ran! But I didn't kill him! I just—" He stopped. His mouth twisted into a perplexed frown. Then a new instinct took over, the instinct of his vocation: a reporter zeroing in on the pulse of a story. "Wait a second . . . What do you mean before *you* found him? Were you there as well?" His eyes narrowed. "Hold on . . . I know your face. You . . . You're that kid that overheard Connie and me! I saw your face when we got away."

Uh-oh. "Thank you for your time, Mr.—"

"Oh no, you don't." Frank was quick. He hurled himself out of his chair and shoved Li back into his. "Don't move. I haven't decided what to do with you yet."

In his fist, he squeezed the brass paperweight.

Oh crap. Oh crap. Oh crap. Now Li was the one doing the math on escape routes.

Frank started muttering under his breath. "I can't let you get away. You know too much. I've said too much. Connie'll kill me. Unless . . ." His scarred face looked more and more like it had been chipped out of rock. "Unless I get rid of you."

"Mr. Dixon, I—"

"Shut up. You should know better, kid. Don't push me." Frank's knuckles popped as he throttled the fatal football. "You don't understand what I've had to do to keep this paper alive. I've had to beg and plead and scrape. I've drained my 401k. I've had to cut my own salary just to keep paying my high-profile staff. And on top of everything else, there was our mayor's little Freudian slip, Oscar's threats, and my wife is thinking about a separation. I can't handle it anymore. I'm not going to let you be the fuse that blows up everything I've done."

Frank flung his arm back, ready to drive the paperweight into Li's skull.

"Now, now . . . let's not act rashly, Frank."

The paperweight clattered on the ground. Frank retreated, his eyes huge. His hands flew to the collar of his shirt, and he made these strange, gurgling sounds as if the collar tried to strangle him.

Li's hammering heart ground to a halt. He felt a cold spot slide down his spine. That new voice was deep and rich, the hum of a cello. A slim hand folded around his shoulder.

Li fought not to look at Constance Henderson.

"Hello, Liam. I'm surprised to find you here. Though perhaps not *too* surprised." Her voice felt like black ice pressed against his ears. "And Frank, dear, you're letting that temper get away from you again, aren't you? Probably blabbed every secret in your heart by now. You should work on that."

Frank's words garbled in his throat, sounding like a new language. The language of terror.

"Now what am I going to do with both of you?"

Frank and Li gulped in unison.

She barked at Frank, who tried to recoil into the paneling along the wall. "You're a worm, Frank. A spineless, gutless, hopeless worm. You could have ruined everything, all because you have the constitution of a wet square of tissue paper. You're a failure. I'll deal with you later, and you'll be lucky to end up editing bathroom graffiti at this rate."

A whimper escaped from the ex-editor-in-chief.

Constance's fingernails dug into Li's shirt. "And Liam, you've been a naughty boy. You could have been at home studying or spending time with your little friends instead of sadly decomposing in a ditch by the highway." Her voice sharpened, ice over steel. "Morley, take this young man out of my sight. Don't hurt him until you're well out of town. I never want to see his face again."

Oh crap! Oh crap! Oh crap! What am I going to do?

Li's heart thundered in his throat, and sweat poured out of his palms. Morley, a scruffy weasel of a man with sharp eyes matching his gray stubble, had prodded him out of the office and forced him into *The Gazette's* utilitarian parking garage. Cars slumbered in the midafternoon lull. The sound of their footsteps reverberated off the barren concrete walls. The place was deserted, empty as a tomb.

Except for a killer and his victim.

Come on, use your brain, Liam! Think! THINK! But the blood seemed to drop away from his head and into his feet, making them want to run, to take a dangerous risk. No doubt Morley would open fire if Li even got a foot too far away.

Does he have a gun? He didn't when he broke into my apartment. But who's to say he doesn't have one now?

The panic tried to drown his rational thoughts. *Do it. Run. He'll kill you. Get out. Flee. Get away. Do it or die.*

Morley didn't touch him or talk. But he followed Li at such a close distance that the boy could smell the sour stench of whiskey oozing from him. No more than the length of a single shoe.

Are you just going to let him kill you?

Li's merciless brain played out the scenario. Forced into Morley's or Constance's nondescript car. A drive to a distant highway. Then murder. Constance would finally lose her current headache.

What could he do? Scream? Screams were quickly silenced. Morley was right on his tail. So close.

Too close?

An idea wriggled into his head, a stupid, hastily cobbled-together, probably fatal idea. It would give him a second—maybe less—of leeway. Was that enough?

Do it or die.

This is the stupidest thing I'll ever do. He took a nerve-settling breath, fortified his spirit with a thought about saving his mother and sister from any more grief.

One final breath.

He stopped walking. Just stopped.

Morley was so close that he bumped into Li. There was a milli-second—no more—of shock, of displacement, of confusion at what just happened. The millisecond Li needed.

Li bolted, diving behind a parked car, his heart shifting from his throat to his ears. He found it difficult to breathe.

Morley chuckled. "Cute, kid. Very cute. Go on. Keep running. You'll just wear yourself out."

Li's hands were slick with sweat. Daring not to breathe, he collapsed to his stomach and started crawling, like a soldier under barbed wire, beneath the cars. His body became sticky with oil as he scrambled through the patches under leaky undercarriages. Sweat dripped into his eyes. He prayed to whatever deity would listen to him.

Morley's footsteps ambled along, echoing in the empty garage, echoing in Li's ears. He was still so damn close. "Come on, kid. Hide-and-seek can't last forever."

Li knew this wouldn't last. He'd run out of cars. Slowly, he began to double back, crawling on his knees and elbows back to the first car. He hoped to confuse his killer.

"Come out, come out, wherever you are."

Now what? Li peeked out from his hiding spot. Morley's feet were only three cars ahead of him. Not good. How would he get out of this?

He thought of his slashed sneakers.

The echoes of Morley's steps rang out like the booming ticks of a doomsday clock.

Noise.

Li squirmed out from his hiding place. Adrenaline bellowed in his brain, making him dizzy. He peeled off a sneaker and hoped his throwing arm from high school baseball hadn't lost its touch.

He popped up, a panicked jack-in-the-box, and chucked his shoe at a sedan parked across the way. Its car alarm wailed. Quick as a blink, Li dived under his car and watched Morley's feet turn and walk toward the howling vehicle. Morley started whistling, his pace calm.

Li flung himself to his belly and shuffled under his line of cars.

"Aww, cute job, kid. But you'll run out of shoes before I run out of patience."

Li crawled as fast as his speeding heart could take it. He needed more noise, more confusion. Risking it, he grabbed his other sneaker and tossed it at another likely vehicle in a neighboring section. Its alarm shrieked. Then another car. And another. Soon the garage was a riot of noise. People had to hear it and investigate. They had to!

Morley's feet froze at least eleven cars behind Li. They were waiting.

Li would be forced to run for it. His options were fading.

He barely heard over the screeching cars, "Where are you, Liam? Come out and play."

He could see sunlight streaming through the garage exit. Only a few feet away.

Please, whoever's out there, please take care of Mom and Anna for me. Li swallowed another deep breath.

He dived out of his hiding space and fled toward the exit, hoping all the running he did in baseball would pay off now. Blood surged to his legs, powering them, pumping them like pistons in a galloping engine. Behind him, he heard Morley shout, "You're mine, kid!" His would-be killer's racing footsteps clamored against the concrete, always sounding a mere inch away from Li.

Almost there. Almost there. Almost there.

Li ignored the stabbing pains in his socked feet and the fact his heartbeat felt like nothing more than a raw, sustained note in his chest. He gave no attention to the idea that Morley could jump in his car and run Li down like a stray animal. He burst into the sunlight and pounded his screaming legs in the direction of the police station.

CHAPTER 16

Oscar's Secret

"Detective Hughes!!!"

"Liam? What the—? What's wrong?"

Li had exploded into the station, having sprinted the whole mile or two from the parking garage. The dispatcher threw herself out of the chair with a shriek when he burst in—saturated in sweat, smeared with oil, eyes enormous and frightened, blood leaching through his white socks. Having spotted the detective, Li called out to him and then collapsed on the floor, clutching the stitch in his side, sure he would never force enough oxygen into his body. Morley wouldn't need to kill him, because he was sure a heart attack would happen. Black spots danced in front of his watering eyes.

The police were quick and efficient. Li had been peeled off the floor, water dabbed on his face and poured into his body, first aid applied to his feet. They gave him a towel to wipe off the smudges of motor oil on his skin. As doctors were summoned, the officers perched him on a chair in front of Detective Hughes' desk.

Detective Hughes, his buckeye-brown eyes wide and bewildered, kneeled next to Li, making sure he stayed hydrated and awake. "Liam, what in God's name is going on?"

"Constance ... Morley ... tried ... kill me ..."

"Breathe. That's it. Keep breathing. What's this about killing you?"

The whole story came out, wheezing, fragmented, but there. Life and color started to seep back into Li's cheeks, but the strain and fear in his face didn't ease. His eyes bounced like a ping-pong ball around the station, searching for hideouts. Constance could be here. Lying in wait. A hunter in her blind. She could be anywhere. She could be—

"They're not here, Liam. But she did call with a 'tip' saying she suddenly remembered seeing a man matching your description having an argument with Oscar on the night he died. That, of course, conflicts with all the other testimony we have."

"Maybe she's trying to frame me as well as kill me." Li's voice sounded like sandpaper.

"Drink your water, Liam. We'll get you checked out and drive you home."

"NO! Morley could be there!"

"We can't keep you here forever. Liam, I told you to keep your nose clean. And now you're in danger. Why on Earth would they want to kill you?"

"Because I know their secret. Mayor Marshall Henderson is a bigot."

Detective Hughes arched an eyebrow. "Pardon?"

Li gulped water and launched into his story. "That's the starting point. After the Bauer riots, Juliana Esposito from *The Shorewood Gazette* interviewed the mayor about his response to the whole thing. He responded with the belief that the restuarant's staff deserved to be tormented! He was as racist, if not more, than Oscar himself. This is one of the most diverse cities in the state and, if his bigotry got out, it would spell the end of his mayoral career. Particularly since he lied to his constituents about his feelings. And an end to his career would mean an end to Constance's power as Mrs. Mayor.

"She put pressure on Frank Dixon, so he changed the final article to reflect positively on Mayor Henderson. Pure censorship. Then he fired Juliana because she knew the truth. The whole thing was a big cover-up. Oscar got suspicious and found out about Frank's and Constance's lies. He blackmailed them, not for money, but to make them squirm and to provide leverage for his plans, such as resigning from the paper. Then I got nosy and found out as well. That's why they want to get rid of me. To shut me up for good."

Detective Hughes' eyes broadcasted the struggle within him, hovering somewhere between reproach and worry. "You've certainly been enterprising with these unofficial investigations of yours. So you're saying they could have killed Oscar to keep him quiet?"

"It's a possibility. They were certainly willing to kill me. But I don't know ... Frank confessed everything he did when he panicked, and he didn't mention Oscar's murder."

"That's not exactly a testimonial to innocence, Liam."

"Is ... Is there something we can do, Detective? I ... I'm scared."

Detective Hughes stood. His eyes softened for a moment. "Okay, give me a minute." He picked up his telephone receiver. "Lou? It's Tony. Can you check those archives of yours and tell me what you know about a man named Morley? Uh-huh ... uh-huh ... That bad, huh? Suspicion of murder? I see. And an outstanding warrant. That certainly makes things easier. Thanks, Lou." He hung up. "Looks like this Morley is a nasty character. You must have just scraped by with your life. We'll send officers out to your place to check. And you can stay until we get word back from them."

Li melted from exhaustion and relief.

Detective Hughes studied the hurt and terrified boy. "Now Liam, I have to insist you stop snooping. You could have been killed today. Why do you insist on putting your life in danger? Why are you trying to hunt down a murderer?"

That perked Li up. "Because there's a friend of mine who is frightened and regrets the mistake he made. Reuben did not kill Oscar. All he did was leave that package. He didn't hurt anyone. In fact, I think, when Oscar died, Reuben was working with me. But he doesn't know what's going to happen to him. He's sinking into remorse and that could hurt him and his boyfriend worse than any physical pain. I can't let him suffer. Not after he saved my life."

His eyes glinted like twin pools of winter ice.

Detective Hughes pushed out a frayed sigh. "Liam, I don't want you to get killed. It's dangerous."

"Have you learned anything new about Oscar's—?"

"No." That one word carried the force of a million bullets.

"Detective—"

"No. No more questions. Never again."

Li wanted to protest when Adam poked his head into the cubicle. "Hey, Tony. I managed to trace the doctor Kathryn saw after the Bauer incident. Apparently, she went to Los Angeles to see him, which is why I never got a line on what made her sick." Detective Hughes tried to signal to Adam to keep quiet, but the Wolf was too keen on the scent. "She saw an allergy specialist."

Li's eyes swelled as if he just saw the fabric of reality tear open. He ran his fingers through his short black hair, his habit when disparate ideas and images were slamming together in his head. The stormy night. The coat. The collar. The move. The resignation. The dinner. The grocery store. The list in the lining of his pocket. The cane. The missing groceries. And Oscar's personality.

All the puzzle pieces formed a neat and tidy picture.

Li started to mutter. "That's it. Oh my God, that's it! That explains everything!"

Detective Hughes and a shocked and chastened Adam stared at him.

"Um, Liam? Is everything okay?"

Li jerked to his feet and drilled his laser-bright eyes into the detective's face.

"Oscar Lindstrom planned to murder his wife."

"It fits. It all *fits.*"

Li sank back into his chair, almost dazed by his own revelation. The two policemen shared a look that suggested they wanted to summon a special kind of doctor for Li. The kind with a soothing tranquilizer.

Detective Hughes cleared his throat. "Liam? Do you mind illuminating us on this theory of yours?"

"It's not a theory, Detective. It can't be. It has to be the truth." A sober, mature determination set his jaw and strengthened the conviction in his eyes. "All along, we were confused by how Oscar was in two places at the same time. It seemed, didn't it, that two stories were tangled together. And there *were* two stories. Oscar's plans and the plans of the person who killed him.

"Oscar had two core tenets of his personality. Firstly, *he was a perfectionist.* After his first wife, the wife he loved most of all, passed away, he became obsessed with finding the perfect mate to replace her. He married Constance because she was efficient, organized, and detail-oriented, making her a generally faultless commander. But he didn't care for her independence. Hence their eventual divorce. Oscar wanted a wife who would wait on him hand and foot, a Stepford wife. And in Kathryn Lindstrom, he found what he wanted. He believed she was flawless.

"But we forgot about the *second* tenet of his personality: *Oscar was a critic.* Like I said before, a critic to his soul. Criticizing people brought him happiness. He loved finding the flaws in everything around him. He would tell his son 'perfection can be perfected.' Perfection was an ideal to strive for, but not something anyone could achieve. That would give him billions of opportunities to point out the faults of the world. Until he met Kathryn. He believed her to be the perfect woman.

"And you know what happened? She annoyed him! Because he was unable to satisfy that second key factor of his personality. He wanted to criticize her, but he couldn't find anything wrong with her. So he grew more and more irked by her presence. Eventually, he settled on the idea of eliminating her from his life. Sounds like an old adage, doesn't it? Those who find perfection are often dissatisfied."

Detective Hughes interrupted. "So he decided to kill her? That's hideous. That's insane. Why not get a divorce?"

"Because Kathryn would never leave him. She adored Oscar, truly and deeply. Kathryn Lindstrom is a mothering soul who wanted a man to take care of, to spoil, to coddle, to baby. She didn't want to be a wife, so much as a nursemaid or mother. In Oscar, she found a man she could coddle and care for, and I think she wouldn't dream of divorcing him. And Oscar knew that. Plus I think Oscar might have gotten a horrible kick out of devising the 'perfect' crime. Another chance for him to assert his idea of 'superiority.'" Li grimaced. "Disgusting, isn't it?"

A frown tugged at Detective Hughes' lips. "Completely. But I still can't see how he devised this murder."

Li's eyes glossed over as he delved into his imagination and memories, drawing up vivid pictures of what he believed happened. "It started when Kathryn got sick at Bauer. She must have eaten something that disagreed with her." He nodded at Adam. "You said she saw an allergy specialist, and that's when it hit me. *Kathryn Lindstrom is allergic to white pepper.* Violently allergic, I'd say. And I don't think she knew she was allergic until she ate the white pepper sauce on her dish during that last dinner at Bauer. No one at the restaurant learned what happened because she saw a doctor in LA, and by then it was too late. Oscar destroyed them, but silently held on to the knowledge of his wife's allergy.

"Do you see where I'm going with this? After they learned the truth, Kathryn would eliminate white pepper from the house. When Oscar decided to murder her, he realized her deadly allergy could leave him virtually blameless if he planned properly. But he had to get white pepper. Hence the visit to a grocery store. Remember the grocery list he had? There was the entry *G-W-P* for *ground white pepper.*

"And think about where his body was found! *Crouched by the pepper section of the spice aisle.*"

The detective raised his hands. "All right, all right . . . Granted if all of that is true, how on Earth did he think he would get away with it?"

"His enormous ego probably made him believe he couldn't make a mistake and that the crime was infallible." He rolled his eyes. "In any case, he planned carefully. He studied many stores before settling on Esther's Family Grocery, satisfied with it probably because it's not the most secure or high-tech supermarket in the world. Then he began cutting off all ties in town. Submitting his résumé to other newspapers. Buying a new house. Resigning from his old post. Getting ready for a big getaway, I'd wager. I wonder . . . was he planning to write a fourth book? Do you know anything about that, Detective? A synopsis, a title, anything?"

"He planned to call it *Clean Plate.*"

Li clapped his hands once. He beamed. "That's it! A clean plate! Or better yet, *a clean slate.* Oscar wanted to start over, to take his life in a new direction. So he decided to clean his plate, ending with getting rid of the woman who had started to irritate him.

"The list of groceries might have been his one moment of criminal vanity. Hiding the murder weapon in plain sight, so to speak. Burying the truth in a pile of nonsense. Laughing at the cops maybe. He probably even left the list lying around, overly confident in his plans. Jason told me how his father had a bad habit of leaving evidence of his affairs lying around his office, preening that no one was that observant. So why not thinly concealed evidence of his planned murder? Then he set the wheels in motion. He waited for the perfect night—cloudy, no moon. He announced to his family his intention to stay in his office, went to said office and placed that silhouette of himself in the window to give him an alibi, slipped on a big coat with an upturned collar to hide his face, and then snuck out when everyone else was occupied, leaving his trademark cane behind. He wanted to stay inconspicuous. He walked to Esther's Family Grocery and went immediately to the spice aisle. His sole purpose was to acquire his murder weapon, which explains why he didn't have any other groceries with him."

Adam jumped in. "And just as he was crouching down to grab the pepper, someone killed him." He blushed when his superior glanced at him.

Li nodded. "Exactly. And that's where Oscar's murderous plans came to an end and another's continued to work." He tented his fingers, his eyebrows knitted together. "Oscar's plans do manage to clear away some of the clues, but not all of them. Like the bag of sugar on the floor near his body. Or the scanner in the toilet. Or the fact no one saw anything amiss that night."

Detective Hughes, who had been taking covert notes while Li spoke, posed a question. "Do *you* have any interesting theories about that, Liam?" Just a shade of scorn worked into his tone.

Adam drummed nervous fingers on Detective Hughes' desk. "Um . . . I think I have an idea, Tony. Since he was killed trying to get a murder weapon, maybe someone killed him specifically to *stop* him from getting that weapon."

"Then it could possibly be Jason Lindstrom. He did love his stepmother."

Li's eyes snapped into focus. He jolted in his seat. "Wait! What?"

A smile unfurled across the detective's dark chocolate skin. "Something you've missed, Liam? I noticed that Jason had an affection for his young stepmother. An affection far more serious than—"

Li shook his head. "No way. He didn't love her. He hated her. Perhaps hated her more than Oscar."

The smile died. "What was that?"

"Jason hates Kathryn. A lot. Because she never stopped his dad's abuse. She just stood there and watched Oscar torture his son without stepping in to stop him. She was an apathetic bystander, most likely because Jason was not her own child, therefore not her responsibility. Jason loathed her, because she never helped him. But he was conflicted because she never did anything outwardly to hurt him. She was motherly and kind and never lifted a finger against him. That's what Jason meant when he told me that 'Kathryn wouldn't hurt someone like that.' That is, by violence. She'd hurt people by simply ignoring them when they needed help. So whenever he blushed or became awkward about her, it was because he had trouble reconciling his anger at her neglect and her sweet, generous nature. I imagine he wouldn't be too upset if she died . . . or, at the very least, disappeared from his life altogether."

The detective scowled. "Well, there goes another theory. You're certainly adept at making them and discrediting them, aren't you, Liam?" He drove his chin forward. "The trouble is that we still don't have a solid piece of evidence as to who killed Oscar. Not a single clue. Not even *you* have a name to put to the murderer, Liam, and you seem to burst with ideas."

Li's brow pleated with a tight frown. His gaze was remote. His brain churned through the information, winnowing away the answers they had and focusing on the remaining questions. A pattern emerged, rising from the mess of this mystery. Li's silvery-blue eyes shone like dawn on a misty morning.

Why did no one notice anything amiss that night?

How did the bag of sugar get involved?

What was the story of the fatal scanner?

Who murdered Oscar Lindstrom?

Li thought he knew.

"I have an idea who it must be, Detective. But you need evidence. If you look closely, you should be able to find it. Because the key to this whole mystery is that Oscar is the only victim. There were no more dangers after he was killed. Once he was dead, our murderer's agenda was completed. This wasn't a murder out of selfish greed, but out of charity, so to speak."

"Charity?"

"Yes. And I think if we told one particular person the truth, our killer will come quietly."

The suspect wasn't at home. Li, riding along, suggested they try the Lindstrom house.

Kathryn met them in the foyer, ever-present apron around her waist, broom in hand. But her eyes were nonplussed. "Li? Detective? What's this about?"

When asked, she revealed the suspect was upstairs in Oscar's office, an interloper in his private kingdom, helping Kathryn pack away her husband's belongings.

While the police informed Kathryn about their intentions, Li crept up the stairs. Inside the office, Li saw the murderer bury Oscar's books inside a box. The murderer turned to face Li, expression baffled. "Um ... can I help you?"

"It's over."

There was no mistaking the import of those words. They were heavy and filled the room with echoes, the last gong of a funeral bell. The murderer flinched, eyes wary. Then they sank into nothingness, a blank stare.

"I see. Does ... Does she know?"

A heartbroken cry answered from downstairs. The wail of a wounded widow.

The murderer sighed. "That answers that, then. I did my best."

Footsteps on the landing. The office door slid open, and Detective Hughes, his face an official mask of duty, sauntered inside the room. His voice held the weight of centuries of combined police tradition.

"Tom Delancey, you are under arrest for the murder of Oscar Lindstrom."

CHAPTER 17

Beginning, Middle, and End

"Li, you have to tell us everything! What happened?"

It had been a few weeks since the arrest. Li sat on a chair in Reuben and Noah's apartment with his two friends. Fernando Rodriguez and Sarah Johanson, a lively young woman in a bold summer dress and a sheer rainbow scarf wrapped around her bald head, had joined them. Both couples were snuggling in their respective seats, that near shave with the law still fresh in their heads. Li had been staying with Reuben and Noah while he was a witness in the trial against Frank Dixon, John Morley, and Constance Henderson. Just until the nightmarish ordeal was over.

The police found Morley lying in wait at Li's apartment. He had been loaded with enough weapons to furnish a grassroots militia. On his arrest, he sold out Constance without batting an eyelash. At the same time, Juliana Esposito released her *real* article about the mayor, shattering his reputation and any future campaigns. It had been several weeks of scandal and upheaval, so much so that Oscar Lindstrom's murder nearly vanished from public view.

But not from police view. Tom Delancey confessed everything and was currently making a home for himself in prison.

"Come on, Li!" Noah insisted, his arms wrapped stoutly around Reuben's waist. "Quit stalling. How did you figure it out?"

Li, shy before his audience, quelled the urge to shuffle his feet, since they were still bandaged from that Hail Mary sprint. "Well, you see, it turned out to be just like I thought earlier. Kathryn Lindstrom was the beginning, middle, and end of this murder."

"How so?"

"She was the motive. Tom Delancey loved Kathryn, loved her with all his heart. It was as simple as that. There always seemed to be a close bond of friendship between Tom and Staci and the Lindstroms, despite their insistence that Oscar had no one in his life he considered a friend. So why would they associate with the

Lindstroms? Since Oscar didn't care for others, Jason didn't have friends, and Staci seemed to be nothing more than a temporary fling, who did that leave? *Tom knew Kathryn*. We could even trace their friendship back further. Kathryn said she lived in Northern California. Tom used to write for the *San Francisco Chronicle*. I think Tom met Kathryn in San Francisco and fell madly in love with her. But she didn't love him, because she wanted a man she could mother. When she married Oscar and moved to Shorewood, he followed her, unwilling to lose her.

"I think the biggest clues came from Jason Lindstrom. He described Tom as 'the perpetual bachelor' complete with beer signs and singing bass. Rather stereotypical, don't you think? Like overcompensation, an assertion that he *was* a bachelor rather than a man pining for a woman. But the clue I like best is the position of his house."

"His house?" Reuben asked. "What do you mean?"

"I'm mostly referring to his front window. It had an okay view of Oscar's office window, *but its best view was of Kathryn's flower beds*. I saw those flowers as the green light at the end of Daisy's dock in *The Great Gatsby*. Jay Gatsby gazing at the dock of the faraway woman he loved. I believe it was a similar experience for Tom Delancey, a chance to see Kathryn from afar. He bought that house to be as close to her as he could."

Sarah laced her delicate fingers with Fernando's solid ones. "If it hadn't led to so much pain, it could have been romantic. How did it all end with murder?"

Li nodded to her boyfriend. "That's where Fernando was a big help." Fernando looked like Li had accused him of being Kathryn in disguise. "He remembered that there were *three* people at the table when Kathryn got sick. One was Oscar. Another was Kathryn. The third wasn't Jason, because he didn't go to these dinners. So the *third* person at that dinner knew about Kathryn's allergy to white pepper. Kathryn would have told him. I inferred that it was Tom Delancey. He often had dinner with his colleague; more chances to spend time with the woman he loved, I'd wager.

"So Tom knew about the allergy. Oscar decided to kill his wife, who irritated him with her 'perfection' of all things, with this same knowledge. Oscar got cocky and left the incriminating list of groceries out in his office, confident he'd hidden his intentions from everyone. But Tom, who would sometimes be in the office as Oscar's colleague, saw the entry *G-W-P* for ground white pepper on it and suspected Oscar was up to something. Everyone knew Oscar had something big planned. As big as murder. We can't be sure when Tom believed Oscar would kill Kathryn. It may be that he thought Oscar was going to hurt her somehow, his feelings probably colored by jealousy and a deep desire to get rid of the horrible man she married. Whatever it was, Tom would not allow Oscar to harm Kathryn."

"So it was a case of stopping Oscar before he got the white pepper," Noah said.

"Exactly. Just like Officer Schafer-Schmidt said. Tom knew Oscar would need to go to a grocery store at some time and kept a close watch on him. He saw Oscar go into Esther's Family Grocery, witnessed his satisfaction with the place, and made his own plans to stop him. And they were ingenious in their simplicity." Li's eyes shimmered like new armor. "It bothered me like crazy that no one saw anything amiss that night. In a store that empty, anything out of the ordinary would be noticeable. The problem was the weapon: *a scanner*. Customers do NOT handle those tools. If any of the customers handled the scanner, it would be noticed. But since everyone said it was a normal night and nothing seemed out of place, *then the person who handled it had to be the type of person who was expected to do so.*"

"Whoa whoa whoa." Reuben held up a hand. "Reverse. Rewind. Back up. Care to repeat that in English?"

"A handheld supermarket scanner is an *occupation-specific* weapon. Think of it like ... a nightstick to a police officer. If a *civilian in civilian clothes* carried around a nightstick, people would notice it. Because it wouldn't be right. It would be unexpected. But if a police officer carried one, no one would pay any real attention to it. It would be typical and expected. Provided one thing: *the officer would have to be in uniform.*

"See what I mean? In order for the killer to escape detection carrying around the fatal scanner, *he would have to look like an employee at Esther's Family Grocery!* And that was easy! We wear a *uniform,* a very simple uniform to acquire. White button-up shirt, black slacks, black shoes, black necktie, and the crowning touch: a brown apron. All very easy to get. Tom's only real danger was getting the apron, which was the evidence we got on him before his arrest. A receipt for an apron matching the ones in our store."

Fernando was an inch away from falling off the edge of his chair. "Then what happened?"

Li had a sudden vision of himself as an oral storyteller of long ago, a crowd of people huddled close to him and the fire to hear the ancient tale. This section had a sizeable contribution from Detective Hughes. "Tom and Staci got home from the baseball game at a quarter after six. While Staci sat by the front window being a convenient witness to Oscar's alibi, Tom went off to 'work on his article.' In reality, he changed into his employee disguise, waited for Oscar to leave around a quarter to seven, and followed him to Esther's Family Grocery. At seven o'clock, Oscar arrived at the supermarket, Tom close behind him. As Oscar went to the spice aisle, Tom discovered the scanner on a shelf, probably one left behind by Lazy Leo. It made a sturdy weapon of opportunity and furthered his disguise.

"Tom went to the aisle next to the spice aisle: pasta. Through the perforated backing of the shelves, he could see Oscar biding his time for the perfect moment to grab the white pepper. When Oscar crouched down, Tom used a box of pasta to tip over a bag of sugar on the opposite riser. The sugar fell, hitting Oscar on the head and stunning him. Just enough to scramble his thoughts so he didn't cry out. Then Tom scurried around the corner and used the scanner to finish the job. All his outdoor activities gave him the requisite strength to commit the murder.

"He had to act quickly. He raced to the public restrooms in the back corner of the store, stuffed the scanner in the toilet and flushed it to wash off fingerprints and any trace evidence, slipped off his apron, and left by the back doors. In the alley, he balled up the apron and tossed it aside, so it wouldn't be found in his possession." Li's eyes sparkled as he looked at Reuben. "I think Bill liked his new cat bed."

Reuben's jaw dropped. "You mean . . . that's *the* apron?"

"I'm pretty much positive it is."

"Holy cow. What happened after that?"

"Not very much. He went home, changed, and went to dinner with Staci. No one tied him to the murder. His connection to Oscar was tenuous, no witnesses saw him at the store that night, and his motive was purely the welfare of Oscar's wife. That's why I didn't suspect him until later." Li's gaze became contemplative. "I started changing my thinking when I realized that Oscar was the only victim so far. It seemed to me that whoever killed him had no intention to kill anyone else. And that was the case. Once Tom got rid of Oscar, all his problems were solved. Kathryn was saved . . . and free to marry again. Maybe even marry her unknown savior . . ."

Li thought about the remaining Lindstroms. Kathryn had moved back home to San Francisco with the intention of never setting foot past Modesto ever again. Jason had left too, after finding some old friends from his school days. The last letter he sent to Li said he found a job and was attending college as a journalism major. The picture sent with the letter showed Jason with a full smile and a healthy glow to his cheeks.

Li thought he would survive after all.

Reuben, still reeling, shook his head. "What a crazy week that was. You saved our butts, Li. If you didn't believe Fern and me, I . . . we . . . it would have been really ugly." A shadow flickered on his face. It was chased away when Noah kissed him on the cheek. "You're a hero, Li. Thank you."

Li's face flushed pink. "Um . . . you're welcome. I . . . I don't know about *hero* . . ."

"You are, Li. Leave it at that." Reuben settled further into his seat with a sigh. "I am so glad I left that place. Terrible vibes. This

new job is much more in my wheelhouse as a business major."
Noah gently elbowed him in the belly. Reuben blushed. "Oh, sorry,
Li. It was total and complete crap what Leo did."

"Don't worry about it. I wasn't surprised."

Shortly after the multiple arrests, Leo pulled Li into his office
and said how he was sorry this had to be such bad news, but that
he felt he had hired Li too hastily and was afraid Li's "adventures
with law enforcement" wouldn't reflect positively on the family-
friendly mission of Esther's Family Grocery. Never mind the
murder.

Layman's terms: Li was out of a job. Again.

Noah intervened. "We'll help you find another job as soon as
possible. We owe you big-time, Li. Anytime. Anyplace."

"Guys, guys . . . It's okay." Li lifted his hands, and his smile was
broad. "Turns out one of my earlier contacts got back to me for a
job opening. I start next week."

The other four cheered, congratulated him, patted his back,
called for a toast.

Sarah asked the all-important question. "So where will you be
working, Li?"

"Clerk at That's How I Want to Die Mystery Bookshop." Li
shrugged. "I know it's not the most glamorous work, but hey . . . a
job's a job."

About the Author

 Daniel Stallings's love of Golden Age detective fiction inspired him to update the classic murder mystery for the modern age in his first Li Johnson mystery, *Sunny Side Up*. In addition to writing mysteries, Stallings works in theater as a producer, director, and actor. Combining his interests in mysteries and theater, Stallings operates Mastery Mystery Productions, which produces custom interactive mystery game events. He currently serves as President of the Eastern Sierra Branch of the California Writers Club. Stallings lives in the city of Ridgecrest in California's Mojave Desert.

CPSIA information can be obtained
at www.ICGtesting.com
Printed in the USA
JSHW032033300920
8393JS00001B/26